My Turn

My Turn
by Roz Avrett

ARBOR HOUSE • New York

Copyright © 1983 by Roz Avrett

All rights reserved, including the right of reproduction in whole or in part in any form. Published in the United States of America by Arbor House Publishing Company and in Canada by Fitzhenry & Whiteside, Ltd.

Library of Congress Catalogue Card Number: 83-70482

ISBN: 0-87795-476-3

Manufactured in the United States of America

10 9 8 7 6 5 4 3 2 1

This book is printed on acid free paper. The paper in this book meets the guidelines for permanence and durability of the Committee on Production Guidelines for Book Longevity of the Council on Library Resources.

For all those wonderful people who said, "stop writing those wonderful TV commercials and start writing novels:"

Olivia Altschuler, Jack Avrett, Titina and Noël Barber, Nina Bourne, Virginia Shook Alexander Dexter Dexter Berry Cordner, Barbie and Bill Claggett, Joan and Frank Ginsberg, Mary and Shelly Holzer, Mort Metzler, Jocelyn and Jack Mickle, Peter Nord, Mara and Paul Palmer, Alexandra Penney, H. Melvin Philpott, Russell Rhodes, John Siddeley, Rita Picker Silton, Norman F. Stevens, Jr., Denise Thorne and Barbara and Alan Woltz.

And to Natalie Schafer for introducing me to Gloria Safier. And to Gloria Safier for everything, especially my brilliant, incisive and *patient* editor, Eleanor Johnson.

And finally, to my son, Jerry Reynolds, who has always encouraged me to write...mostly checks.

CHAPTER ONE

At thirty-seven, Jill Harrington still worried that she'd be arrested if she tore the "Do not remove under penalty of law" labels off her pillows and mattresses. She worried that she might be run over and They'd discover the safety pins in her minimizer bra. She worried about black cats, getting her period in a white skirt and lightning striking twice. During thunderstorms, she'd put on her husband's high rubber trout fishing boots and cower in the back of the garage, far from windows, fireplaces and TV sets.

But today the weather was perfect. She didn't have to leave the house and face the dreaded shopping mall. The neighbors with the black cat had gone away for two weeks, taking the cat with them. Today, she could devote all her energy to worrying about The Bills. Would she *ever* catch up?

She mixed herself a scotch and soda. Only two bottles of soda and one of scotch left underneath the sink. She hated its being kept there but Ian had insisted. "Reverse snobbism," he said. Jill regarded the last bottle. That was it—until Ian got another job.

What had gone wrong? All she'd ever wanted was a lovely

home and a life and some money to cushion the blows. She fixed herself a second scotch. What the hell. What was two hundred calories more when she already weighed one-fifty? What had become of the strawberry blonde with the wasp waist in the Bachrach wedding portrait?

She switched on the radio. WQXR usually cheered her up. There was a commercial about how easy it was to get money from the nearest Citibank Cash Machine, twenty-four hours a day. She longed to grab an axe and attack her nearest Citibank Cash Machine, wherever the hell it was. Chop it open. Rob. Steal. Pillage. God, maybe she was losing her mind.

She turned back to The Bills. Before Ian had been canned, she used to sort them: Food. Utilities. School. Stores. Doctors. Dentists. She'd toss out last month's Bills and replace them with this month's Bills. Then, she'd select those with the most urgent threats and pay them. Nowadays, she just closed her eyes and reached into the pile. Whatever her fingers touched, she paid. She'd keep going until Ian's unemployment check ran out.

So far, she'd turned up two letters stating that "this was a fourth warning," plus a curt note from her gynecologist requesting that she drop by his office to see if something couldn't be worked out. She hadn't even been to her gynecologist in three years.

"Why me?" Why couldn't Ian get a job?

Not just any job, but one which Ian felt was in keeping with their lifestyle on Badger Hollow Lane.

A few months ago, in desperation, she'd suggested to him that he start driving a cab at night in New York City, leaving his days free to continue the job hunt. After closing the bedroom windows, Ian had turned on her.

"What if the girls' school found out I was driving a cab? What do you think they'd say?"

"They'd probably say thank God those Harringtons are paying at last. The school doesn't give a good goddamn where the money comes from so long as it comes."

Ian had thrown a chair at her. She'd thrown it back. "Have

you any idea how humiliating it is when everybody knows your parents don't pay their bills?"

"It's just that I don't want it bandied about that I'm out of a job. A man has a sense of pride, Jill. But then, how could you know about that?"

"All I understand is how hard it is to face the headmistress at one of those ditsy teas when we've sent the school five hundred instead of the five thousand we owe. I understand that, Ian."

Ian had had jobs in the past. Nothing earthshaking, just respectable, although she had to admit it had been downhill since he'd been editor of his college newspaper. Ian was a snob, but he seemed to be a bitter failure at everyday life. It made him rotten company, except in bed. At least that was one thing he was good at.

She shook her head in disbelief. How could Ian have let this happen to her and the girls? Maybe it was her own fault. That's what her Aunt Peggy had suggested. Why hadn't she let well enough alone? Why had she urged Ian to ask for a raise? That's when the advertising agency had let him go. And the magazine. And now, Ian had been fired from his job selling advertising space at the Yellow Pages. If only she'd let sleeping dogs lie, Ian might still have been muddling along with the phone books.

Twelve years ago, when Ian had asked her to marry him, he'd made it quite clear that he wasn't cut out for Madison Avenue or Wall Street or any other rat race. He liked comfort, good books, crossword puzzles, backgammon. He liked chess, the opera, the eighteenth century. He had no use for railroad schedules, nine-to-five days, port or transit authority. He was just treading water until his grandmother, Rose-Delia Harrington, joined twenty generations of Harringtons at the great haggis banquet in the sky.

Rose-Delia had invested heavily in Sears Roebuck stock in the Twenties and had managed to hang on to it through the Depression. In the Fifties, she'd converted it to tax-free municipal bonds, and now she was worth more than eight million

9

dollars. She was eighty-three. And Ian was her only living relative.

When Jill had first stared into Ian's heavily fringed blue eyes, Rose-Delia's assets had been overshadowed by his arresting good looks, his lean, well-muscled body and lovemaking that went beyond romance to caveman passion. When Ian had slipped his mother's round four-carat Tiffany diamond onto her finger, Jill had started to cry. She'd told him that all she'd ever wanted was a loving husband and two children and that she'd inherited her mother's genuine Tudor house in Westchester. She'd do his shirts. Give up her advertising career and indulge in any kind of sex he wanted, except group.

He'd snorted that there were no genuine Tudor houses in the United States, and if they were going to live happily ever after, she'd better read up on history and architecture.

Jill closed her eyes and stabbed at one of The Bills. She opened her eyes and read aloud. "Ah, Gristede Brothers, Groceries," she said. "One hundred-eighty dollars. Past-due. Please remit. Protect your credit." When had she paid them last? Two months ago? Three? Four?

She wrote out a check for twenty-five dollars, and noted on it "on account." On account of that's all I've got. Tears sprang to her eyes. "Why me?"

Why couldn't all this have happened to someone else? Why not those smug Clarkes next door with their three color TV sets, Betamax, video games, Knabe grand? Those Clarkes, who sent their children to public school and ate fast food for dinner? Who made love on Sunday mornings with the shades up?

She always worked so hard. With the girls. The garden. The house.

Mummy and Daddy had paid sixty-five thousand for it and today it was worth more than three times that much. Maybe more.

Hadn't she refinished the floors herself? No workmen could have lavished care like that. Hadn't she painted the walls and sanded them and painted again until they shone like dull, heavy satin? Petit-pointed the seats for Mummy's old, fake Louis XV dining room chairs? Made the toile draperies by hand? Made the girls' clothes herself, except, of course, for the hand-me-downs from Ian's cousin in Buffalo who sent Harris tweed suits no matter what the season?

She gulped her scotch and reached for another Bill. Only this time it wasn't a Bill. She tore off the end of the envelope and pulled out a piece of scented pink stationery. Pumpkin Endicott-Osborne. Her college roommate. Pumpkin had been living in London for years and now she was opening a branch of her decorating business, Department of the Interior, in New York. Could they have dinner? Or lunch? She'd give a call on the morning of the twentieth.

Jill looked at the calendar on the refrigerator. "Oh, God," she moaned, "*this* is the morning of the twentieth."

She couldn't let Pumpkin see the kitchen table strewn with bills or the sewing machine or the sink full of dishes. Or *her*. Pumpkin, all legs and blonde hair. Pumpkin, who had a six-figure income, size six blue jeans and a floor-length sable coat. Thirty-eight-year-old Pumpkin who had the looks of a twenty-eight-year-old, the energy of an eighteen-year-old. Pumpkin, the flawless.

The insistent ring of the telephone sliced into Jill's gloom. Maybe she wouldn't answer. Maybe she'd pretend she was out. Reluctantly, she reached across The Bills and picked up the receiver. "Hello?" She felt a lift of expectancy. Maybe someone would tell her that she'd won a million-dollar sweepstakes.

"Is that you, Jill?" She recognized Pumpkin's Locust Valley lockjaw instantly. "I was positive I'd gotten a wrong number."

"Yes! Pumpkin, where are you? This doesn't sound like a long distance call."

"Short distance, love. Very short. I'm in Westport. Had to pick up a few things for a job I'm doing. You did get my note?"

"Yes."

"Well then, how about lunch? Twelve-thirty?"

"Lunch? Well, yes, of course. Let me check and see what's in the fridge," she said gaily, as though she weren't on intimate terms with the three cans of tuna, loaf of protein bread, two eggs, soggy green pepper and carton of skimmed milk, not to mention the pork shoulder, Lean Cuisine TV Dinner and leftover meat loaf in the freezer.

"I won't hear of it," laughed Pumpkin. "Why don't you jump into your car and whip over here. There's a wonderful place called Chez Pierre on Main Street. Do you know it?"

How long ago had she and Ian eaten at Pierre's? Their sixth anniversary? Before Beth was born? "Oh, yes. It's heaven."

"See you there. In about an hour. I'll ring Pierre so we're sure to get a table."

"I'll hurry. I'm not exactly dressed." Jill regarded her robe. By no stretch of the imagination could it be called a peignoir. It was maroon flannel and looked as though it had weathered a long bout of alcoholic invalidism.

"Throw on *any*thing. I'm dressed for antiquing. I hate shops to get the idea that I can afford their silly prices. Bye-bye."

The last time she'd seen her, Pumpkin had been wearing a red suede shirt, cavalry twill pants, jodphur boots and her engagement ring. All ten carats of emerald-cut Art Deco perfection, turned under, of course, to prevent its being snatched.

Jill tore upstairs and flung open her closet. What would be the least humiliating? The gray suit? The tan plaid skirt? The green shirt with the tie? They were the only things she hadn't remade for the girls or that hadn't fallen apart.

She slipped out of the robe and into the green silk shirt. The middle button barely held. She pinned it with a large, strong safety pin. Thank God the shirt had a billowly tie. She tied it and anchored it securely over the gap. Then she poured herself into the tan plaid skirt. The zipper almost made it to the top. But the hook didn't work at all. She pinned the skirt closed with two safety pins and struggled into her camel's hair blazer. The blazer hadn't buttoned in years but it did serve to conceal the makeshift waistband. She'd borrow one of Ian's belts just in case the safety pins didn't prove as strong as they looked. Ian's waist was thirty-two inches. So was hers.

Her feet refused to slip into her pumps, so she floured the toes with baby powder. It didn't help. The only shoes that fit were her Gucci loafers. Once her feet had been elegant, slim and dainty. Now they looked like boiled Italian sausages.

She regarded her purse. It was older than most high school students. She stuffed it back into the drawer and dropped a lipstick into her jacket pocket. She did the same with the car keys. She gave herself one last check in the full-length mirror.

Did she look like the wife of a Scottish laird about to tramp the moors? A New England intellectual with a mind fixated beyond the transitory? Eccentric rich, perhaps?

No. She looked like a bag lady.

Savagely, she jerked the rubber band from her pony tail and attacked her shoulder-length strawberry-blonde hair with a brush. Loose, her hair rippled into soft waves, framing her face. Not a trace of gray. Deftly, she lined her lids with Elizabeth Arden *Storm Cloud* pencil. She'd been out of mascara for a year, but she did have some blush left. She patted the former sites of her cheekbones. Then she smeared Vaseline Intensive Care Lotion on her parched hands. Maybe Pumpkin wouldn't notice that she hadn't had a manicure since before the first Children's Crusade.

Chez Pierre's. Jill remembered it as a movie set. Intimate. Fragrant with fresh seasonal flowers. Aromatic with the mysteries of a French kitchen. Lights that made everyone over forty look ten years younger.

As she walked up the tiny, steep steps, Jill prayed that it had lost none of its magic.

What was she going to say to Pumpkin? Her head was swimming from the scotch. And the race to get dressed hadn't helped. But how could she get through lunch without at least one Bloody Mary?

She pulled the door open and stepped inside. A waiter sped toward her.

"Do you have a reservation, madame?" His eyes narrowed as he took in her costume. Or was it her imagination? "I'm afraid we're booked today. Completely booked."

"I'm meeting Mrs. Osborne." Jill smiled broadly, in an effort to look friendly. His expression told her it hadn't worked.

"Follow me, please," he sniffed, turning on his heel.

Jill followed docilely. As they neared Pumpkin's table, her ancient loafer caught on one of the ancient floorboards and she landed full force in the lap of a small man drinking red wine. It splashed. On him. On her. All of her safety pins instantly gave way.

Pumpkin grabbed Jill's arm, laughing. "You really like to make an entrance, don't you? Are you hurt? I'll tell Pierre we're suing for personal injuries."

"I'm so sorry," Jill wailed, patting the man's arm. "I hope your suit is okay."

"Yes, yes, but I'm afraid some spilled on you, my dear."

"I guess I ought to wear my glasses," Jill offered. She had never worn glasses in her life. "I'll send you some wine. Please ask the waiter." Pumpkin pulled Jill over to their table.

"Well, now that that little trauma is over, what'll you have," asked Pumpkin, her giant Nile green eyes roaming Jill's outfit.

"A vodka martini, very dry, with a twist." It would probably make things worse. If that were possible.

"Well, what's up? What are you doing with yourself in the backwoods?" Pumpkin asked, her eyes riveted to where the jaunty bow of Jill's blouse had come undone, revealing yet another safety pin and an inch of shiny beige Minimizer bra.

"Oh, the usual. Trying to make ends meet. You know."

"And the girls? I haven't seen them in ages."

"They're both at Laurel Hall. Wendy would like to spend next summer in France. And Bethy is toying with the idea of visiting her great-grandmother Harrington in Palm Beach." Jill sipped at her martini. Her words seemed echoed in her ears. Was she being loud? She had been brought up to think that anything—incest, murder—was better than being loud.

"And Ian? How *is* good old Ian?" Pumpkin inquired, her voice oozing curare.

"Same as always," Jill gave what she hoped was a sigh of bliss.

"But what are *you* doing?" Pumpkin was tireless. "Where's your life going? I mean, I haven't seen you in three years. Or is it four? You must have more news than that."

"What have you been up to, Pumpkin?"

"We're talking about you, remember? Don't try to shit your oldest and dearest friend. What's happening?"

"Ohh, I've been working in the garden. Puttering. Keeping the *maison* up to snuff. Menus. *You* know."

How in hell could Pumpkin know? Pumpkin would never know. Suddenly Jill felt very protective of Pumpkin. She didn't want her to know.

"Puttering, huh? And resenting the shit out of Ian."

Jill winced and took another sip.

"Come on. What's the handsome and provocative Ian doing? Besides providing you with a no-frills fuck?"

"Looking for a job."

"The last time I saw you, Ian was looking for a job." Pumpkin signaled the waiter for another round.

"He did have a job. For more than two years. Then, he asked for a raise. It's all my fault, Pumpkin. I told him to. If he hadn't asked for a raise, he wouldn't have been fired. I should have kept my big mouth shut."

"I probably shouldn't ask you this, Jill, but what *is* Ian's fatal charm? He's terrific looking, but that doesn't cut any ice at the bank."

"I know. You've always thought Ian was a consummate horse's ass. You even said so once."

"I guess I did. I'm sorry." It had been after Ian had tried to drag Pumpkin away from a party and into the back seat of someone's car.

"Ian is what used to be referred to in our youth as a sex machine. That really turns me on. Christ, Pumpkin, I couldn't have admitted that a few years ago. You almost have to be middle-aged before you can discuss sex without a giggle."

Pumpkin couldn't believe what she was hearing.

"I also think you have to be in your thirties before you have any fun. It's worth a wrinkle or two." Jill smiled broadly.

Jill? Having fun? With a sex machine?

Other than her ex-husband, Stephen Osborne, Pumpkin had never been to bed with anyone a second time. "Go on," she encouraged, stabbing her ice cubes with a tapered coral nail.

"You won't believe this, but the more trouble Ian had with his various jobs, the better he got in bed. He thinks I'm the most glamorous woman in history. He calls me Helen. Juliet. He thinks I'm some kind of goddess."

Pumpkin stared at Jill. It was impossible for her to imagine herself in Jill's place. Ever since her divorce, Pumpkin had controlled her life. It had taken discipline, and at times, it had torn her apart. But she was in control.

"You've got to learn how to control your life, Jill, rather than vice versa."

Did Jill even have a clue what she was talking about?

"I guess I like being married."

"So much so that you're willing to put up with..." Pumpkin hesitated. It was crucial to choose exactly the right word. "With... humiliation just so that you can sign yourself Mrs. Ian Harrington, occupation, homemaker?"

"It's not so humiliating, Pumpkin." Jill's voice caught.

"Okay, then. Who have you seen from school lately? College? Advertising? Name two besides me."

"Just you."

"You're afraid, aren't you? Afraid to let them see what happened to the prom queen. Admit it, Jill. It's the first step on the road to recovery. Like admitting one is an alcoholic."

"You know, sometimes I worry about that, too. Can we order?"

Jill turned to the menu. Everything sounded fattening. But she wasn't even hungry. She was depressed. Damn Pumpkin.
"You win, Pumpkin. Everything you said is right. Things stink. They couldn't be worse. I don't care so much for me, it's the girls. If things don't get better, it looks like they'll have to drop out of Laurel Hall. They're never going to have the things you and I grew up expecting to have. It kills me to see that."

"When you walked in, Jill, I sensed you were playing Miz Scarlett done up in Miz Ellen's portieres."

"I don't want to borrow money, Pumpkin, just some of my old self-confidence." She took a hefty slug of her martini. "And maybe even my old self. I guess I lost it somewhere." She reached into her pocket for a Kleenex and found one, fused into a tight, hard little ball. She blotted her eyes with the napkin.

"I don't know what to do about Ian. Or the girls. They would love to go to Europe but there's no way we could afford it. As it is we're so far behind on the tuition at Laurel Hall I'm half afraid the school won't take them back next semester. Beth couldn't care less. She calls it—and I quote—a 'stuck-up shit palace.' She's her father's daughter, all right. But Wendy, my darling, loves Laurel Hall. I never have to beg her to do her homework. I never have to ask her to do anything. Her room is neat. Her drawers are neat. Beth and Ian, that bastard, gang up against her."

"What about Ian's famous grandmother? Couldn't she give Ian an advance on his inheritance? Or even just a loan? What does she have to spend money on at her age, anyway? Isn't she in her eighties?"

"Rose-Delia is eighty-three. And she feels fine. Very involved with charities in Palm Beach. The last time we saw her, she said, 'Ian, charity didn't begin at home, it began in Palm Beach.' She believes in standing on your own two feet."

"Well, Rose-Delia and I have a lot in common. Why on earth don't you get a job? The girls are in school all day. You've got no excuses anymore. And Ian *is* around a lot."

"Get a job?" Jill laughed, "If one more well-meaning friend tells me to get a job, I think I'll commit suicide."

"Jill, it's not as though I'm suggesting that you go out and hook. Anyway, you gave up a promising career. Didn't you get a promotion and a raise your first year at Philpott Associates? As I recall, they loved you."

"Promising at twenty-five is ancient history at thirty-seven. What advertising agency would hire an old bag like me? And what would I wear for an interview? Omar's out of the tent business. Pumpkin, I don't even know how much subway fare is anymore. Can't we change the subject? Let's talk about you."

"Don't, Jill. It won't help."

But Jill persevered. "What made you divorce Stephen, Pumpkin? I thought he had everything—rising young attorney, political aims on the horizon, greatest running back in Princeton history. Isn't he a partner in his law firm?"

"Guilty of all of the above. I guess we were both too busy with other things. He worked a lot. Weekends. Late at night."

"But you weren't into decorating then. What were you so busy doing? Planning the menus? Weeding the rock garden? Shopping? Puttering?" Jill hoped she didn't sound too harsh. But Pumpkin wasn't leveling with her and they both knew it.

"Touché." Pumpkin looked away. "Do you remember him at all, Jill?"

"Vaguely. I thought he was hard to talk to, but I only saw him at parties."

"He only talked to men at parties. At dinners, when he was forced to sit between two women, it was damned difficult for him. He couldn't wait for coffee and dessert so he could go into another room and go back to his football and law practice. Women seemed to be crazy about him but he was scared one of them might touch him and some sexual nuance would osmose through the sleeve of his dinner jacket."

"Naive me. I just thought I bored him. I didn't know a damn thing about football or law."

How could Pumpkin have lived with that? She was an artist. Sensitive. Vulnerable. Anxious to please. So much like her. What had happened?

"How long were you married? Before the separation, I mean, not the final decree."

"Two years. Before the mast." Pumpkin stabbed a leaf of Bibb lettuce vinaigrette.

"Funny, I thought it was longer."

"So did I. How many years is it for you, Jill? Ten? Eleven?"

"Twelve and a little more."

"Christ. And you're still speaking."

"It hasn't been *all* bad, Pumpkin. I've had some wonderful times with Ian."

"Okay." Pumpkin tossed her a look she couldn't decipher. Suddenly she felt defensive.

"Come on, Pumpkin. You can't stop now. So you and Stephen were both too busy to bother about being married. Since when is that grounds for divorce?"

"Stephen was an incurable snob. But not like Ian. He was more of a location snob than an intellectual snob. He used to say, 'I know there's intelligent life outside of our zip code. I work with it. I don't have to drink with it, too.'"

"Ian might have said something like that, but he wouldn't have meant it." Ian loved to hang out with people who belied his preppy upbringing. His favorites were horse-playing apartment building superintendents. He also adored the company of a drunken poet or writer *manqué*. Anyone he could look down on.

Pumpkin put down her salad fork. She'd hardly eaten anything. "Aside from posturing in front of others, Stephen wouldn't communicate with me.

"When I'd call him at the office, even if it was something important, he was in a meeting. Always. I'm sure it was the truth but for God's sake all meetings aren't matters of life and death. I just hated being put off. The idea that those assholes in the office took precedence over *me*—well, I just couldn't stand it after a while."

19

Pumpkin dabbed at her coral mouth. "How about some more wine as long as he's up?" She nodded to the waiter.

At least Ian had never put *her* off. He'd just sneaked around, devious and crafty, laughing as she licked her wounds.

"Stephen delighted in putting me on hold. Talking to a brick wall is no fun, Jill. You asked what he did...specifically. Well, being married to Stephen was like being married to an absentee landlord. He left me notes, cassettes with instructions. He delighted in taking the car and leaving me marooned on Saturday, in the country."

"What was he like in bed?" She still felt funny asking that.

Pumpkin winced. "Slightly less interesting than he was at dinner parties. At least he didn't talk about football."

"Oh." What was there to say now? If she'd been on the telephone, she would have pretended someone was at the door.

Pumpkin didn't seem to notice Jill's embarrassment. "He used to make me feel so guilty that I stopped being crazy about him. Everyone else was. His mother, his brother, his secretary, the senior partners, his dental hygienist. It was an impossible situation."

"What was impossible? He didn't like to talk to women at dinner parties? He didn't like to talk with you on the phone? He took the car? Those are just symptoms, Pumpkin. What was the problem?"

"Coffee? Espresso?" Pumpkin's eyes avoided hers.

"Come on." God, if someone asked her about Ian she could catalog faults faster than an auctioneer. A dark thought struck her. "Pumpkin, was he violent? Did he ever strike you?"

"Of course. But I didn't want to get into that."

"We *are* into it. Why did he hit you?"

"He said he didn't mean to. It just happened. He was exhausted. He was drunk. He was overwrought. I was stupid enough to believe him—until he broke my arm."

"Broke...your...arm?" Jill put down her fork. This was unbelievable.

"The right one. In two places. And separated my shoulder."

"How, for God's sake?" With all of his weird behavior Ian had never hit her, never even tried. He was too much of a coward.

"With the dictionary."

Jill stared at Pumpkin. "The dictionary?"

"Well, we were arguing about how to spell a word. He looked it up and he was wrong. It pissed him off. So he threw the book at me, so to speak."

"But how could a dictionary do so much damage?"

"Remember that giant one we had in the library? It was on a stand. It must have weighed forty pounds. He really heaved it at me. I put my arm up to protect my face. The impact knocked me down. When I tried to get up, he kicked my arm out from under me and walked on it. Then he kicked me in the shoulder. It seemed like the more he kicked, the more turned on he got."

"What did you do? How'd you react?"

"Very calmly. And believe me, Jill, I don't know how I stayed calm. I said, 'The Bar Association would love to know about this. So would Ballantyne, Clifford.' That's his law firm. He ran out of the room, out of the apartment. I didn't see him for two weeks."

Jill was stunned. She never would have expected this from that quiet man at the dinner party. "Christ, Pumpkin, I'm so sorry. I had no idea."

"No one does. Not even my lawyers. And I want to keep it that way. Whatever Stephen's troubles are, he worked hard for his career and he deserves it."

"What if he marries someone else? Would you warn her?"

"So far, he hasn't. He's devoted his life to the firm. What ever else he does is none of my business."

"Well, what do you think made him act like that?"

"*I* think he was jealous of me. My shrink didn't necessarily disagree. You see, he had to have me but he wanted to keep me to himself. He hated that I could talk to men *and* women, that I actually enjoyed parties. Also, it didn't exactly thrill

21

him that I was making noises about going into interior design."

"Well, at least Ian isn't jealous of me and my squaw role in society," Jill smiled.

"Don't be too sure. Now, what about you? We've digressed."

Jill wondered how Pumpkin could sit there calmly, talking matter-of-factly about a subject that usually made headlines in the *Post*. How could she be dispassionate about something so personal? So horrible? She wondered how she would react if Ian tried that on *her*.

"Am I that boring, Jill?" Pumpkin waved her hand in front of Jill's eyes. "Let's get back to *you*. What's your next step? *I* think you ought to give Madison Avenue another swipe. Forgive me for saying it, but it seems like you're in a depressing rut. God, today seems to have brought out the truth serum for both of us."

"I hope you're not going to give me a lecture about aging gracefully."

"Nope. I just think you've got to change your image of yourself."

"What do you mean?"

"Well you just referred to yourself as a 'squaw.' Somehow, Jill, I don't think that's where it's at, as they say. That simply isn't how to face life in the Eighties."

"Maybe not, Pumpkin. But you're in a visual business ...and I used to be in one. By no stretch of the imagination do I look like a Madison Avenue tycoon stepping out in my Valentino."

Jill gulped the dregs of her wine. Damn, she wished there were more.

"Jill, please don't misunderstand me—" Pumpkin began, but Jill interrupted.

"And don't tell me about all my middle-aged wisdom, understanding, courage, knowledge, and all that crap. Maybe I *do* have some of those virtues but what are they going to do for me? They sure as hell aren't going to pay the kids' tuition."

"It's what *you* have to do for *you*, Jill. My advice—and I don't care if you don't want to hear it—is for you to go back into advertising. What have you got to lose? It's the practical place to start. Decorating was the only thing I knew. It saved my life. Advertising is the only thing *you* know, Jill. Maybe it could save yours."

"But, Pumpkin, I'm so out of it. Oh, I guess I know some things. Like how to have the whitest wash on the block. How to cut grease. Prevent embarrassing underarm odor. How to cook. I even looked into opening a cooking school in my kitchen but it's against the law. You know, zoning. No offensive aromas of *coq au vin* or *blanquette de veau* are permitted to pollute the air of Badger Hollow."

Jill tore open a roll and slathered it with butter. "I guess I was relieved. I hate to cook. I only learned to keep Ian happy. And most of the time he's not home for dinner so the girls and I eat the whole thing ourselves. And, as you can see, that's the last thing I need."

"I have it, Jill," Pumpkin said, plucking the roll from Jill's fingers, "why don't you come back to New York with me for a few days? Get away from it all? Re-think things. I'm sure Ian could cope."

"I'm not so sure. And the girls? Beth would love it. But Wendy would be lost—and I'd miss her, Pumpkin."

"I'm sure you both would survive. How could they begrudge their hard-working mother a little vacation?"

"Ian doesn't think I do anything. You just don't know Ian," Jill began.

"Oh, yes I do. I'll bet you haven't had a vacation in...three years?"

"Six. Know what we sound like?"

Pumpkin shook her head. She'd never had a conversation like this in her life.

"Two C's in the K."

"What?"

"Two cunts in the kitchen. You've seen a zillion commercials like this on television. There's a woman alone, struggling with a seemingly insurmountable problem. She can't figure out which detergent to buy or which toothpaste is tougher on bad breath or which cooking oil fights cholesterol best or which toilet paper will turn her husband on. Then her next-door neighbor comes to the rescue. Convinced beyond the shadow of a doubt that the neighbor's favorite product will insure complete happiness, C number one tells C number two that she'll buy it. Hence, two C's in the K."

"That's revolting. Worse than all those crotch sprays put together." Pumpkin waved for another round. She'd have lots of black coffee later.

"Those commercials are called 'slice of life.' You don't have to be Anna Freud to understand *that*." Jill giggled.

"Okay, then, Jill, what about a slice of life, Manhattan-style?"

"You know," mused Jill, ignoring Pumpkin's invitation, "I feel as though I've lived through every 'slice of life' commercial on television. I live in the kitchen, you know. It's where the action is."

"Jill, you'd have a ball in New York."

"I'm dying to visit you, Pumpkin. God knows I could use a change of scene. But I'm afraid of Ian. He gets so jealous."

"Well, no one ever accused him of rampant maturity." Pumpkin slicked on a ribbon of coral lipstick.

"I suppose I *could* stock the fridge. Some TV dinners and Chunky Soup," said Jill timidly. She did want to go to New York. More than anything in a long time.

"I know," said Pumpkin, "let's take them a couple of ducks from right here. Gourmet treat. Less guilt for mother. You'll be back in two days, so what's the big deal?"

Jill stared into her lap. "I want to go, God knows..." she began, biting her lip.

But Pumpkin didn't hear her. She was busy ordering the ducks, more coffee and the check. She handed her American Express card to the waiter.

Jill had never had an American Express card. She had never had any kind of credit card. Ian didn't believe in credit. He'd always paid cash for everything, even their Buick.

"If you can't afford to pay for it, you can't afford to buy it," he'd always said, a philosophy he claimed had been instilled in him by his grandmother, Rose-Delia.

Until this moment, it hadn't really bothered Jill. But she realized now that if she had a Visa, she could treat Pumpkin to lunch. She could have the dent taken out of the back fender. She could buy some clothes that fit. She could hold up her head in the supermarket.

"Okay," Pumpkin said decisively, "let's go." Jill felt a surge of excitement. She was actually going to spend two days and nights in New York. For the first time in almost twelve years! Two whole days and nights of doing something besides feeling depressed.

She hadn't felt so exhilarated since she'd played the lead in Smith College's production of *Rebecca*.

CHAPTER TWO

*P*umpkin's penthouse, floating high above the East River, was a far cry from Jill's Tudor house on Badger Hollow Lane.

"It's dazzling, Pumpkin. Absolutely dazzling," Jill sighed.

"Wait till I'm finished. I've only been here a few weeks, you know. Haven't even started on the dining room."

The dining room? Jill had never been in an apartment with a dining room before. She tiptoed past a white satin loveseat. "That looks like a Winslow Homer. And, my God, that's a Hopper, isn't it?"

"Right on both counts. Now, let's have a drink and get down to business. Perrier? Fresca? Tab?"

"Scotch, thank you. And what business? I thought I was here for a fantasy trip. To see how the fabled Pumpkin Endicott-Osborne lives. The reality behind the myth."

"I'm referring to the business of what you're going to do with the rest of your life."

"But I know exactly what I'm going to do with the rest of my life," Jill said resolutely. She smiled at Pumpkin.

"Sit around waiting for Ian to get yet another lousy job, take out the garbage and drive you to orgasm?"

Jill winced. She had to admit, after twelve years, orgasms were still Ian's greatest talent.

"You've got to start moving your butt, Jill," Pumpkin barked, pouring a scotch into a brandy snifter. "You've got to crawl out of the mud forever." She thrust the glass toward her.

"And how do you propose I do that? I mean, without a benefactor, I couldn't even make it from Badger Hollow to Beekman Place."

"I can't believe I'm hearing this. Jill Hodges Harrington, former prom queen, former valedictorian, former best-dressed and most-likely-to-succeed."

"That's it. *Former.*"

"Jill, you've got to take the bullshit by the horns." Pumpkin rose from the white pigskin Regency side chair and extended her arms dramatically. "And *I* am going to help you. You are my project."

"But Pumpkin," Jill said forlornly, "I'm not an apartment. You can't just redecorate me."

"Want to bet?" grinned Pumpkin. "In two months, you won't recognize yourself. Come."

Pumpkin's bathroom was right off her bedroom. It was equipped with a three-way mirror, sunlamp, massage table, sauna, whirlpool, exercycle and mini beauty salon.

"Okay, Jill, strip to your panty hose."

Jill looked stricken. "Panty hose?"

"Right. You are going to face yourself just as I do. In that uncompromising mirror." Pumpkin flicked a switch. The room flooded with unkind fluorescent light.

"Christ," moaned Jill, "where'd you learn your technique? The KGB?"

Pumpkin stalked her with a tape measure. "Hold out your arm."

"Upper arm, sixteen inches." Pumpkin jotted the information down as she spoke.

When all of Jill's measurements had been duly recorded,

Pumpkin directed Jill to take a good, long look in the mirror. "Your past and present, Jill. Now we shall go to work on your future."

Who was this lump? This gelatinous blob?

"You've got to shed thirty or forty pounds. I'm not really sure how much. We'll take it ten at a time. And then, we'll have your hair restyled. And we'll give you a pedicure. Then a manicure. And a resumé."

"Resumé?"

"Right. In two short months, you are going to hit the pavement. You are not going to make cheesecake or pies. You're not going to cater weddings or Bar Mitzvahs. You're going to have a career—and an attaché case."

Jill's voice quavered. "Pumpkin, be realistic. I can't get a job. I can't even get an interview. And I don't think I can type anymore."

"I was referring to a job where you type your own work, not other people's. A career. Okay?"

"Pumpkin, you don't know how hard this is for me. I have to talk to myself just to make a shopping list...just to get to the supermarket."

"Talk to yourself?" Now what was Jill trying to hand her?

"Not out loud, exactly. It's the same thing I did when I had to pass the swimming test in college. Remember the five-pound rubber brick and how everyone had to dive into the deep end and bring the brick back up?"

Pumpkin nodded, expecting the worst.

"Well, to get through the rubber brick parts of my life, I have to talk to myself. Now do you understand?"

"Exactly what do you say to yourself, Jill?"

"Well," Jill hesitated, "things like 'OK, Jill, you're going to take this list and you're going to go out into the driveway and get into the car and turn on the ignition. Then you're going to drive the one-point-two miles to the shopping center. Then, you're going to park the car. Lock it. And go into the supermarket. Then, you're going to get a cart and start pushing it, beginning on the left with the bread, rolls and muffins.'"

Pumpkin stared at Jill in disbelief.

"Listen Pumpkin, if I hadn't had too much to drink I would never have admitted this. I know it sounds crazy."

"Don't give it another thought. Your dreaded dark secret is safe with me. But now we've got to move it. Neville is picking us up in twenty minutes. We're going to the Four Seasons for dinner, so we have to look glamorous."

"Neville?"

"My newest best friend from London. Neville Leopard, Lord Russelshire. He and I are in business together, sort of."

"How can *I* meet Lord Russelshire? With my safety pins and ratty camel's hair blazer? Oh, Pumpkin, it's hopeless."

"Nonsense."

"But I've been under so much pressure lately. All I want to do is go to bed and watch TV."

"You're never going to go to bed and watch TV again. Ever. You're going to wear my tent dress. For obvious reasons. And pink panty hose. And my pink shoes. You used to be able to wear my shoes."

"I hope they're sandals and they stretch and that the heels aren't over half an inch. I don't want to fall and break my hip."

Pumpkin thrust a pair of pink cobra ankle-strap sandals with four inch heels toward her. "These should do. Now, at the Four Seasons, I want you to order a grilled fish. Don't touch the rolls and butter. And pretend you hate dessert. It's easy. I do it all the time. If you can't stand it, go to the ladies' room until they take the dessert cart away."

Guilt pricked Jill's body. "Pumpkin, do you think they're all right? Do you think they like the ducks? I really shouldn't be going out with you and Lord What's-his-name."

"Hurry up," snapped Pumpkin. "Neville is probably walking into the lobby right now. And he hates to be kept waiting."

"Pumpkin, you don't understand, do you?"

"What?"

"How lousy I feel having run away from home on a lark. I'm supposed to be a responsible adult."

"You *are* a responsible adult. On holiday. About to go to the ultimate responsible adult restaurant for some stimulating conversation with two other responsible adults. Hurry up."

Resigned, Jill slithered into Pumpkin's tent and cobra spikes. She splashed herself with Chanel 19. She was enjoying herself and that made her feel even guiltier than enjoying Ian's peculiar brand of lovemaking.

Voices in the foyer. Pumpkin's suddenly an octave lower, and a bass-baritone telling Pumpkin how devastating she looked. When had Ian told her she looked devastating? Ever? The sharp ring of the telephone blanked out Lord Russelshire in mid-compliment. It was probably something dreadful. It usually was when the phone rang.

"For you, Jill," Pumpkin trilled.

"Mother, you've got to come home immediately," cried Wendy. "The most awful thing has happened. Hurry." The line went dead.

CHAPTER THREE

"*Oh, Pumpkin*, I feel as if I've been washed up on the banks of the River Styx," Jill sobbed on the phone from Badger Hollow. "Yesterday, when the girls got home from their music lessons, the kitchen was in flames. *Engulfed*. The idiot, Ian, had put the ducks under the broiler. The *broiler*, Pumpkin. Then he wandered off to the public library. Lately, he's always there. Anyhow, the oven caught fire. The heat from it set the wallpaper off, which somehow shorted out the refrigerator. The kitchen floor is gone. Totally. And what wasn't burned was ruined by water and smoke." She blew her nose. "What am I going to do now?"

"What is Ian doing?" Pumpkin asked guardedly.

"Sitting in the yard reading John Donne. He says the house smells too awful. It's affecting his sinuses."

"Jill, you've got to get a lawyer."

"A lawyer? I need a contractor. A painter. A paperhanger. A fairy godmother, maybe. The last thing I need is a lawyer."

"Well, then, you need someone to give you orders. That's me, and my orders are: Pack some things. Grab the girls. Hop on a train. The girls can sleep in my dining room until the other guest room is ready next week."

"I can't do that. The girls would miss school."

"Then enroll them at Laurel Hill as boarding students."

"Laurel *Hall*, Pumpkin. Laurel Hill is a mental institution. And besides, I can't afford to enroll them as boarding students. And I don't even have the money for three train tickets."

"I'll send a limo up. It'll be there in an hour."

"But what good would that do, Pumpkin? I know you're trying to help me, but it isn't going to work." Her voice rose on a wave of hysteria.

"Jill, stop worrying. I'll lend you the money. How much is it?"

"Somewhere around eight thousand. I've got all that back tuition, remember?"

Pumpkin didn't remember. "Okay. I can swing it. You can pay me back when you get your job and in the meantime, you can work for me. The fascinating world of interior design awaits you."

"It won't work."

"Of course it'll work. But you have to want it to."

"I do, but I don't want to abandon my children. I don't even want them around that maniac anymore. Look what happened when I took one evening off. A conflagration. And it could have been worse. Suppose they'd been burned or suffered smoke inhalation. You're not a mother. You wouldn't understand." Jill's voice shook.

"I've got it, Jill," Pumpkin said calmly. "Ask the girls. My guess is that they'd love to board. Back in the Dark Ages when I went to Miss Webster's, the boarders always had more fun. There was more—well, camaraderie after classes."

"Well, I guess you have a point. The girls might be a lot happier boarding. It would keep them away from that pyromaniac and free my conscience."

"Good."

"Pumpkin, you're playing on my nerves, which are currently dragging across my sodden living room carpet. You've caught me in a weak moment, so I'll take orders."

"Call Laurel. Tell them you want an appointment to enroll the girls. Find out how much. Call me back. I'll be there with a check. Then, we'll pack and we'll be back in town in time for dinner. Neville was devastated last night."

Suddenly, Jill felt hopeful. "Sounds great. I'll call you back in a few minutes. And Pumpkin," she added, fighting back tears, "thanks." She hung up and thumbed to Laurel Hall in her ragged little address book.

"Jill, you can't pack up and leave, just like that." Ian gave Jill a long, sullen look. "What am *I* supposed to do?"

"I'm not exactly packing up, I just need to get away for a few days. I don't have the strength for all of this at the moment."

"You know what you have, Jill? Terminal feminine itch! You just can't let well enough alone. You and those goddamn feminists don't know a good thing when you've got it."

"I'm sick of the situation, Ian."

"Sick of the situation, Ian," he mimicked her. "What situation, exactly, my darling?"

"The one you've created." Jill's face burned. "From now on, I refuse to let you do this to me and to Wendy and to Bethy."

"So you're going to shuffle off to New York with that bitch-goddess friend of yours and get a job because I am driving you away from home. Gentle, charming me. Scholar. Humanitarian. Aesthete."

Did Ian really believe that?

Jill watched in horror as he got up, sauntered to the window and stared at the kitchen table in the yard.

"I haven't changed one iota since we got married. I told you that I didn't want to bother with the Rat Race. I still don't. And you know why. When Rose-Delia kicks off, we won't have to worry about a thing."

"Feeding your children and your wife right now, today, is the issue, Ian."

"You don't exactly look underfed, pet."

This time she wouldn't play into his hands.

"You know I'll get a job, Jill. Christ, I've sent out nearly four hundred resumés. You've seen me sitting by the telephone."

"It seems to me that you could spend more time job-hunting and less at the library."

"The library is my only recreation. And it's almost free."

"I've begged you to change careers. I've suggested that we move away from New York so that you could be a big fish. I've said over and over that I'd go back to work. The girls are in school and they have after-school activities. Music lessons. If you supervised their homework..."

"Jill," Ian yawned, "why are we going back over this again?"

"Christ, Ian, why do you have to fight me every step of the way? I thought you loved me."

"You said it. Loved. Past tense. You're a nagging bitch, Jill. You've turned into a harridan." He sighed, closed his eyes.

"You bastard. I wish you were Jason Picker."

"Jason Picker? That midget faggot?"

"Jason Picker is the most charming man I've ever met."

"Jason Picker is a dilettante. A teacher of high school English who mistakenly believes he can direct inept middle-aged broads like you in bad, dull plays for the Community Theater. In *A Doll's House*. What a laugh!"

"It was *Gaslight*, you bastard." Jill picked up the Waterford crystal table lamp Ian had given her for their tenth anniversary and hurled it across the room. Ian stepped aside, and the lamp crashed through the window, landing beside the kitchen table in the yard.

"Cocksucker," Jill shrieked.

"Jason, yes. Me, no." Ian smirked.

"You're jealous of Jason Picker. *He's* written a novel. He's had a wonderful career. He's in *Who's Who*. You wouldn't catch Jason Picker putting cooked ducks under a broiler and traipsing off to the library. Jason Picker is a gentleman."

"Just don't bend over in the gentleman's room."

"Ian, you *are* a consummate horse's ass. Pumpkin was right."

"Ahh. The sainted Pumpkin. You won't find any moss growing on her ass."

"Or her bank account."

"What an enlightening conversation we're having. First, the riveting Jason Picker, who hires lithe young boys to break in his tweeds. And now the scintillating Pumpkin Endicott-Osborne, decorator to fast-food society. God!"

"You're jealous of Pumpkin, too. You've always been jealous of my relationships. Every single one. You're probably jealous of my relationship with our daughters."

"Really, Jill, I think you should lie down."

"You've insulted my friends. You can't even stand to have me speak to them on the phone. I suppose it's your own quaint way of keeping me pregnant in summer and barefoot in winter, or however that saying goes. I wish Daddy were here. He would have something to say to you."

"Your father loved me. So did your mother. *I* was the one who finally took their aging daughter off their hands, remember?"

"Twenty-five is hardly aging. This is not the seventeenth century, Ian, although I know you wish it were. And it may interest you to know that I did go to bed with Jason Picker. Lots of times. At the Community Theater. In the star's dressing room."

"How did he measure up? No pun intended."

"Ian, we've got to discuss the kitchen. It's going to cost almost seven thousand to put it back together. You totalled it, you know."

"How easily you sink into the mundane, my dear."

"First, there's the sub-floor. We have to have a new one. In short, it's almost like adding an entire new room. I'm going to get a job, too. I don't give a damn what you say. I'm borrowing the money from Pumpkin to pay Laurel Hall. The girls are going to board there. And while I'm at it, I might as well borrow the money to fix the kitchen. Pumpkin offered."

"I don't want to borrow a red cent from that cunt. I'd starve in the gutter first."

"You are not borrowing a red cent from that cunt, as you so graciously put it. *I'm* doing the borrowing. The floor has to be replaced. Suppose we sell the house?"

"Sell the house? Can't you commute to this wonderful new job in Never-Never Land? The mythical career that's meant to pay off the national debt you've incurred?"

Jill said nothing. There was nothing more to say. She'd made up her mind. All she needed was the strength to follow through with her plans.

"Where am I supposed to live, Jill?"

"You wouldn't be the first person to get an apartment through the *New York Times*. After all, Ian, it *is* my house. My parents left it to me." It was the first time in twelve years she had ever reminded Ian of that.

Ian looked forlorn. "So you keep reminding me. Well, I guess that's that." He paused.

Jill felt the old guilt return. How could she leave this pathetic creature on his own?

He came toward her, holding out his arms. "I didn't really mean it. You never mention that it's your house. I'm sorry. I worship you, Jill."

How many times had she heard that? But it still worked. She hesitated.

He pulled at her bra right through her blouse. The safety pins gave. He ripped off her blouse and bra. Her pink-and-white breasts flopped free. His hands were fondling her with an urgency that made her quake. She responded instinctively, confounded by her weakness. She wanted him. His penis, bloated and purple, stabbed through the hole beneath the string of his pajama pants.

Jill stared at it, like she was watching a movie.

Was she this desperate for love? To be Mrs. Ian Harrington?

Maybe Pumpkin was right. Maybe she'd put up with anything for this.

In one determined motion, Ian pushed Jill backward onto the sofa, plunged into her and came. Jill sighed. That was it. If she never went to bed with a man again, this would be the last time she'd let Ian touch her.

"How does that compare with Jason Picker?" He stood up and dried his penis on her discarded blouse.

CHAPTER FOUR

Jill stared into the full-length mirror at Alex & Walter's Physical Fitness Studio. One hundred twenty-eight pounds, poured into a black leotard, stared back at her. Only eight pounds and she'd hit one-twenty, the mystical, magical number that had eluded her since before Wendy's birth.

When Jill had confessed her inability to stick with a diet, Pumpkin had replied, "Fine. Try them all."

She'd gotten diarrhea from the fruit diet, bad breath from the protein diet, constipation from the egg-and-grapefruit diet. Now she was on the broth diet and in two days, it would be the broiled-fish-and-tomato diet.

Now she had the energy of a ninety-year-old carp nestling in the mud at the bottom of a mountain tarn, but she looked great.

Wearily, she pulled off the leotard and tights and stuffed them into her tote. All she had to do was get dressed and walk—briskly—back to Pumpkin's. Every muscle in her body ached. She longed to take the Fifty-Seventh Street crosstown bus. But what if Pumpkin found out? And somehow she knew Pumpkin would.

For the past eight weeks, Jill had been on a regimen the Army would have been proud of. Exercise at home the second her feet hit the floor in the morning. Three bites of breakfast. A brisk walk to Pumpkin's office, "Department of the Interior," ten blocks away. Run errands. Deliver lampshades. Scoot all over with swatches. Eat two bites of lunch. Run around all afternoon with wallpaper and floor plans. How could so many people afford to spend so much money on décor?

Then, on to Alex and Walter's gym at four-thirty every afternoon for a private workout with Alex himself. In five days, he had Jill swinging from the trapeze, leaping onto the parallel bars, hanging from the rings with her legs over her head. She couldn't believe it.

She walked out onto West Fifty-Sixth Street, determined to avoid the temptation of bars, restaurants, delis and bakeries.

"It's been worth every sacrifice," she confided to Pumpkin.

"Sacrifice? Giving up Hostess Twinkies and Instant Café Vienna was a sacrifice? How about Kool Aid? Was that a sacrifice, too?" Pumpkin had snapped. "Those people in Jonestown didn't have to add any cyanide, you know."

Jill leaned closer to catch her reflection in a window. Gone were the bags under the eyes, the puffy cheeks, the blotchy skin. With a clear, smooth complexion, deep blue-green eyes, and high cheekbones she was—yes—beautiful.

Last week she'd thrown her thirty-eight C Minimizer bras—safety pins and all—into the incinerator. They reminded her of the day she'd dumped all her maternity clothes into the Goodwill bin in the supermarket parking lot.

She'd spoken to the girls twice a week. They both loved boarding at Laurel Hall, especially Bethy. They couldn't wait for the first big weekend in New York.

She had not spoken to Ian. He had written her several garbled letters telling her that the kitchen had been fixed and that he had learned how to make coffee. He rambled on about his philosophy, and something about his plans to sing in an opera and hike across Montana. As far as she knew, the longest walk Ian had ever taken was up to a window in the unemployment office. Once, his strange, wild dreams and labyrinthine ideas had intrigued her. Once, she dreamed of laying bare his secret side. Now, she yawned just thinking about him. Pumpkin was right. She had to get a divorce.

Jill dove into Pumpkin's old green cashmere turtleneck and shook out her short strawberry-blonde curls. Her second day in New York, Pumpkin had dragged her to Monsieur Augustin, who'd slashed nine inches from her pageboy and curled the remaining wisps into a cap of glistening ringlets. When she'd gotten the courage to open her eyes, she'd gasped. Her face had never been so round! If nothing else, this haircut would keep her on a diet.

"Do not worry, Madame Osborne's friend," Monsieur Augustin had purred, "in two weeks you will kiss zee mirror."

Jill leaned closer and did just that.

Ian was sprawled on Pumpkin's charcoal pigskin sofa, struggling with last Sunday's *Times* crossword. He always gave himself half an hour to solve it before he plunged into a deep depression. A half-empty bottle of Dewar's stood on the floor beside the sofa.

"Ian. Well." What was there to say except "what the fuck do you want now?" But Jill thought better of it. Pumpkin was having people in for drinks at six o'clock.

That morning, Pumpkin had promised that it would be a great party. "You'll have a fabulous time. Everyone will love you. It'll be a real ego boost. All sorts of interesting people. A couple of advertising buddies who may just be looking for a glamorous copywriter. Good business contacts. A headhunter. A real estate tycoon. And, Da-Da, a movie star of an account man from one of the hot agencies. You'll devour him if he doesn't devour you first. You can play prom queen all over again. Whatever you do, don't be late. Wear my silver gauze dress and the Maude Frizon shoes. The silver and purple ones. Tonight is *important*." Then, Pumpkin had fled with a bolt of three-hundred-dollars-a-yard chintz under her arm. All sorts of interesting people. And Ian. Dirty button-down shirt with only one button. Corduroy trousers that could walk by themselves. No socks. A pair of Hush Puppies from the tombs of the Caesars. Pale blonde stubble glistening on his cheeks in the diffused light from the Tiffany lamp.

"I need a hundred, Jill," he said thickly, "then I'll be on my way."

She watched him as one watches an exotic animal at the zoo. She had actually slept with this man. For years. Gone down on him. Suffered through having two children with him. And if someone asked her who he was, she'd have to answer: "I have no idea."

"A hundred?" she said weakly. She had well over a hundred in her bureau drawer. Pumpkin had put her on salary, and paid her in cash, since her first day in New York.

"Just give it to him, stupid," her little voice said. "Give it to him right now and get him the hell out of here before Pumpkin gets home. Before the guests start to arrive."

Jill marched to her room, pulled open the top drawer of a highly-polished Biedermier chest and took out ten crisp tens. She counted them twice before returning to the living room where Ian was guzzling from the bottle of Dewar's.

"One hundred dollars." She thrust the bills toward him. He made no move to take them. She scattered them across the crossword puzzle. "Excuse me, Ian, but I must dress for a party."

"Thanks," he mumbled putting down the bottle. "Party, huh? Here? Lots of faggots and dikes. That's what New York parties are all about. Been to plenty of 'em. Can't believe you left my bed for faggots and dikes."

Panic gripped Jill. As thin as he was, Ian was a head taller than she. She couldn't possibly use force to get him out of Pumpkin's living room. What would Pumpkin have done? But Pumpkin would never be in this mess.

Quietly, Jill turned and started down the little hallway,

back to her room. Why risk being late for the party? She slipped out of her sweater and jeans.

In fifteen minutes, Jill had done her face the way the makeup man at Elizabeth Arden had taught her. Two more minutes for panty hose and shoes. Thirty seconds to zip into the silver gauze dress and Pumpkin's David Webb crystal necklace.

When she returned to the living room, Ian had slid off the sofa and was wedged between it and the cocktail table. She had to get him up and out. But how? She could hear Pumpkin's housekeeper, Tansy, joking with the bartenders. Any minute now the first guests would be arriving. She wanted to kick Ian with her Maude Frizon spike heels.

"May I help?" asked a clipped voice from the shadows near the fireplace.

Jill spun around. Noël St. Martin! She recognized him from his photographs in "W." One of the most famous painters in New York. He wore a black Persian lamb blazer, white flannel trousers and gold reflective contact lenses.

"This... person seems to be in his cups," Jill said flatly.

"Salmonella, perhaps?" Noël suggested. "You must be Jill Harrington. Pumpkin speaks of no one else. Why has she hidden you away for so long?"

God forbid Noël St. Martin should find out.

"Pumpkin tells me that you have decided to trade the joys of bucolic motherhood for the challenge of the Big Apple." Noël winked. The lenses sparkled.

Jill smiled with confidence. "Could you help me lift him?" She gestured toward the sleeping man.

"Let's get the old boy into Tansy's room for the duration. I hear he's been giving you and your daughters a rough time. I'll take his shoulders and you grab his feet."

They inched Ian's dead weight through the dining room, into the kitchen where Tansy was making eyes for the salmon mousse from sliced stuffed olives.

"Hel-lo, what does we have here?" Tansy exclaimed. Although she had been born on St. Kitt's, in the West Indies, and reared in Harlem, Tansy somehow managed to sound just like Scarlett's Mammy.

"Look lak this gennelmum needs ter sleep it off. Doan you fret, Miz Jilly. He's goin to be awright in mah room. Ah'll keep mah hands off'n him," she laughed. Her big belly shook. So did her wig.

"Oh, Tansy, thank you. I don't know what I would have done with my—husband. He's been a real pain lately."

"Thas one thing husbins kin be."

"I think I only stayed married so long because we had the girls... my daughters."

"Shucks, chile, that ain no reason to stay married. I had mah girls long 'fore ah met the Revrun Mosbry. Took me years to decide. Ah said to mahself, Tansy, you got these heah chillun, you got ter git them a papa. So's ah did. Ya know, Miz Jilly, there's a lid for evry pot an you goin' fines yours."

It was a way to look at things.

Anorexic women gleamed and slithered like lizards across the room. Dresses of metallic cloth, sequins, and bugle beads moved close to hiss at each other's cheeks and then away into new territory.

Jill was in a daze. This had to be a movie. At least a miniseries.

Jill met Lucy Farrington, the actress who had made her stage debut shortly before World War I and was now on *Love Boat*; Maggie Sletzer, the doyenne of Manhattan real estate; six twittering painters of far less renown than Noël St. Martin; Selena Markingham, *the* literary agent; Countess Vanna Pijarski, the Russian decorator, Pumpkin's biggest rival; and finally, Sallie Moreton. Sallie was to cuisine what Pumpkin was to interior design. And she used Pumpkin's parties as test kitchens for her newest creations. Tonight, there was baked Brie to be eaten with small slices of apple, caviar-and-cream cheese lollipops and tiny eggs Benedict, made with quail eggs. There were no raw vegetables—definitely "out."

Jill was struck by all these successful women. She'd never been to a party like this on Badger Hollow Lane.

"I sense that you're about to ask the identity of the apparition bearing down on us," said Noël St. Martin.

A tall, thin woman with larkspur hair and a flutter of bangle bracelets was working her way through the crowd like she was running for office.

"She's certainly captured the Mother Theresa of Calcutta look," Noël said with a grin.

"I think she scares me," whispered Jill.

"I know she scares me," Noël confided. "Her name is Charlene Whitrock. She's an associate creative director at one of those big-business advertising agencies. DDB or BBDO or BD something or other. They all sound like vitamin pills. Better brace yourself, Jill. She's looking for a copywriter and Pumpkin has been promoting you like crazy. Hope you're wearing armor under your Halston."

Charlene Whitrock bulldozed her way toward Jill, elbowed Noël St. Martin to one side and clamped Jill's arm with the force of a tourniquet. Is this what Pumpkin meant about controlling your own destiny?

"Pumpkin's told me all about you, Jill," oozed Charlene. "She convinced me that you could do a lot of good for me and for yourself, of course, in my group at BDK&C."

Jill was taken off guard. How should she respond? She hadn't worked in twelve years. But BDK&C was the fourth largest agency in the world. She'd wanted to work there, years ago, when she was struggling along at dumpy little Philpott Associates.

"How do you do?" Jill said coolly, extending her hand. "I haven't worked since 19..." She hesitated. "My reel is..."

"Already seen your reel. Pumpkin sent it over by messenger yesterday. With your resumé. I know more about you than the CIA. Now be a good girl and come over to my office around eleven tomorrow morning."

"But tomorrow is... Saturday." Jill felt weak. This was all

too much. And the girls were coming in for their big weekend in New York.

"You're damn right it's Saturday, love," barked Charlene. "I get more done on Saturdays and Sundays than on any other days of the week. No phones. No interruptions. No distractions. My secretary comes in to make coffee and type. We'll talk." Charlene crept a sinewy arm around Jill's shoulders. Something cracked. Cartilage? Bangle bracelets?

"I'm not sure I can handle this," Jill said to Noël. "I think I'm in over my head." What did Noël St. Martin care? *He* didn't have to worry about a job. Or the girls. Or a drunk soon-to-be-ex-husband probably trying to scratch his way out of Tansy's room at this very moment. She dreaded seeing Ian at the end of the party. "Shit," she murmured.

"You can handle anything," Noël slurred, listing slightly. "All you have to do is *act* as sensational as you look."

Jill didn't feel sensational.

"Wing it," Noël added. "Do you think I got famous through sheer talent? No one does, my dear. Work your ass off. And you will if you go to work for that old cunt, Charlie Whitrock."

Noël sipped his martini. "The world belongs to those who persevere," he belched. "If you come in second, you might as well come in last." He bent down and kissed Jill on the cheek. "I tell myself shit like that all the time. Keeps the old ego churning. Think I'll have a final martini before they send my liver to Arizona."

Jill stood alone watching the guests funnel into the foyer and out into the hall.

A navy chalk striped suit, looking as if it were still on its hanger loomed toward her. A citrusy cologne scented the air, along with Pumpkin's Rigaud candles. The breast pocket handkerchief was creased into three perfect, snowy Alps.

"Forgive me, Jill," a voice said warmly. "I've been trying to get through this crush for an hour."

"I'm Keefe Neuman," he began, "and Pumpkin..."

"Has told you all about me," Jill finished with a laugh.

She studied him. Height: six. Weight: one-sixty. Hair: black-shot-with-pewter. Eyes: blue-gray. Age: somewhere between thirty-five and fifty. Roles: president; oil magnate; pilot; breaker-of-hearts.

"Nice to meet you, Keefe." The girlishness of her voice surprised her. "That's an unusual name. Keefe."

"It's really O'Keefe. Worse, huh? My mother was *Abie's Irish Rose*, so to speak. May I get you a drink?"

She'd been doing so well with her Perrier. What the hell. "Scotch and soda, please."

At nine-fifteen, the party slammed shut. No one was left but Noël St. Martin and Keefe. Noël sat upright in an oyster silk bergere. Pumpkin wiped an ice cube across her forehead. Jill stared out the window. Keefe moved toward them with three scotches and one martini on a tray. He smiled.

"How are you liking New York?"

Jill didn't know what to say. She didn't want to sound like a hick. "You know, I didn't quite believe Pumpkin when she told me that the party would be over before nine. I thought we'd be shoveling them out at midnight. That's how it is in the suburbs."

It was the first time Jill had been able to choke out the word. Ian had always insisted on calling Badger Hollow "the country," something it hadn't been since the first half of the nineteenth century.

"Well, Jill-O, how'd you like your coming out party?" asked Pumpkin, stuffing the last of the caviar lollipops into her coral mouth. Why was it that her lipstick never seemed to wear off or smear onto her teeth?

Before Jill could answer, Keefe bent to kiss Pumpkin on both cheeks. He shook Jill's hand and parked his glass on the marble mantelpiece. "I'm on a plane to the coast first thing. Good luck with Charlie, Jill."

"Charlie?"

"Charlene Whitrock. Don't let her yap at you. She's all talk. I'll buy you a drink. Soon." His pinstriped figure disappeared into the foyer.

"Well, well, well! I guess we liked our coming out party," Pumpkin laughed. "I see we've made a conquest."

Jill felt her face warming. He *was* damned attractive.

"Well, out with it. What do you think of him? O'Keefe Neuman, the Brooklyn Adonis."

"He's perfectly charming," Jill said a bit too quickly. She didn't need Pumpkin grilling her. She was worried about tomorrow. Charlene. The interview. What to wear. What to say. And there was something about Keefe Neuman. First she'd wanted him to go. Then she'd wanted him to stay. It was all too confusing.

"I see you broke down and had a drink," Pumpkin accused.

"I almost made it. Almost. But unlike you, Pumpkin, I was born two drinks under par."

Pumpkin laughed. "Good line. May I steal it?"

"Steal away. But it doesn't sound like you. *You* emerged from the womb liberated. You're Lucy Mott. Emma Goldman. Susan B. Anthony."

"Hardly Susan B. Anthony," Pumpkin drawled. "Susan B. Anthony founded the Women's Christian Temperance Union." Pumpkin sank into an oyster silk pouf. "Incidentally, where is the fair Ian? Not that I give a rat's ass."

As if on cue, Ian materialized, and leaned heavily against the side of a delicate Chippendale breakfront. He was still wearing the button-down shirt but his corduroys had given way to a pair of faded blue boxer shorts. "I have an announcement to make."

"Shit," Jill muttered. What next?

"You are looking at the next Don Giovanni. We open in Vermont, I think. Maybe New Hampshire. Whatever. Anyhow, we open somewhere in four weeks. And it's going to be the greatest production ever mounted." He lurched against the breakfront. It wiggled. "We're doing it in modern dress. T-shirts. Jeans. Running shoes. Sweat suits. I've been practicing for months."

"Why, Ian, I didn't know you sang," Pumpkin yawned.

"I sing like Caruso. Corelli. Pavarotti. I was in the Yale

Glee Club. I tried out for the Met."

"But you dropped the spear." Pumpkin fixed herself a drink. "The way we're doing *Don Giovanni* is very interesting. The Don loved fast women... right?"

Pumpkin, Jill and Noël nodded.

"And what goes with fast women? Fast cars! The Don would love fast cars if he were here today."

Pumpkin added an extra splash of scotch. Twelve years of this? Poor Jill. No wonder.

"And what goes with fast women and fast cars?" No one said a word. "Fast food!"

Pumpkin gagged on her drink.

"*Sooo*, we're setting the opera in a Burger King. *Là ci darem la mano, là mi dirai di sì,*" he bellowed, and pitched forward, taking the Chippendale breakfront with him.

Pumpkin, stony-faced, intoned from the depths of the pigskin sofa, "One Tang Dynasty pottery bull, one pair of Ch'ien Lung cloisonné dogs, four sixteenth-century Venetian goblets and three panes of original glass. And that's just the bottom shelf."

"Oh, Pumpkin, what can I do?" wailed Jill.

"Get Tansy, if she's still up, and a dustpan and brush."

"Up? Up? De walls of Jer-i-cho come tumblin' down and ya want ter know if ah's up."

"Listen, Jill, if that cocksucker tries anything tomorrow," Pumpkin indicated the sprawling Ian with the toe of her bronze pump, "you have my permission to zonk him over the head with this." She handed Jill a 600-year-old gray porcelain vase filled with white tulips. "And by the way, Jilly, how did you ever let Ian get the upper hand? He seems to have no control over his own life and all the control over yours."

"If I knew the answer to that, Pumpkin, I wouldn't be standing here like an idiot, owing you millions. Plus my life."

"Relax. Everything is covered under my insurance policy."

"And what about one Mr. Harrington?" They'd almost forgotten Noël St. Martin was still there. He rose unsteadily from his chair. "Is he covered, too? Pumpkin, my love, may I sleep in the library? I think you ladies might need some masculine protection."

"By all means." Pumpkin began picking up the shards. Jill and Noël tried to move Ian. It was harder than before the party.

Ian opened his eyes. "Ah, the great artist. Shall we discuss the Mannerism of El Greco? The neoclassicism of David? Or perhaps Fauvism is more to your liking? Matisse, *peut-être?*"

"Shh, Ian, I think we should get you to bed." Jill was bone tired. "You've had a busy day."

"I have it," Ian cried with renewed strength, "Pointillism. *Aimez-vous* Seurat?" His head fell sideways and he passed out.

Tansy, Noël, Jill and Pumpkin dragged him slowly to the Louis XVI daybed in the dining room and Jill covered him with a mohair throw.

"One last thing, Jill," said Pumpkin, pretending to yawn, "don't fall in love with Keefe Neuman. You won't get anywhere. No one does." I couldn't, she thought.

"It never crossed my mind," Jill replied. Fall in love? That was at the pit of her priorities. Things had been a hell of a lot easier when she had had only The Bills to worry about.

She opened the door to her room. A snoring lump lay across the bed. The years broke over her in a punishing, asphyxiating wave. Gently, she nudged Ian's shoulder. Nothing. She squeezed her eyes shut. This had been the most exhausting day of her life. How had Ian found the stamina to get in here? Twenty minutes ago, when they had deposited him in the dining room, it seemed impossible that he would be able to move a hair before morning.

"Why are you waking me up, you sadist?" he grunted. "You're delighting in this when you know I have a heavy day tomorrow."

So he hadn't passed out after all. He probably hadn't even been drunk. Another of Ian's little jokes. Jill sighed.

"I gave you the hundred dollars. Why don't you leave?"

"Where would I go? The Plaza? The girls arrive at eleven tomorrow and we're going bicycling in Central Park."

"Ian, you promised to leave." Desperation edged her voice.

"And we all know that I've never broken a promise in my life. You are a moron."

"Well, it's about time you kept a promise. Because if you don't, Ian, this time I'm getting a divorce."

"Jill, I'm really bored with your terminal case of feminine itch. Itching to leave home. Itching to get a job at that advertising agency. And now, you're itching after that Neuman character. Don't deny it. I heard your beloved Pumpkin: 'Don't fall in love with Keefe Neuman.' Well, you goddamn well better not fall in love with Keefe Neuman or I'll see that he gets a pair of cement shoes."

"I don't think it's any of your business anymore." Jill glanced at her watch. Would this horrible evening never end?

"I should think you would be tired. All those pseudo-celebs."

She refused to let Ian sidetrack her. "If you are serious about bike riding in Central Park, which I doubt, I don't think it's a good idea. There are two million bikers in New York and last year, over three thousand of them were killed or maimed."

"And the latter group was here for cocktails this evening."

"*I* wouldn't ride in Central Park."

"You wouldn't ride a bicycle in the lobby of this building if the doorman held you on."

"Ian, don't you read the papers? God knows you spend enough time in the library. Bicycling is dangerous. Especially if one has never ridden in the city."

"Eating is dangerous. Drinking is dangerous. Water is full of poison. Perrier is loaded with salt. Half the soft drinks are contaminated; the other half are brimming with caffeine. And booze, is... well, you name it. You might as well live in a plastic bubble. Which is exactly where you have been living, my love. You know, I'm very curious about this trial job of yours. This re-stab at a career." He grinned.

"Ian, if you take the girls out on bikes, I'm going to get a divorce. Now get the hell out of my room." Jill began opening windows and turning out lights.

"This is not your room, Jill. This is Pumpkin's room. It's tarted up in a most obscene manner. Looks like a bad set design. That woman doesn't understand the meaning of the word 'classic.'"

"Good night, Ian."

"Good night, Jill. See you after the bike rides." He made no move to leave. "Since you're soon to be rich, I'll let you spring for lunch."

"I forbid it, Ian." Jill's voice quivered.

"We're not going to ride through the South Bronx, only in Central Park. The muggers and rapists have no interest in the park on a Saturday morning. Even you should know that."

"Ian, I'm their mother."

"And I'm their father. At least, that's what I've been led to believe. If you don't want us to go, stay here and stop us. No one is forcing you to go kneel at the scaly feet of dried-up-old-what's-her-name."

"Charlene Whitrock. And it's called an interview. Something you wouldn't understand, of course, eschewing them as you do."

Ian kissed her wetly at the base of her throat.

"Ian!" Jill recoiled. But in spite of herself, she wanted him to want her.

"Jill, have you thought of seeing a psychiatrist? Hanging out with all those alcoholics is making you wiggy, you know? Alcohol is far worse for the brain than it is for the liver."

What the hell was he talking about? She'd practically gone on the wagon since she escaped his clutches. "Advice for you to follow, Ian. Now, let me get ready for bed."

"Be my guest." He propped himself against four peach satin-and-lace pillows. "And you know what else? I think you've lost too much weight. You were a hell of a lot sexier when you had that Rubens look."

"Okay, Ian, if you won't leave, I will." Jill grabbed a pillow and marched out, slamming the door behind her.

"You don't know what you're missing, you bitch!" she heard Ian hissing through the door.

Jill nestled down into the Louis XVI daybed, and fell into a deep, dreamless sleep.

CHAPTER FIVE

Charlene Whitrock's office had all the warmth of a cryogenic lab.

White enamel walls and ceiling. An enormous steel sofa with charcoal patent leather cushions. A stainless steel and bronze conference table that doubled as a desk. Ice-blue spotlights aimed from hidden recesses overhead.

The only touch of life came from the Venus's-flytrap into whose spiny jaws Charlene would pitch tiny bits of raw beef at the end of meetings. Charlene glanced at it. She'd give it a treat. Later. After the Harrington girl arrived for her interview.

She scanned Jill Harrington's resumé for the third time. Nothing wrong with her background. Good schools. English major at Smith. Five years' experience with the tiny-but-chic Philpott Associates. They were still running one of her campaigns.

For some reason, she'd quit after she'd married Ian What's-his-name. Harrington. Why? Wonder what he did? Two daughters at boarding school. And Pumpkin Osborne's address. So. She was divorced. Or separated.

No wonder Pumpkin was anxious for Jill to get a job! Both of them at their ages, living in a girls' dorm.

She'd liked what she'd seen of Jill. She seemed pleasant. Conservative. Probably wouldn't make trouble. Anglo-Saxon good looks. Thirty-seven. But she looked much younger. All of this was extremely important to the client Charlene had in mind: the Country Kitchens Company.

It was a hundred-year-old stuffy family business that should have been a dream account, but instead sent any agency people assigned to it first to booze, then pills. Brodhead Kincaid had turned it over to Charlene, saying that he didn't understand them, and until they came out of the ninteenth century, he wasn't even going to try.

In the past year alone, Country Kitchens had gobbled up nine copywriters and six art directors. But none had been successful on this account. Country Kitchens was not a "challenge"—meaning an impossible account that netted a large profit, with overbearing junior management and watchdog senior management—and it wasn't a boutique account—one everyone fought to work on because it was fun, required imagination and almost paid for itself. Country Kitchens was in a class by itself, which was the only thing about it that made Charlene's heart soar. If she'd had one more like it she, too, would have resorted to booze and pills.

Country Kitchens claimed they wanted flamboyant work. Commercials that would be on the lips of everyone at smart cocktail parties. They wanted awards. Dazzle. Sizzle.

But after approving commercials at the storyboard stage, they'd whittled down the costs until they were taking their own photographs in a cramped New Jersey studio. They did their own casting for television and hired their own directors. And who could stop them? After all, they *were* the client. So much for dazzle and sizzle.

In their own immortal words... "There are more Country Kitchens in country kitchens, city kitchens and suburban kitchens than any other kitchens in these here United States."

Charlene had tried for ten years to get them to replace that slogan. She'd given birth to a daughter, gotten a divorce, had a hysterectomy and gone totally gray. The Country Kitchens slogan had endured.

"I must be going senile," Charlene thought. Working on this account was like doing the Australian crawl through rubber cement. What made her think Ms. Jill Harrington of Badger Hollow could save her ass? And yet instinct told her there was something about Jill.

Jill did have several advantages over other copywriters at her level: she was at least ten years older than everyone else, wouldn't make incessant demands for raises, a larger office or one with a window. Charlene sighed. God, she needed a vacation. Maybe she could take a week off next month.

Jill Harrington wouldn't complain about working on weekends. She needed the money. She needed the work. She had two daughters at a fancy boarding school and a husband, or ex-husband, lurking somewhere in the picture.

Where was Jill, anyway? Five minutes late! Bad sign. It was never too early to discover a shirker. If Charlene was going to spend her weekends locked up in the office with advertising plans, then she was going to make goddamn sure whoever worked for her would be there, too. She buzzed for Bammie. Three times. Dammit, where was she?

"Yes, Charlie?" Bammie's voice squeaked over the intercom.

"Coffee, please. And bring a pot and an extra cup." Her voice easily carried into the outer office, but Charlene loved playing with the intercom.

She peered into the mirror of her blush compact and frowned. Suddenly it occurred to her that with her unnaturally blue hair, her sunlamp bronzed complexion and the grape ice lipstick, she looked vaguely like a Weimaraner. "Shit," she muttered.

Bammie Pomino appeared in the doorway. She was wearing a T-shirt, with *Breathless* outlined in gold studs, and tight white velvet jeans.

"Bammie, I wish you wouldn't wear that shirt in the office."

"But Charlie," she groaned, "Breathless is your most successful new product. It's the hottest perfume since Opium."

"It's just that I think that it's not very professional office attire."

Bammie rolled her eyes. "Charlie, you sound just like my mother. When she first went to work, they wore gloves and hats in the summer. And there wasn't any air conditioning."

"Coffee, please. And no more T-shirts."

Bammie Pomino was the only person at BDK&C under fifty who wasn't terrified of Charlene. That was because she was the only one who knew how shy, burnt-out, and lonely Charlene really was. Bammie answered her mail, ordered her groceries, even bought her underwear. And in return, Bammie was invited to all of Charlene's dinner and cocktail parties, where she played dutiful daughter to perfection, taking coats, emptying ashtrays, whisking away coffee cups. All before settling down with a bottle of Chivas supplied by Charlie. She had a job with great perks. So why bitch about the fucking T-shirt?

"You got it, Charlie," she called. "Mrs. Harrington is here."

Jill stepped forward, her heart somewhere between her teeth and her discreet single strand of pearls. Her gaze rested on Bammie's *Breathless* chest.

Bammie smiled. "We've been expecting you." She leaned against the silver mylar-covered door, holding it wide open. Once Jill was inside, she closed it silently.

Charlene liked all interviews to be taped so that she could listen to everything that went on and could replay the tapes over and over, searching for intonations, evasions, and vulnerabilities. It was her favorite pastime.

Jill sat rigid in her chair, waiting for Charlene to make the first move. Pumpkin had warned her about the blue spotlights, but they still unnerved her.

She studied Charlene's face. It was absolutely immobile, except for the lower jaw, which jerked loosely as she spoke. Like the jaw of a medical school skeleton. Her skin, translucent and yellow around her violet eyes, was lightly mottled and finely wrinkled. Despite moisturizer, makeup, mascara and eye shadow in half a dozen shades each expertly blended into the next, her skin looked like a paint job over already-peeling paint. Her hair was cut into a severe Dutch Boy.

You had to hand it to her, Jill thought. At least Charlene had opted for drama, rather than the two-piece dresses and lacquered navy straw hats of her mother's middle age.

"I'll come to the point, Jill," Charlie croaked. "I'm not going to ask you why you want to work for BDK&C. Or, for me, for that matter, because I'm sure you don't know. And I'm not going to ask you how much money you want." Charlie reached for a cigarette. "Smoke?"

Jill shook her head.

"You need as much as it takes to pay for school and clothes and an apartment and then some." Charlie exhaled. "What I am going to ask you is: How would you like the chance to work on one of our most challenging and prestigious accounts?"

Jill felt the room shift beneath her. "Why yes..." she began, before realizing that Charlie didn't expect an answer.

"It's the Country Kitchens Company. They've been with the agency for thirty-five years. I'm sure you've seen their ads?" Jill flushed with pride. Here was her chance.

"Better than that, Mrs. Whitrock, I've just had a Country Kitchens kitchen installed in my home. It's lovely." She caught Charlene's wince at "Mrs. Whitrock."

"Please call me Charlie. So, you have some first-hand knowledge? That's more than anyone else in my group has. What made you select a Country Kitchen?"

"We had a little fire in the kitchen and things had to be replaced." Instantly, Jill realized that was the wrong thing to say. She hurriedly went on, "And there I was, faced with any number of solutions. I shopped around and Country Kitchens had the most interesting choices, the prettiest floors." Actually, she'd done the whole thing on the telephone with Mrs. Fenwick of the Badger Hollow Tile and Linoleum Shoppe, but Charlie would never know. Jill's throat went dry, her palms suddenly clammy. "I have the Provençal in green and pink."

"My dear Jill, you sound as though you're working for the company already. Believe me, no one else has ever walked into this office and shown such unbridled enthusiasm."

Unbridled enthusiasm sure beat the shit out of smoldering hostility. Jill smiled to herself.

"Thank you, Mrs. Whit—Charlene. I'd love to be a part of BDK&C."

Charlene studied Jill. What *was* this girl's line? Some sort of weirdo boarding school tact? She *was* different!

"I've looked at your print ads and your reel, Jill. They're a little dated but that frozen pie campaign is still running. How do you think you'll like working with twenty-five-year-olds? Twenty-year-olds, even?"

"You mean I won't be working with you?" Jill asked, quaking. One twenty-five-year-old could eat her alive.

"Of course you'll be working with me. But you'll also have to work with an art director in my group. And a producer. And the people at your level of experience are all in their twenties."

"Okay. That's terrific." Jill tried to sound enthusiastic.

"It's really too bad you dropped out, Jill. But then, I guess, lots of people do. To find themselves and all that." Charlene had never felt the need to find herself.

"I didn't exactly drop out, Mrs. Whit—Charlie. I quit when I got pregnant. Ian didn't think I should work."

Ian must be some winner, Charlene thought. Odd that Pumpkin Osborne hadn't mentioned him. "Ian sounds right out of *Life with Father*. He actually insisted that you walk away from a promising career to make tuna casseroles?" Charlene had never even eaten a tuna casserole.

"He didn't exactly insist, Charlene. I thought I wanted to be a wife. Right after I had Wendy, nine months, to be exact, I had Bethy." Jill swallowed. "And I guess you know the rest."

"Well, only what Pumpkin has told me, though you know how she can condense *War and Peace* into three sentences. But I don't mean to pry." Charlene leaned back in her chair, lit another cigarette and smiled encouragingly.

Outside, Bammie choked on a huge gulp of hot coffee. Charlene had no shame. How many times had she heard Charlene get the interviewee to bare his or her soul?

"I didn't really want to leave advertising," Jill continued. "I guess I did it to keep the peace. But I did resent Ian for it. He thought my working made him look like a failure. As it's turned out, he is, I guess. It's taken me a long time to face it. Sometimes I think if it hadn't been for Pumpkin, I never would have."

"It's funny how fate twists and turns us around," Charlie sighed. "In spite of our plans, it seems like it's the accidents that steer our lives."

Bammie couldn't stand it anymore. But Charlie was right about accidents. If Charlie hadn't slipped on the ice one freezing night and Bammie hadn't been the only person on the block and hadn't gotten Charlie home to a warm bed, Charlie would have frozen to death and Bammie wouldn't have this great job. She'd still be at the telephone company, listening to customer complaints.

Jill looked directly into Charlene Whitrock's cold eyes. What she saw there didn't frighten her anymore. "I'd love to work on Country Kitchens or on anything else you think I'd be right for. And I do know why I'd like to work at BDK&C—because I'd be working on things I understand. I'm sure I've spent more time in kitchens than anyone else in your group."

"Including the fancy fag gourmet cook! Okay." Charlene rose. This time she didn't feel like giving her plant a treat. "When can you start? Is Monday going to give you cardiac arrest?"

It was really happening. The end of one life and the beginning of another. Jill couldn't believe it.

"Monday sounds terrific," she said, her heart pounding.

Charlene pumped her hand. "Come right here to my office.

A little before nine. Bammie and I will get you settled in. You can meet your art director. Now, do you have a lunch date? I'd be delighted to spring for a bite."

"Oh, thanks, but I'm meeting my daughters." Jill paused, then asked shyly, "Would you like to join us?"

Charlie couldn't stand children, except for her daughter Kimberly who was twenty-four and lived in Paris. "No, dear. You enjoy yourselves. We'll have plenty of time once you're here. Bammie and I will grab a burger. Now, scoot. I'll see you on Monday."

As Jill walked out the door, she felt a wave of relief. She wasn't ready for lunch with Charlie. And she wanted to savor this moment alone. Someone needed her! At last. After all those years feeling useless in her Badger Hollow kitchen. It was just a start, but it was all *hers*. As she signed out of the building, she snapped out of her daydream.

Would Ian and the girls have finished their bike rides by now? She glanced at her watch. She had time to take her portfolio back to Pumpkin's before lunch. She hailed a cab. To hell with walking fast *or* slow. She wanted to celebrate with Pumpkin and the girls. Please make Ian have gone. Anywhere. She couldn't bear to look into those insinuating eyes or listen to those *sotto voce* insults. And she especially didn't want him to touch her. Ever again.

Only Tansy was at Pumpkin's when Jill arrived. The living room somehow seemed forlorn in daylight. The afternoon sun glared at motes of dust, random fingerprints on the mirrored walls, gazed unflinchingly on flowers past their prime, ashtrays that had barely been wiped clean. Tansy was shoveling ashes out of the cold hearth, sniffling.

"Tansy, where is everybody?" Jill was disappointed she had no one else to share her conquest with.

"Ohhh, Miz Jilly, they's out. They's gone. Miz Pumpkin and Mr. Noël. They's...they's..." She gave in to loud, wracking sobs. "They's..."

"Gone where? Where, Tansy?"

"To de Roose-velt Hospital. Ahm 'sposed ter tell you to go there. Ahm 'sposed to take you if you cain't go by yerself. You 'sposed to go to de emer-gen-cy room. Fifty-Ninth-an-Ninth," she howled. "Roose-velt Hospital, Miz Jilly."

"Who's sick, Tansy? What happened?"

"Acci-dent."

"What happened to Pumpkin?"

"Miz Pumpkin's fine. Acci-dent."

"Tansy, what accident? Who's hurt? When did it happen?" Dear God, what the hell was Tansy talking about?

"Ah gots ter take you..." she began, weeping.

"Just tell me what happened, Tansy. *Who* is hurt? Tansy?" Jill grabbed Tansy's soft, big shoulders. "What happened?" Panic swept over her. "Please."

"Miz Pumpkin and Mr. Noël an de Lawd were havin' a cocktail. Half hour ago. The phone rang. 'Hel-lo,' ah says. 'Miz Osborne's resi-dence.' An some gal tells me that it's Roose-velt Hospital an we got ter git over there now. Somethin' real bad has happened. Come to the emergency room. Then, Mr. Noël gits on the line. An Mr. Noël, he say, when Miz Jilly git heah tell her ter come to Roose-velt Hospital. That's all ah knows, Miz Jilly."

It wasn't Pumpkin or Noël or Lord Russelshire. Maybe it was Ian. Or—God, no, she prayed—one of the girls. She heard her voice, oddly cool. "You stay here by the phone, Tansy, in case anyone calls. And try to calm down. Tell them I'm on my way."

Tansy nodded. "Ah'll do jest that. An ah'll have myself a little taste of bourbon. Tha's okay, isn't it? A nice taste would sho hep." But Jill didn't hear her. She was already out the door.

Of course it was something Ian had done. It always was. Had he fallen off his bike? Probably. Had he let his medical insurance lapse? Likely. Just when something was finally going right, he had to screw things up.

By the time the cab pulled up outside the entrance to the

emergency room, Jill was seething. A little while ago she'd been so happy, just sitting in Charlene's inhuman, ridiculous office, letting herself be told she was a dropout. Now this. Whatever it was. She paid the cab and dashed inside.

She was standing in a cavernous, sterile waiting room. People, most of them shoeless, were slumped in orange plastic chairs. The air was heavy with smoke and the odor of ancient urine. Pumpkin, Noël St. Martin and Lord Russelshire huddled in a far corner, close to the only window. Their faces were drawn. Pumpkin had no lipstick on. Lord Russelshire slouched against the wall. Noël stared out of the gray window.

Jill wiggled through the mass of sour bodies. "What's happened?" she gasped.

Noël put his arm around her. It felt hard, comforting. "Maybe we should dash across the street. There's a bar just across Ninth Avenue."

"I don't want to go to a bar. I want to know what Ian's done now. Where's Wendy? And Bethy?"

"Darling," Pumpkin said hesitantly, "something horrible has happened." She put her arm around Jill on top of Noël's.

"Won't somebody tell me something? *Please?* What is it?" It felt like the room was spinning.

"We think Bethy is in shock," Noël said, "but we really don't know anything concrete. We're not *family*, so the hospital won't tell us anything." He shook his head.

"And Wendy? What about my darling?" Jill's voice was shrill with panic. "Is she in shock, too? They fell off those goddamned bikes, didn't they? Didn't they?" Jill jerked savagely on Pumpkin's arm.

"Yes, my dear, I'm afraid they all had nasty falls. But that is absolutely all we know." Lord Russelshire's expression was kind.

Jill was terrified. *God, don't let me lose control.*

"There was a bus... the Seventy-second Street crosstown," Pumpkin began, her voice shaky. "Somehow, Wendy got between the bus and a car, an out-of-town driver. That's sort of what happened. But, Jill, I promise, that's all we know. We're not keeping *anything* from you."

Jill scanned their ashen faces. "Wendy's dead, isn't she? And Ian's alive. That's it, isn't it?" She sat down with a thud in an orange chair.

"Jill, sweetheart," Noël pleaded, "we just don't know yet. Don't think the worst."

She was determined not to faint. She let herself go limp, took long, deep breaths.

"I'd like to see them, please," she heard a voice say. Was it hers? It was so calm, the same voice that asked to see gloves at Saks, steaks at Gristede's. "Please."

"I think we have to wait until the doctors are through. 'Til they've moved them out of emergency. They said it might take a little while. In the meantime," Russelshire said in a monotone, "we could just nip across the street to that pub."

"Yes," Pumpkin whispered, "we're not doing anybody any good here."

The policeman stationed outside the double glass doors to the emergency room unlocked them and nodded to a young intern in a white lab coat. Together, they looked around the room. "Mrs. Harrington?" the policeman said. "Is there a Mrs. Ian Harrington here?"

Jill turned toward him as a young woman—a girl, almost—with a dirty little boy clinging to her hand jumped up and started toward the double glass doors. "My name is Juliet Harrington," the woman said softly.

"But *I'm* Mrs. Harrington." Jill's clear voice rang out over the transistor radios. "Mrs. Ian Harrington. There must be some mistake." Jill turned pleading eyes to Pumpkin. "Tell them that I'm Mrs. Ian Harrington."

Pumpkin started toward the door, pulling Jill by the hand. Noël and Lord Russelshire followed helplessly behind. "Officer! Doctor!" she announced, "this is Mrs. Harrington. H-A-R-R-I-N-G-T-O-N. Her husband and children are in there. We're here to see what has happened. I'm Mrs. Osborne, Mrs. Harrington's sister. What's going on?"

"Will Mrs. Harrington please come with us?" the intern said coldly, ignoring Pumpkin's glare.

The young woman with the filthy child stared insolently at Pumpkin and Jill and retreated to the orange plastic chairs. Jill followed the intern through the double doors. The policeman locked the doors after them.

"There couldn't be two Mrs. Harringtons, could there? I mean, both here, at the same time?" Jill knew it was a ridiculous suggestion. But who was that woman?

"In New York? Sure. Let's see if you can identify your husband, Mrs. Harrington. Then we'll know for sure, right? He sustained a nasty fall from his bicycle. Too bad you didn't make it here earlier."

"I'm sorry," Jill mumbled. Why was she always sorry? Why should she be? If anyone should be sorry, it was Ian.

"Here we are." The intern dragged back a dingy curtain. Ian lay on a high, narrow table. His mouth was slack, his mocking eyes closed. His arms lay limply at his side.

They had cut off his jeans and sweater. Everything but his green boxer shorts was in shreds in a bloody shopping bag marked "patient's belongings."

"I know you're there. I know you're there," he repeated monotonously. His breathing was shallow.

"He's been saying that since we brought him in," the intern told Jill. "We did an X-ray series. Nothing actually broken. There may be some internal bleeding, but I don't think we'll have to go in. I'm betting it will stop on its own. He'll be with us for a few days though, maybe a week. We'll know more when we get the results from all the tests."

"Oh." Jill sighed. She really didn't care. She couldn't feel anything. But what about Wendy? And Bethy?

"And my daughters, doctor. Where are they? Are they here?"

Ian groaned. "I know you're there, my sun. I know you're there, Juliet."

Jill stared at him. What was he talking about?

"Juliet, my love."

"It's Jill, Ian. Jill."

"Juliet, my sun..."

"Yes, Ian. Jill is here. Your wife," she said squeezing his arm lightly. "We don't have a son, Ian. We have two daughters, Ian. Wendy and Bethy."

"Wendy and Bethy?" He seemed suddenly alert, agitated. "Beth. Where's my Beth? And Wendy? You've got to find Wendy, before it's too late. Good Christ, get Wendy." He began to sob.

Jill was terrified. Where was Wendy? She turned to the intern.

"Beth is okay, Mrs. Harrington. Shock, of course. But you can take her home. We've checked her over." As if she were a car.

"She was at least thirty feet from the accident. She wasn't hurt. Physically, that is. It's the shock."

"Doctor, why won't anyone around here tell me the truth? Where's Wendy?"

"Mrs. Harrington, there was a collision between a bus and a car running a red light at the corner of Madison Avenue and Seventy-Second Street. However, your daughters and your husband happened to be there at the same time. Apparently Beth was trying to keep up with her father and older sister. Thank God, she couldn't. She'll be all right. And so will your husband. But Wendy...Wendy didn't make it. I'm so sorry. I know how much it hurts, Mrs. Harrington. I lost a son."

The intern dropped his gaze to his feet for a moment, then lifted his head. "But there was nothing anybody could do. It was just a terrible accident."

"Accidents," murmured Jill. The intern stepped forward.

"Mrs. Harrington, Bethy needs you now." He patted her arm. It occurred to her that he was probably overworked. In a hurry.

Jill could hear the sirens screaming across Fifty-Ninth Street.

Nothing made sense. An accident. Like the ducks in the broiler. She hadn't eaten anything since the one caviar lollipop at the cocktail party last night. Where was Wendy?

"The nurse will be in, Mrs. Harrington. She'll help you out. Just a minute or two."

Help her out. Who could help? It was all her fault. If she hadn't been with Charlene Whitrock, none of this would have happened. She didn't give a shit if Ian ever got out of the emergency room.

"I'll take you upstairs now, dear." A plump nurse held her arm. "We can get the paperwork started. You and the Mister have a joint account? Maybe you could write a check on that until we can get the medical insurance straightened out?" In one hand, she held a "patient's belongings" bag; in the other, Beth's hand. Beth was sucking her thumb.

Jill couldn't endure the noise much longer. But Bethy was here. She had to be strong. "Bethy, I'm going to take you home now." She reached to take her in her arms.

"It's about time, Mother." Beth looked as though she'd been having a lovely day in the park. Her cheeks were pink. Her pale hair shone. An Instamatic camera hung from a cord around her neck. Jill didn't know Bethy owned a camera.

She folded Beth in her arms. "Oh, Bethy. We've got to find Wendy." She fought back tears. Never cry in front of a child, she thought. It makes them insecure.

"Mrs. Harrington," the nurse said, "you can see your daughter, though Mr. Harrington has already made the identification."

"Identification?"

"She was DOA. I'm sorry."

DOA. That was Pumpkin's expression for "drunk on arrival." The words melted her resolve not to cry.

"I don't want to see Wendy, Moth-er," Beth whispered.

"Of course not, darling. Of course not." Christ. She had to stop crying.

"Can we go to the Japanese restaurant now, Mother?"

"Bethy, not now," Jill hushed.

"If Wendy hadn't been showing off for Daddy, she never would have ridden into that bus. She was always doing everything you told us not to do."

"Beth, please."

"She's in shock, Mrs. Harrington. Take her home. Put her to bed. Give her one of these every four hours." The nurse handed Jill a paper envelope fat with tablets.

"Can't we please go to the Japanese restaurant? If you won't take me, Daddy will," Beth whined.

"Daddy can't go anywhere. Daddy had a bad fall. He has to stay here. In the hospital."

"Daddy was trying to keep the bus from squashing Wendy."

Jill moved Beth toward the door. Where would she find the strength? Somewhere. "Thank you," she bent closer to read the name on the nurse's pin, "Mrs. Nuncio. Now, where do I go to fill out the papers?"

"To Admissions. But you must ask your husband to sign a paper—a release. A power-of-attorney, you know, so you can take care of the bills. They'll explain it all to you. Bye-bye, little Bethy."

Pay the bills! And then it dawned on Jill. Mrs. Nuncio thought they were rich; or at least able to pay their bills. After all, Jill reasoned, the accident had happened on Madison Avenue and Seventy-Second Street, not exactly in Harlem. And by no stretch of the imagination did they bear any resemblance to anyone outside in the waiting room. Ian was another matter though.

"You're so mean, Moth-er. No wonder Daddy doesn't want to live with you anymore. Well, *I* don't want to live with you, either. If we can't go to the Japanese restaurant, I want to go back to Laurel Hall. I love it there."

"Bethy, you don't know what you're saying. You're in shock."

Jill leaned against the wall, trying to collect her thoughts.

"Mother, I'm perfectly okay. I've got the whole thing right here." She tapped the Instamatic camera around her neck. "Just like TV news. Live coverage. The instant I saw something happening, I started snapping. I've got seventy-two color shots. Daddy. The car. Wendy. The bus. Everything!"

Jill gaped at Beth in horror; this was the child she had carried for nine months. Agonized in labor over. Tried to love. Ian's genes must be stronger than dirt.

"Beth, I'm going to ignore that. And as soon as possible you and I are going to visit a doctor for you to talk to."

Beth had always been so sweet, so helpful. Who was this person?

Jill inhaled deeply and reached out to hug Beth. She jerked away. "I hated Wendy. You loved her more. So don't hug me. I hate you."

"Bethy, Bethy, I didn't love Wendy more. I didn't."

"You always loved Wendy more. Wendy is like you; I'm like Daddy," she said proudly.

"Not true." Jill tried to smile. All true.

"Wendy got the best things. The ballet lessons."

"But you hate to dance."

"The best shit clothes from those cousin creeps in Buffalo."

"Beth, not now. Please." Please, not now. "You know Dad and I don't have much money." Money. Christ. What the hell was she going to do?

"Then how come Daddy bought me this camera? And this sweater? Feel. Cashmere. *And* designer jeans for Wendy. Daddy has taste."

"Hush, Bethy. Wendy's..." The word tore at her throat... "Wendy's dead. Don't you care?"

"I know, Moth-er. But Daddy didn't love Wendy. He loves *me*. And Mom, you're wrong. Daddy has plenty of money. He charged everything on his American Express card. So there." Beth stuck out her tongue.

American Express? Ian didn't have any credit cards. Beth must be deeper in shock than they thought.

"Mother, face it," Beth trilled. "You never even used my name. I was just one of the 'girls.' We weren't Siamese twins, you know. I hated being one of the girls, and I hated Wendy because she made me one of the girls. I hated Wendy. Hated. Hated. Hated." Tears streaked her face.

Why couldn't it have been Beth? What a horrible thought. Why couldn't it have been Ian? Stinking, selfish, Machiavellian Ian?

Jill shoved Beth aside and moved to the table where Ian lay, now semiconscious. She grabbed his slack arms and shook them as hard as she could, an animal shaking its prey.

"Wake up, you goddamn son-of-a-bitch. Wake up. I don't want you to miss one second of what's in store for you."

She grabbed the plastic ice water pitcher from the beside table and doused Ian with its contents. She was bashing him with the empty pitcher when the young intern silently slipped his arm around her from behind and plunged the tranquilizing needle into the soft flesh of her upper arm.

Jill awoke muffled in a cotton fog. Her mouth was dry. Her teeth were slimy. Someone was slumped in a chair near a window.

"Wendy?" Jill whispered. "Wendy, dearest?"

Instantly, Jill felt a cool hand on her throbbing forehead.

"Jill, I'm here." Pumpkin. Jill tried to sit up. But the fierce pain in her head threw her back against the pillow.

"Pumpkin, what time is it?" But she didn't care. It was just something to say. What difference did it make? What difference did anything make without Wendy? God, how she loathed Ian. Why hadn't they let her kill him?

"Children aren't supposed to die, are they, Pumpkin? I can't live with Wendy's death. I feel so guilty and lonely and scared. Help me, Pumpkin." Jill's voice was meek.

"She'll always be your daughter, Jill. Remember that." Pumpkin spoke carefully, softly.

"How long does it take to stop loving someone, Pumpkin?"

"You'll never stop loving her, Jill. Only after a while it won't be so raw."

"Are you sure it'll get better? Have you ever loved anyone

that much, Pumpkin?" Pumpkin smiled. If Jill only knew.

"It's odd that you should have to ask me that, Jill." She rose from her chair, and sat on the edge of Jill's bed.

Her lipstick had disappeared. Her hair was shoved behind her ears. Her mascara had run into what was left of her blush. For the first time in her life she looked her age. She gazed helplessly at Jill.

"I've loved you for twenty years."

For twenty years. She'd never mentioned it. And now, it seemed, was not the time. But maybe there never would be a time. Jill stared thoughtfully at her friend.

"Oh, Pumpkin. I didn't know. I wish I could love you the same way."

There was a long, silent moment as Pumpkin held Jill's gaze. And then the moment was lost. Jill cleared her throat.

"What did they give me?"

Pumpkin moved off the bed. "Sodium pentathol, my dear. It's not very exotic, but it sure knocks you to the old parquet."

"I feel like I've been in a coma."

"It's early the next morning, which means Sunday, and just as soon as you talk to the shrink, we can leave."

"Psychiatrist?" More quacking. How much more could she take? And what was she supposed to say besides "I'd like to kill my husband, thank you very much."

"Someone on staff here. He's been in a couple of times, waiting for you to wake up. Seems you were pretty wild yesterday. By the time we'd taken Bethy home to Tansy and tucked her in, and got back here, you were out cold."

"What did I do?" Suddenly she thought of all the times she'd telephoned a Badger Hollow hostess to thank her for her tiresome parties, only to be informed of something mortifying that Ian had done or said. "Did I kill him?"

"Who?"

"Ian."

Pumpkin laughed. "Not quite. Your weapon was a plastic water pitcher. An empty one. Not exactly lethal, my dear."

Jill felt like laughing. Or maybe crying. "Let's get out of here, Pumpkin. Let's go *do* something. Something besides talk."

"There is one thing... we... have to do. Find Ian's medical insurance. He told the nurse that it's in a drawer in his desk. Out in Badger Hollow."

"Christ," Jill remembered. "I was supposed to sign some papers and give them a check."

"Done. Everything is all set."

"What about Ian?" Even his name tasted sour.

"He's going to be here for a week, maybe more. He has a concussion, internal bleeding, which they've almost managed to stop, and a separated shoulder."

"Add to that a separated wife. As soon as I can face it, Pumpkin, I'm getting a divorce. I think I can face it now. I certainly can't imagine anything else after what he's done."

"You can face anything so long as it's finite," Pumpkin said, ringing for the nurse. She had to face something. And it wasn't finite.

Had Jill understood any of what she'd said? Since their freshman year, Pumpkin had loved Jill, but she had never been able to tell her. Jill was beautiful and strong. No man had ever made Pumpkin feel so happy, so loved. She had given up trying to find one who could. But now her secret was out. And she knew for certain that Jill would never feel that way about her. Could she live with it? She'd have to.

CHAPTER SIX

ill unlocked the kitchen door and was knocked breathless by the stench. "Smells like a mattress fire in a flop house," sniffed Pumpkin. Even the smell of new plastic from the recently installed Country Kitchen didn't help. Jill and Pumpkin wandered through the kitchen.

Every inch of counter space, including the floating butcher block table in the center of the room, was littered with wine bottles, beer cans, glasses. Cognac bottles, framboise bottles, Cointreau bottles, poire bottles, port bottles. All empty. Pumpkin gave a low whistle.

"I think you'd better call a landfill. I was under the impression that our pal Ian was stone cold broke."

"No one knows better than you, Pumpkin."

"Johnnie Walker Black? Rèmy Martin? He must have a rich uncle in the closet."

"You know there's just Ian and his grandmother, Rose-Delia."

"Merely a figure of speech, darling." Je-sus. Ian had been

on some binge, thought Pumpkin. Everything liquid. Not one dirty dish. Did he ever eat?

"Have you ever seen such a mess?" Jill was shocked. She thought of Wendy, sitting at the kitchen table. Wendy standing with the refrigerator door open after school. Would the hurt ever stop?

"Soon you won't have to worry about it anymore. First, you're going to get Ian out of your life. Then you're going to get this *house* out of your life."

Jill looked around. Whose house was this, anyway? Was this where she'd cooked? Drank? Sewn the girls' clothes? Prayed for Ian to come home?

"We're not going to find Ian's medical insurance in the plastic French provincial cupboards, Jill." Pumpkin steered Jill toward a set of swinging doors.

The dining room was dark, except for one tiny bulb still burning in the chandelier.

How like Ian to wander out, leaving the lights on for days. The shades were at half-mast.

It reminded Jill of her grandmother's dining room after her funeral. Mildew. Sticky plates. Dull forks with dried egg between the tines. Goblets that had never known the benefit of spot-free dishwashing detergent.

Jill turned her back and walked through the center hall to the living room. There was her "good crystal," left by Mother. God it was ugly. Why hadn't she ever noticed that before?

She reached for one of the ugliest of the goblets, the Lilliputian size, and held it up to the light. Its base was crusted with port. Only a desperate person would resort to drinking from this. She tossed it into a wastebasket. Then, automatically, she started shoveling cans and bottles in after it.

"Jill, come *on*. No more conditioned response. No more Super Mom."

"But Pumpkin, who'd want to come to a messy house, let alone buy one?"

"Tansy and her niece will come up tomorrow and take care of things. There's plenty of time..." Pumpkin almost said, "before the funeral." But the look on Jill's face stopped her.

Jill noticed the broken pane where she'd hurled the Waterford crystal at Ian. A shirt cardboard had been placed over the jagged hole. Each new reminder made her stomach hurt.

"Pumpkin, Wendy's gone. But I still can't really believe it. What's wrong with me?"

"You're still in shock. You'll believe it later, little by little, and I'll be here to help you." Pumpkin paused. She'd always be there.

"Bethy hates me," Jill spoke softly.

Pumpkin's long, silken arm slid around her. "We're going to get what we came up here to get, Jill. And then we are going back to my apartment and try to get on with our lives."

But the house had drawn Jill back under its spell.

"Major medical. Didn't Ian say that that stuff was in his desk? In the library?"

Jill nodded and mutely followed Pumpkin.

If anything, the library was worse than the kitchen or the dining room. More styrofoam coffee containers. More glasses. A foot-high bed of ashes in the fireplace grate. Pillows, books and papers piled on the floor. Books open on the sofa, their pages stained with circles of red.

Directly in front of the fireplace, a book lay open upside down. "A-*ha*," Pumpkin drawled, "'J. Wilkes, Essay on Women, 1763.' *Now* I know whence cometh Ian's ideas. Listen to this, underlined in green ink: 'Life can little else supply, but a few good fucks and then we die.' How eloquent."

"Do you suppose that's what that smarmy bastard's been doing in here? On my favorite sofa?" Jill loved to say 'smarmy.'

"Probably not. I'm sure it's all part of Ian's fantasy life." Pumpkin wasn't sure of anything except that she wanted to get the hell out of this charnel house. She couldn't breathe.

"Okay," Jill said with resolution, "let's go." She started pulling open the drawers of the desk and dumping the contents on the floor.

Out tumbled notes on the Cavalier poets and quotations

from Shakespeare, mostly scribbled on disintegrating cocktail napkins. Telephone numbers. Packages of condoms in a variety of shades and textures.

Good God, Ian had never used those things with her! Jill had been on the pill until she forgot and they'd had Wendy and she hadn't gone back on fast enough to stop Beth.

"*The Rake's Progress*," laughed Pumpkin.

"Oh, Pumpkin, I don't know what I would have done without you. A few minutes ago, I was contemplating suicide and now I almost feel like laughing. Maybe I'm turning into a maniac-depressive." Jill grasped the handle of the bottom drawer. It was locked. "What do you suppose is in here?"

"Let's get a screwdriver and a hammer and find out," Pumpkin said. She loved a challenge. And she was relieved to see Jill's spirits lifting. "I don't know about you, but I haven't had such a good time since I used to snoop through my parents' drawers. I used to pray that they'd go out early so I wouldn't be too sleepy to sneak into their room and have a field day."

"You did that?" Pumpkin would never cease to amaze Jill. The idea of even walking into her parents' room still terrified her.

"They were both having affairs and thought no one knew. It was an absolute riot. Mother was involved with an old college flame who'd never gotten over her. And Pop was pounding the liver out of his secretary of the moment. He used to trade them in every two years, like his Cadillac."

"That must have been hard for you."

"Oh, it wasn't so bad. Except for the letters. I'd never seen letters like that before. Still haven't."

Pumpkin slid the screwdriver along the top of the drawer and gave it a loud slam with the hammer. The wood splintered. "Oh, shit. Sorry, Jill."

"That's okay. I always hated that desk, anyway."

Pumpkin hit it again and the drawer sprang free. It was a file drawer the depth of three ordinary drawers. It was filled with bundles of letters held together with rubber bands.

Jill lifted out the top bundle. "Do you think we should?"

"Is the Pope Polish?" Pumpkin reached for a second bundle. There must have been hundreds of letters.

Jill opened the top envelope and extracted a much-folded piece of bond typing paper. Her hands were shaking almost as badly as her voice. "Pumpkin, I think it's a love letter." She handed it to Jill. "Read," she commanded. "My love," Pumpkin began,

> before we met, my life was one long unaspirated yawn. —A series of minor mishaps, banal banter. You've brightened my dusty corner. —Compared to you, D. H. Lawrence knew nothing of wanting. —Nothing of the pitch of exquisite anticipation. And you, my lover, are the only fulfillment that has ever lived up to my anticipation. — Knowing that you love me, no matter what, I could climb the Matterhorn barefoot. Until later, when you, O cruel knight, cut out my heart and offer it up to Eros. Helen.

"Period. End of quote."

"If anyone ever wrote that to me, I'd change my name and move to Salt Lake City. Good God, look at this!"

What had seemed like bundles of letters were actually bundles of bank credit cards. Visa cards and Mastercards, neatly stacked and tied with string. A couple hundred thousand dollars in credit!

"I thought you said Ian didn't believe in credit!" Pumpkin said, paving the top of the desk with plastic cards. "It's amazing. What do you think was going on in his head?"

"Honestly, Pumpkin, all I know is that he'd always told me he didn't believe in credit," replied Jill, diving for the drawer. "That lying, laying son-of-a-bitch."

"How many do you think are here? Let's count them."

"I'll get a tray. We'll take them into the dining room and spread them out."

Pumpkin spread out the cards while Jill screwed new bulbs into the chandelier. "Christ, I've never seen anything like it.

Ian should be able to make *The Guiness Book* with this haul."

"But isn't it illegal or something?" Jill asked. "I didn't know you could have more than one Visa and one Mastercard. Are they stamped with different names? You know, aliases?"

"Nope. They all seem to be 'Ian Woodside Harrington.' And sure, it's legal. Stephen used to be on the legal staff of Citibank, or was it Marine Midland? Anyhow, that was before I married him."

"Oh," Jill said quietly. All those goddamn credit cards right under her nose the whole time.

"I have six Mastercards and a couple of Visas myself. Just in case. That must have been in the back of Ian's mind, too. *But* your credit has to be pretty good to qualify for more than one of each."

Why did Ian need a big cash reserve? Something warned her that this was the teeniest tip of the biggest iceberg.

Jill started counting. Twenty Mastercards. Almost as many Visa cards. And two American Express cards. Bastard. Keeping her at the poverty level, afraid to face the butcher, the headmistress, the garage. Afraid to go to the gynecologist. Afraid to buy a new sweater or a lousy shirt. Afraid every time the phone rang. Afraid of lawsuits. Afraid her creditors would hire someone to give her cement shoes.

Ian was going to pay. But how?

Pumpkin gazed thoughtfully at the credit cards. "Guess what you and I are going to do, Jill?"

"I'm not sure, Pumpkin, but I'd like to make his life as miserable as he's made mine. Just as soon as he gets out of the hospital. I wish to God I'd had something more potent than a plastic water pitcher back there."

"Well, I'm glad you didn't. And you will be, too. Now, let's get practical. You are going to take every single one of these cards and withdraw the maximum amount of cash from each one."

"Can I do that?"

"Why not? It's just what Mr. Ian Woodside Harrington

deserves. I'd love to see the look on his face when he realizes his credit's been drained. Wouldn't you?" Pumpkin's laugh filled the gloomy dining room.

"Then I can pay for Wendy's funeral." Jill toyed with a Visa card.

"And," Pumpkin continued, "it also means, dear one, that you can get an apartment and Bethy can live with you again. It would be the best thing for both of you."

"I know I'm a burden, Pumpkin," Jill said in a small voice.

"That is not, repeat *not* what I meant. Look to the future, Jill. Now you can have everything you deserve. And best of all, there's not a goddamn thing Ian can do to stop you."

"There's one thing you forgot. Maybe two."

"Oh?" Pumpkin was not used to having her authority challenged. "What?"

"The cards are all in his name, not mine. How can I use them?"

"Do you think the cash machines have eyes in the backs of their heads? All you need to know is a personal code number for each and how to push a few buttons. *Voilà!* Nice, clean money and plenty of it. Now, what's the second thing I've overlooked?"

"What if Ian has used up all the credit? Maybe we're counting our cards before they're hatched."

"Here we are," said Pumpkin, grinning, "the code numbers and the monthly statements. A-*ha!* Cleverly sent to a post office box number and not to the family manse, which is how he kept it all from you. Now, read and smile."

Jill took the statements from Pumpkin. Quickly she scanned them. Ian didn't owe any of the banks a penny.

"I can't believe it, Pumpkin. Ian's paid up."

"So you can take out the maximum amount. Beautiful. Now you don't have to get mad, you can get even."

"The Mastercards seem to have a limit of thirty-five hundred," Jill read.

"That's about average. From two thousand to thirty-five

hundred. Very few people get cards with five thousand or more in credit."

"Stephen again?"

"Right. It is handy having been married to a lawyer."

"Which explains why Ian had *so many cards*."

"Miss Marple strikes!" laughed Pumpkin. "I haven't had so much fun since I decorated Noël's four-story studio."

"One thing still puzzles me, Pumpkin. Ian hasn't had a job in recent history, so he's not exactly a great credit risk. How did he get all these?"

Pumpkin studied the cards. It looked as though they'd never been used. "Look, Jill. At the expiration dates. They all say next month. That means they're all at least three years old and he's never used any of them. See how new they look?"

"Cash machines work at night, don't they, Pumpkin?"

"Sure. But night isn't a good idea. That's when the credit card cash machine robbers come out to play."

"Right." Jill wished Pumpkin would go back to Manhattan. Robbers be damned, she wanted that money. She didn't even want to figure out exactly how much—she wanted it and she wanted it now. What was happening to her?

"Let's get the medical insurance stuff, Jill."

"Do you think I should burn those letters, Pumpkin?"

"No. They're not your letters. Simple as that."

"Well, they're in my house, against my will. And they were written to my husband. Besides, I think they're obscene."

"They could be great evidence in your forthcoming divorce from the slave master. Don't do anything rash."

"Pumpkin, do you think I'd want anyone else to read that garbage? It's humiliating! Wouldn't you be humiliated?"

"Probably not. If the one I read is any example of the rest, I'd probably assume the writer was suffering from severe brain damage. If anyone should be humiliated, it's Ian. But I doubt he even understands the meaning of the word."

Jill looked pensive. "You know, I used to feel sorry for myself; now I feel sorry for Ian."

"I'm afraid I can't share your pity. I hate to be a drag, Jill, but I've got to get back to town and change. I can't go out like this." Pumpkin was wearing a black Ultrasuede jumpsuit and bronze boots.

"Pumpkin, aren't you afraid of anything?"

"Afraid?" Pumpkin pondered the word. What an odd question. "Sure. Pain. And the dark. And spiders. I guess pain wins, though."

"Come on. What are you afraid of the most?"

"That one day they'll find out that I never had an original idea in my life. You see, I steal all my interiors from old stage sets. Please don't tell anyone."

Jill pawed at the mess on top of the table. What was *she* afraid of? Not pain. Or the dark, which had been a faithful friend in the days of fat and safety pins. What?

Ridicule. That was it. She'd rather die on the rack. In her dreams, they'd all talked about her behind her back. The teachers. The headmistress. Jason Picker. All of Pumpkin's perfect friends. But she didn't have time for self-pity. There was a lot to be done. Tomorrow, she'd telephone Charlie and tell her that she couldn't start Monday. When *could* she start? Maybe never.

"Jill? Wake up!" Pumpkin shook Jill's elbow impatiently. "Here's the medical insurance. The works. Now, let's get out of here."

"I think I'll stay here and clean up this God-awful mess, Pumpkin."

"Bullshit, Jill." She started stuffing the credit cards into a large Baggie. "Tansy and her niece will come up here tomorrow."

The phone rang. Jill jumped. "Who knows we're here?"

"Ian, for one. Tansy. Beth. Anyone who's seen the lights. A wrong number."

"What if it's that Helen person?"

"Has she ever called before?"

"Not that I know of."

"Then, it probably *isn't* that Helen person." Pumpkin picked up the phone. "Hello, this is the Harrington residence."

"This is Rose-Delia in Palm Beach. Is my grandson's wife there?"

Pumpkin handed Jill the phone. "Rose-Delia." Jill gaped.

"Mrs. Harrington, this is Jill." She tried to envision Rose-Delia Harrington. She hadn't seen her in five or six years. Tall. Bone-thin. Haughty. Still beautiful, though faded. With pale blue eyes that could cut diamonds. Rose-Delia's wedding present to Jill had been a presumably gold bracelet that had instantly turned her arm green.

"Well, Jill, Ian telephoned me. Collect, of course. I'm just shocked about all of this. Needless to say, I'll be up on Tuesday for the funeral. And don't book me into a hotel. I'm not staying. I want to see Wendy. And Bethy. And Ian. How is my grandson? He sounded drugged."

"Ian has a concussion, a separated shoulder and maybe some internal bleeding. No one seems to know how long he'll be in the hospital. Are you sure you want to make the trip from Palm Beach?"

"Of course I don't. It's my duty. Are you trying to tell me that I'm not welcome at my great-granddaughter's funeral?"

"No, Mrs. Harrington." She hadn't changed. "I only meant that it probably won't be a very joyous occasion."

"Funerals rarely are, my dear. Although I suspect that mine will be for Ian. Good-bye." Rose-Delia hung up.

"Just like that. 'Good-bye,' and slam. That bitch."

"Be glad you're not related to her," Pumpkin said, turning off the lights. "Let's go, Jill."

"I'm staying. What if Rose-Delia shows up here? Please try to understand."

"What you mean is that you're too embarrassed to let the old bitch see what kind of idiot her precious grandson is. That's it, isn't it?"

"No, not exactly." Jill couldn't explain it. She just suddenly wanted to be alone here, with her ghosts.

"What about Beth?"

"Bethy likes *you* more than she likes *me* these days. And she *adores* Tansy. They're probably watching TV right now. Go home to your dinner dates."

"What'll you eat?"

"I don't feel like anything. And there's coffee." Jill hugged Pumpkin. "Now, scat and come back Tuesday with Bethy. Maybe I'll come to New York tomorrow." She handed Pumpkin Ian's insurance papers. "Please send these to Ian by messenger. I've got things to get out of my system and somehow I think that cleaning up this mess is the best way to do it."

Pumpkin hesitated. She was dying to go back to New York; but she was nervous about leaving Jill behind.

"Who knows," said Jill brightly, "I may find some more dishy letters from the fair Helen."

And then something struck Jill; something that had been nudging at her for a while. "Pumpkin, do you remember my telling you that Ian called me 'Helen' and 'Juliet' and compared me to the great romantic beauties?"

Pumpkin nodded. She remembered, vaguely.

"Well, I don't think Ian was comparing me to Helen of Troy and Juliet Capulet. I think he thought he was in bed with our Helen of the lurid prose. And in the hospital he kept saying 'Juliet is the sun.' Remember?"

Pumpkin listened carefully. What *was* Jill driving at?

"Ian thought that *I* was Juliet—that girl in the hospital this afternoon with the dirty little boy. The one who stood up when the intern called for Mrs. Ian Harrington."

Dirty little boy? Juliet? The sun? What gibberish was this? "Jill, you'd better get in the car and come right back to town with me."

Impatience set Jill's jaw. "You must remember, Pumpkin. You said '*This* is Mrs. Harrington' and then you said 'These people can't speak English,' implying that was why the girl had gotten confused. Pumpkin, I don't think that girl was confused. She *is* Mrs. Ian Harrington. That shit has another wife! And her name is Juliet!"

"Jill, you're overwrought." But what if Jill were right? What if Ian *did* have another wife? How many other Juliets? How many other Helens?

"Pumpkin, you know I'm right, don't you?"

"I think you're jumping to conclusions." But in Ian's case, she had to admit, anything was possible.

"No, Pumpkin. I'm jumping at *facts*."

"May I use the phone, Jill?" Pumpkin asked.

"Of course. If it's possible. Only the High Lama knows when the bill was paid."

"I'm canceling my dinner tonight. I'm going to stay right here and help you sort this out."

"Absolutely not. Your dinner's much more important."

"Only to the owners of the restaurant." She grabbed the phone and started to dial. The phone was dead. "Shit." She turned to Jill. "Guess the High Lama's trying to tell me something. Are you *sure* you'll be okay?"

"I'll go next door and call you first thing." How can I ever repay you, Pumpkin? You've been like a mother to me, she thought. She felt a pang of guilt. She'd let Wendy down. But she couldn't think about that now.

Pumpkin pecked her on the cheek. "You sure?"

Jill smiled. "I'm sure."

"Okay, then, I'm off..." her voice trailed off and Jill heard the front door slam.

Where should she start? It really didn't matter. She poured some cold water into the Mr. Coffee machine, filled the filter half full and turned it on. This was one time that she couldn't rely on a stiff drink to get her through. By the time the coffee was ready, strong and black, she'd already hauled three garbage bags out to the garbage cans.

She poured a mug and climbed the stairs to Wendy's room. She lay down on the bed for a moment, hugging the pillow in its Miss Piggy pillowcase. When she woke up, the coffee was ice cold and birds were chattering in the sunny garden.

83

CHAPTER SEVEN

he Harrington family mausoleum presented its impassive Ionic face to the glittering autumn morning. It dominated Kensico Cemetery, a sprawling necropolis of relentless bad taste nestled in verdant Westchester County hills.

Jill hadn't been here since Ian's grandfather, MacDougall Moodie Harrington, had been buried beneath his mother ten years earlier. Jill had liked Mac. A drinker and womanizer, to be sure, but so charming. Nothing at all like his wife Rose-Delia, with her extravagant beauty and tight smile.

Please, dear God, let me get through it without breaking down, Jill prayed for the millionth time.

She'd almost broken down Sunday on the telephone with Charlene Whitrock. Charlene had made sympathetic noises and reassured Jill that she was on the BDK&C payroll as of Monday morning, no matter when she felt ready to start work.

Only a few more hours, and she would be alone with her pain. Wendy's friends and teachers had gone, leaving behind only Rose-Delia.

"Good God, how I loathe nature," the Harrington matriarch declared, drawing her pavement-length sable coat closer. "All this business these days about protecting nature is sheer lunacy. Nature is inhospitable to man. As one who survived the *Titanic*, I can assure you that there is nothing endearing about the North Atlantic in April. That's why I love Palm Beach. They know how to keep nature under control." She paused for a breath. A chill gust cautiously ruffled the hem of her cloak.

"Let's get into the car before we join the rest of the family." She nodded toward the mausoleum. "We might as well lunch up here, too. I'm sure there are no restaurants near the Roosevelt Hospital. You do know of some place, don't you? It's been such a long time since I was last here."

Jill nodded. She felt numb. At least with Rose-Delia she didn't have to worry about keeping up her end of the conversation. "Yes. Emily Shaw's. I think you'll like it. The broiled lobster is good."

"I would hate to think you'd take me to a restaurant that I wouldn't like."

Jill stood politely aside, waiting for Rose-Delia to get into the stretch Lincoln with its bar and telephone. "Go ahead. Go ahead," she urged, shooing Jill toward the door. "It's so much easier for me if you crawl in first."

Crawl. How apt. Rose-Delia had always treated Jill like a naughty child.

Jill scooted over to the far window. Rose-Delia sat down with a sigh and began arranging her sable folds.

"Now. What's all this nonsense about Beth's being unable to attend her sister's funeral?"

"Mrs. Harrington, Beth has had a dreadful experience. She was *there*. She saw the whole terrible thing happen. And she couldn't do anything to stop it. That was only three days ago. It could take her years to get over it."

Beth had refused absolutely to go the funeral. "Tell them I'm in shock. I'm staying with Tansy. She's the only person who cares about me." Then she'd locked herself in her room.

Jill hadn't really believed Bethy but had let her stay at Pumpkin's anyway. As a child, Jill had been forced to go to the funerals of great-aunts and uncles she barely knew, been made to kiss their pink sewn-together lips. She vowed that when she grew up, no child of hers would have to go through that.

"As funerals go, that wasn't too mawkish. And not too much noise," Rose-Delia sniffed. "I hate too much music in church."

Jill nodded.

"Very good taste, Jill. I detest carcasses made up for cocktails. No one shall be permitted to deface my remains so that people can skulk around saying 'doesn't she look well, considering.' Disgusting."

Jill listened, dumbfounded. Rose-Delia was talking about her own great-granddaughter!

"I want to hear exactly what my grandson has been up to. My lawyer, Hogwood Worth, says that Ian hasn't had a job in quite some time. Months. Is that true?"

"Longer than months, Mrs. Harrington," Jill answered guardedly, relieved to be off the topic of Wendy. "Almost a year."

"Good heavens! Whatever does he do with himself? Mac went to the office every day until he was eighty."

The memory of her plundered home flooded Jill. "He's been job-hunting."

"Well, it certainly doesn't look as though he's been too successful at it."

"He's mailed out hundreds of resumés."

"Um. And stamps so expensive lately. Then what? He sits there waiting for the telephone to ring? For the world to beat a path to Badger Hollow?"

"Ian reads a lot. English works. Eighteenth century, mostly. Do you know John Wilkes?" Jill prodded cautiously, remembering the "few good fucks" doggerel.

"Never heard of him."

"And he does the crosswords. Daily *and* Sunday. Sometimes he even writes his own puzzles and submits them to the *New York Times.*"

"Really? How lucrative can that be?"

"Not very. He has some unemployment left, I think. And he's managed to keep up his medical insurance. The hospital shouldn't be all that expensive."

"Always thought unemployment was a bad idea. Encourages people to be idlers. They should get rid of it. Be that as it may, things do sound dreadful. My grandson sounds like an idiot. He's a married man with responsibilities. It doesn't seem that he takes them seriously."

"No, Mrs. Harrington, he doesn't." Was Rose-Delia trying to be polite in some obtuse way? Or was she pumping her?

"What you're saying then, dear child, is that my grandson is a lousy provider."

Jill gazed out of the window. Now she was "dear child." Rose went on.

"And that he stinks as a husband and father."

Jill knew that if she tried to speak, she'd cry. The upholstered silence cradled them. Rose-Delia leaned forward and pushed a button. The glass panel shot across, insulating them from the driver.

Rose-Delia slouched out of her sable and leaned back with a sigh. "Now we can talk. Forgive me for not understanding. I want you to tell me everything. I've sensed that your lives haven't been going too well for quite some time. Ian's letters to me sound like the ravings of a lunatic. He wanted me to invest a great deal of money in a production of *Don Giovanni*. Something about a breakthrough in the theater and if Don Giovanni were alive today, he'd have fast cars and fast food. The production was to be in a burger restaurant. Does that make any sense to you, Jill?"

Oh, God. The horrible night Ian had pulled down Pumpkin's Chippendale breakfront, smashing nearly everything in it. "No," Jill said, "and Ian doesn't even sing that well."

"Well, he thinks he does. Like his father before him." Rose-Delia winced at the memory.

To her own amazement, Jill suddenly felt like laughing. "It did sound like a crazy idea."

"So was the *Hindenburg*." Rose-Delia replied tartly. "I hope you didn't give Ian any money for *that* project?"

Rose-Delia's pale lashes fluttered as she assessed Jill's wardrobe. No jewelry. Appropriate black. No furs. Black cashmere coat, edges of the cuffs thin as knife blades.

She'd always thought Jill such a frump. Too fat. No style. No conversation. Now, she was almost chic and extremely lovely. What had happened?

"I didn't have any money to give Ian, Mrs. Harrington. I haven't a penny. Just Ian's unemployment checks. Before that, Ian's jobs. The last one only paid twenty-four thousand. He refused to let me go back to work. But I'm going back now."

"I had no idea!" Rose-Delia sounded genuinely shocked. "All I know was what Ian chose to write me. And you, Jill, never wrote at all. It's sad when families can't confide in each other."

Rose-Delia patted Jill's knee. "Ian wrote that your mother left you quite well off but that you refuse to spend anything for schools or clothes. So I've been sending Ian money. Did you know that?"

Jill's mouth dropped open in disbelief. So that's how he'd gotten all that credit.

Rose-Delia didn't seem to notice Jill's expression. "Ian was so delighted when I made it possible for the girls to board at Laurel Hall he flew down to Palm Beach to thank me and take me out to dinner. I was flattered, I must say." But Jill didn't hear her.

Rose-Delia had been sending Ian money? And she hadn't known a thing about it! All that time she'd been sitting at the kitchen table fumbling with bills and coupons there'd been money? Rose-Delia had no reason to lie. But it was all so preposterous. It all made her look like a fool. She felt her cheeks burning under Rose-Delia's curious stare.

"And, Jill, about the kitchen?" Rose-Delia went on. "That was really too bad. Now that I'm thinking of it let me say that even though I'd always thought you were a bit aloof I never thought you had bad manners. That is, until you didn't thank me for the sizeable check I sent you and Ian for the damages. And the very idea of your napping with a cigarette. Really, Jill! It's so dangerous. The whole house could have gone up."

Jill turned horrified eyes to Rose-Delia. Had she gone 'round the bend? But accusing Jill of having burned her own kitchen! The injustice stung.

Obviously, Ian had lied. There seemed to be no end to his devious ways. Here she was, with her crash course in glamour, her shiny new job, the ninety thousand in cash that she'd gotten from the bank cash machines, and she felt just as desolate as the day Pumpkin had first called her for lunch.

"Mrs. Harrington, I don't smoke. I never have," was all that Jill could choke out.

"What? Never smoked? Ian says you're a chain smoker. He wrote that he feared for the girls' lives because you smoked in bed. That's one of the reasons he was elated when I made it possible for them to board at Laurel Hall."

"Ian started the fire, Mrs. Harrington. He left some ducks... already-cooked ducks... under the broiler and went off to the public library." What did she mean about *her* making it possible for the girls to board?

"Oh?" Rose-Delia's pale eyes widened. "Ian did *that?* Probably lost in thought, studying up on that Wilkes fellow."

"You see, Mrs. Harrington, I was at my wits' end when my college roommate, Pumpkin Osborne—you met her at the church—rescued me. *She* loaned me the money for the school. *She* loaned me the money for the kitchen. Took us into her apartment so that I could get a job. *I* had to try to make things work, Mrs. Harrington. But I guess I don't expect you to understand."

"Understand? It's all quite amazing, really. I wish Mac were here. He'd know how to handle Ian. It's all so difficult, Jill. Being a woman alone."

Rose-Delia could have been a woman alone against Napoleon's army and won.

She flicked a small lever and the bar opened. "I think we need a little restorative nip to help us along with our conversation. Besides, they always take so infernally long to bring cocktails in restaurants, don't you think? Of course, maybe that's the impatience of old age. When one's time is running out, Jill, one's patience is down around one's ankles."

She poured two inches of vodka into each of two glasses, added ice and handed one to Jill. "I'm supposed to drink only sherry but I detest it. Glues my teeth together."

By the time they had reached Emily Shaw's Inn, Jill had confided completely in Rose-Delia. The Bills. Ian's lies. The letters. Helen. Juliet. Bethy's hatred.

It gushed out. She didn't understand how she could unburden herself so easily to a woman she'd spent more than twelve years hating, but now it didn't seem to matter. Maybe there was, in Wendy's death, a resolution of sorts, and Jill had finally found a friend in this remarkable woman. Rose-Delia had lived such an exciting life. Even Mac's dying in her arms—in their suite at Claridge's, in the middle of a telephone conversation with Lord Mountbatten—was glamorous. Could Jill dislike Rose-Delia simply because she envied that life?

On impulse, Jill asked, "Were you ever afraid, Mrs. Harrington?"

"Oh, my goodness, yes. But what an odd question, my dear."

"Pumpkin Osborne and I were discussing fear last Saturday night. I guess it's on my mind. But you! It doesn't seem like anything would scare *you*."

"I have two great fears, my dear. One I face every day; the other only occasionally."

What could Rose-Delia possibly be afraid of? Death? Old age?

"Poverty," whispered Rose-Delia. "And drowning. I've

never gotten over the North Atlantic that April night."

"You? Afraid of being poor?" Had Rose-Delia ever paid a bill by herself? And drowning? Surely she didn't swim?

"There was a time when I didn't have millions. Ah, looks like we're here. I hope the lobsters are good today. I have to get my strength up to face Ian."

"Was it an accident? Your millions, I mean," Jill asked.

"How perceptive of you. Unless Ian has told you? *Has* Ian told you anything about me?"

"No. Just that he had no other relatives."

"I mentioned that I was on the *Titanic*." Rose-Delia sipped the last of her vodka, replaced the glass in the bar, and blotted her lips on an ecru silk handkerchief, the Harrington crest discreetly but distinctly visible in one corner. Rose-Delia gazed off into the distance, back into the past. Even now, ten years later, it still hurt to talk about Mac.

"You see, Jill, I was the maid's daughter. Mrs. MacDougall Harrington, Senior's maid's daughter. Everyone in our party was lost in the water but Mac and I. My mother, his parents, his twin sisters were all drowned.

"I went home with Mac. His was the only home I'd ever known. I was thirteen years old and had what your generation refers to as a 'crush' on Mac. He was twenty-three and worked downtown, on the Cotton Exchange.

"We were married on my sixteenth birthday. And we stayed married fifty-seven years. We had such a wonderful life, Jill. I wish you and Ian could have had a life like ours."

So do I, Jill thought. But it's too late now.

"All during our year-long stay in England, I could barely speak to Mac without blushing. Not without butterflies or blushes or speaking too rapidly and saying all the wrong things. Do you know what I mean, Jill?"

Jill knew all too well. Keefe Neuman had the same effect on her and she was a long way from thirteen.

"But after Mac hauled me into the lifeboat, I never stopped talking. Talking is the secret of a good marriage, Jill. Not sex. Not money. It's talking."

More talk with Ian? Impossible.

"Be thankful for Beth, Jill. And for that nice position at the advertising agency. It's going to save your life in the months ahead. I know."

Jill took Rose-Delia's arm and slowly, regally, they glided toward the restaurant. "When Mac went, Jill, I was much more afraid of living than dying. So I want you to stop trying to be so brave. Women's lib, women's fib. Without money, there are no real choices."

When Rose-Delia dropped Jill off in Badger Hollow, Jill had a check in her bag for one hundred thousand dollars.

Hours later, as she sat alone in her Country Kitchen, Jill remembered the cards that one of Wendy's classmates had collected from the flowers and slipped into her coat pocket. It was only then that Jill realized that she was still wearing her coat.

She spread the cards, like so many little white tombstones, on the kitchen table.

Joan Appleshade, the headmistress. The class. Noël St. Martin. Charlene Whitrock. Ian. Bethy (Pumpkin's handwriting). Pumpkin. Rose-Delia. And...Keefe Neuman.

She'd lost a piece of herself forever. Could she live with that? She buried her face in her arms and gave in to the pain.

She thought of Pumpkin. Had she really loved her for twenty years? Jill was glad her friend had left for London. She needed to think.

It was the last thing she thought of. She didn't even hear the telephone ringing.

After a dozen rings, Keefe hung up. Jill was probably asleep. She shouldn't be up there alone. She was so beautiful, so vulnerable. He had no right to intrude on her grief, yet he had the urge to drive up. She'd think he was crazy. He'd only met her once. Still...

CHAPTER EIGHT

Jill's first day at BDK&C was only a few hours old, but already she felt like she was up to her chin in quicksand. It was all so different from the way she'd remembered her old job at Philpott Associates, twelve years ago.

She couldn't believe the noise. Shouting. Singing. Whistling. No one seemed to speak in a normal tone of voice. Radios blared. And everyone was so young.

Charlene Whitrock had warned her that most of the people she'd be working with would be at least ten years younger than she, but Jill wasn't prepared for high school students.

She wasn't ready for Chip La Doza, her art director, when he appeared at the doorless entrance to her steel-and-frosted-glass cubicle.

Not only was he young, but he was tiny, dressed in a banker's charcoal pinstriped suit. At least it was a change from the others on the creative floor, all of whom looked like they were going to a disco, working on a ranch or acting in a World War II movie.

"Welcome to Boring, Dreary, Kinky and Crappy, Jill." He extended his hand. "I'm Chip La Doza."

He dumped a pile of proofs and tear sheets onto Jill's army-issue desk. "Here we are. Archives. Ancient history. Every Country Kitchens print ad since Charlene Whitrock was a pup."

"Hi, Chip. What's the 'Boring, Dreary' routine?"

Did she sound with-it enough? God, she hoped so.

"B-D-K-&-C. Clever, huh? And people think art directors can't write!"

"Clever is right. To have found me. I can't even find the ladies' room."

"I wouldn't use that word if I were you. The feminists here will stone you." Chip's words tumbled out in little clusters.

Jill smiled again. She was getting sick of smiling.

"Jill, after we review this stuff—God, I sound like an account man—anyway, maybe then you'd like to have lunch with me and we could catch up. There's a little restaurant on the ground floor. Maybe you noticed it? Chez Venezia? On the crummy side, but convenient."

"I'd love to." How phony she sounded. Chip was being so nice, trying to make her feel welcome. "I love Italian." Did that sound better?

"Actually, the only Italian thing about it is the name. It's burgers. And they just recently graduated to table cloths. Now, into the screening room for an hour of the most boring footage ever committed to film or tape, or so I was told by the previous art director."

"What happened to him?"

"*Her.* Charlie got pissed after hearing her talking about transferring to another group, so she transferred her over to the radial tire account."

Jill suddenly felt like she couldn't handle anything. Her new chic image was a myth. She ached to shed her dressed-for-success griege gabardine suit and peach silk shirt for some old jeans. She was too *old* for all of this. Who was she kidding?

"I'm glad we're going to be working together," Jill told Chip as they passed a guy carrying ten pounds of layouts. He was wearing a bright orange Con Ed rain poncho and hard hat and was whistling *What a Friend We Have in Jesus.*

"Blind leading the unsighted, Jill," said Chip. "I'm as new as you are on this account. Got on it last Sunday, when I received the telephone summons from Charlie. Your arrival has saved me from working on the dreaded Bronkhorst Drug account. Hemorrhoid preparations. You are my guardian angel, Jill. We're also going to be working on the Ida-Ho potato account. Gourmet all the way."

"I've used Ida-Ho. Not bad."

"Not bad? Sweetheart, this is BDK&C. You better say you love 'em."

Jill was starving. Oh, for some mashed potatoes drizzled with butter. Even Ida-Hos.

Jill glanced around Chez Venezia. She'd never realized that red came in so many shades.

"Is BKD&C political?" she asked innocently. Pumpkin had already warned her about the office politics.

"Political? Good God! BDK&C is so political that they're all cross-eyed trying to figure out which ass to kiss first." Chip stirred his white wine spritzer.

It was dark enough for Jill to stare at Chip without his noticing. He was twenty-seven, had been an art director at BDK&C for five years. He seemed to hate his job, his life, his parents, his borderline homosexuality. Jill couldn't figure out why he was so cheerful.

"It was terrific of you to ask me to lunch."

"My pleasure." He looked like he meant it. "Now, who else do you know upstairs besides Old Leather Cunt?"

"Old Lea..."

"Charlene Whitrock."

"Just Charlie. And you. I like her, Chip. She's giving me a chance. I don't think you know how much that means to me."

"If she didn't think you were any good, you wouldn't be

here. That's our Charlie. That's business in general."

"Well, *I* think she's great." That's what her instincts told her to say. She sipped her white wine. She longed to grab a piece of Italian bread and slather it with butter. But she knew she could never do that again.

"Listen, babe, Charlie's the Queen Mum compared to some of the talent."

"Ohhh?"

"Wait till you meet Alison Dollberg. And her mentor, Lamont Fredsmith. Those two have the greatest relationship since Pavlov and his dog. They've got about fifty mil in billings sewn up between them. You'll love Alison, Jill. Just your type. She went from assistant account coordinator—that's one grade above elevator operator—to senior vice-president in less time than it takes for a Big Mac to arrive."

"Ohh," Jill said again. Best to be noncommittal and soak up everything. Just listen.

"And then there's Nellie Nellie, a.k.a Ellie Ellie. Wait till you catch his act."

"His? Nellie Nellie?"

"A day without Nellie Nellie is like a day without locusts."

"Why do you say that?"

"Nils Nelson. The only fag I ever met who didn't dress well." Chip La Doza glanced nervously at the sleeve of his impeccable pinstriped suit.

"We seem to have a two-thirty meeting with him. Some sort of tie-in ad featuring Ida-Hos. The memo was on my desk when I got back from the screening room. There also seems to be a meeting on something called 'Country Kitchens Goes Gourmet.' Shouldn't it be 'Country Kitchens Go Gourmet?'"

"Leave sleeping cans of worms lie, Jill. Charlie tells me she's been trying to stop them on that since the advent of the gas range. But that's the way they like it."

Jill peeked at her watch. "Maybe we should order?"

"Right. Don't want to keep the grand old fag waiting. At two-thirty, you'll wish you never left the farm."

Ian would love that. Badger Hollow. The *farm*. It fit perfectly his concept of a mini-estate in big estate country.

"I mean it, Jill, ol' pal. Wait till the presentation."

"What presentation?"

"Any presentation. I can't wait to see your face when Nellie Nellie, who looks like an aging boy marine, lisps in to action."

"Oh, come *on*. No one can be that bad."

"Oh, yeah? You just got yourself a date for cocktails. With me. After work." Chip waved for the waiter.

Was Chip telling the truth? Or, was he posturing for her benefit? Pumpkin's advice had filled her with dread. But then, Pumpkin had never worked for an advertising agency.

"*AND*, my dear, do you know what qualifies Nellie Nellie to act as management supervisor on a food account and a home decor account? Huh? A degree in home ec? A member of *AID?* Can he cook? Of course not. To all of the above. Has he ever set foot in a kitchen? Not bloody likely. And, does he have taste? A prime prerequisite, one might think. No to all of the above."

"But Chip, he must have *some*thing."

"Does he, I ask you, understand the modern American houseperson? Her hopes? Wants? Desires? No, I tell you!"

"Shh, Chip," Jill hushed. "I thought you've never worked with him before?"

"Not on these accounts. But I've worked with him on the tampon account, the bra account, the cake mix account, the panty hose account. This place just loves to put all kinds of weirdo guys on women's accounts. You'll see. It really pisses Charlie off. And she's right. Somebody up there thinks men know best. But in the end, Mother knows best."

Was this true?

"Anyhow, what qualifies Ellie Ellie to work on accounts like these, especially Country Kitchens? You almost got me off the track, Jill," Chip laughed.

Jill shook her head to a second white wine. The first was eating holes in her stomach.

"Mr. Nils Nelson *has*, to his credit, learned the difference between sheet vinyl flooring and vinyl tile. A fucking breakthrough, according to Charlie. She says his arches are higher than his IQ."

"Chip, let's be sensible. Why would an agency like BDK&C—a big, fat, rich, blue-chip international advertising agency, put a guy on an account that he wasn't right for?"

"You won't believe it. The FBI wouldn't believe it. The CIA wouldn't believe it."

"Try me."

"For the past ten years, there have been fifteen different management supervisors on Country Kitchens. Ellie is the first one who hasn't been asked off."

"That's worth something, Chip."

"I have saved the best for last. Know why?"

"Tell me."

"He's the first agency guy who isn't taller than the advertising manager of Country Kitchens. In fact, he's shorter than the ad manager. A short Swede! Frankly, I think *I'm* on the fucking account because I'm a fucking *midget*. Let's order."

"Multi-million dollar businesses don't sink or swim because of the relative heights of the personnel," Jill said finally.

"Jill, even little me isn't creative enough to make *that* up."

For once in his life, Chip La Doza had a captive audience. He leaned across the table. "I'm going to give you some lessons in survival, Jill. You've got to watch out for everyone upstairs. As bad as the account guys are, as absurd as Ellie Ellie is, the women are the worst." He took a deep breath. "And because you're so lovely, Jill, you're really going to have to watch it."

Jill stared at Chip in horror. Where was women's lib? Maybe Rose-Delia *was* right.

"The worst one of all, the queen of the termagants, is Old Leather Cunt. She'll steal your ideas right out of your typewriter. She'll steal your ideas *before* you know you have them. Then months later, pouf! Right on TV. Something she killed or said wasn't creative enough. All of which she has taken credit for.

"You'll go to Charlie. Maybe in tears, although I wouldn't

advise it. She'll invite you to lunch. Give you a two peso raise. You'll end up apologizing for having bothered her."

"But she seems so sincere." So had Ian.

Chip shook his head. "And then there's FiFi Woolverson. She'll try to get you into her group, away from Charlie. She tries it with every new writer. Her group is known as the walking wounded. Stay away."

Chip took a gulp of his ice water. "FiFi never does any work in the office. But *ne-vair*. Comes in late. Lunches late. Usually with someone she wants to pump the shit out of. Goes home early. The next day... *voilà*! She appears with the problem solved and half a dozen good commercials."

"I don't think I could work at home," Jill began.

"FiFi Woolverson, whose middle name is The Vintage Whiner for obvious reasons, can't either. Her husband does all of her work at night. Barry Pozner. Ever hear of him? Major talent. She thinks no one knows. *Everyone* knows."

"Isn't there something illegal about that?"

"Look, they pay FiFi fifty and change. BDK&C would have to pay Barry Pozner three times that if he worked here, which he probably wouldn't. So, the way things are, BDK&C gets *his* work at *her* price. Now who's stupid?"

"Things like that only happen in movies."

"Godzilla meets Charlie Whitrock. And that, dear Jill, is only Chapter Uno.

"How about a chili burger, *garni*, with raw onions, mozzarella and plenty of guacamole? I'm having the ribs."

"Executive salad," Jill ordered without conviction. Ian would hate her asking for executive *any*thing.

"Now, for the acid test, Jill. Do you honestly believe that your beloved Charlie will ever give you a break? See that you get a grown-up woman's raise? Or promote you?"

"Why not?"

"Charlie will not promote you. You'll get pissant raises. And lectures. She will explain how she has put her (a) head on the block (b) ass on the line (c) both to make them cough it up for you."

"I had no idea. Twelve years ago, advertising agencies were serious places. You worked hard together. Did your best. Helped your clients. All that American dream stuff my husband says died a malignant death."

"Advertising agencies *are* serious places, Jill. *Too* serious. That's why we're always trying desperately to have fun—with greed, envy, and fear—the supreme motivators of human nature!"

Jill listened intently. When she was at Philpott she wouldn't have understood any of this. She'd fancied herself the pink tornado, taking Madison Avenue by storm.

"If today is confusing, Jill, wait till tomorrow."

Jill laughed.

Was it BDK&C that had made Chip so neurotic? If so, how could *her* sanity take it? But then, if Ian hadn't driven her over the edge, the Byzantine politics of the agency probably wouldn't, either.

If someone had told her four months ago that her life would change completely, she would have told them they were crazy. And yet, it *had* happened.

Here she was, sitting in a minus-four-star restaurant, hanging on every one of Chip La Doza's not-too-well-chosen words. But at least she was in New York, not Badger Hollow. And she had a job.

It was all because of Pumpkin. Pumpkin coaxing, encouraging, patting her on the head. It had been difficult during the three grueling months, and in retrospect it seemed almost impossible. How could Chip ever understand what she'd been through? How could Chip, who'd never even been married, understand about Wendy? Maybe it didn't matter if he did.

Jill knew it was a mistake to take everything he said seriously. Most of it—on the surface anyway—seemed like utter nonsense.

Grown people, advertising superstars, just couldn't behave the way Chip painted them. Anyone with an IQ above ten knew that.

But then, anyone with an IQ above ten wouldn't have believed Ian for twelve minutes, let alone twelve years.

God. *Twelve years.*

In twelve years, Shakespeare had written *Troilus and Cressida, All's Well That Ends Well, Measure for Measure, Othello, King Lear, Macbeth, Timon of Athens, Pericles, Cymbeline* and *The Winter's Tale.*

In twelve years, they'd built the Colossus of Rhodes. In twelve years, Napoleon had conquered most of Europe.

In twelve years, all she'd done was push two screaming babies into being and cooked thirteen thousand meals, give or take a few hundred hamburgers seared by Ian in the backyard.

Where would she be twelve years from now?

Would her hair look like Charlie's? Would she still know Chip? Would it make any difference what went on at BDK&C? Would anyone love her?

Chip straightened up and began fiddling nervously with his tie.

"Don't look now, kid, but Bonehead's making an entrance. Betsy Bloomingdale must be picnicking at his table at Le Cirque. And with him is none other than Charlie Whitrock, dressed to the eights."

"Bonehead?" What now?

"That's our not-too-secret name for Brodhead Kincaid. The president and CEO."

"The 'K' of BDK&C?" What was a CEO?

"That was Bonehead's father, Grayson Palmer Kincaid, the ultimate WASP. Flushed his dentures in the head on his yacht and drowned trying to retrieve them." Chip yawned.

"He left Bonehead with all the trappings of your average, insufferable rich kid. But, Bonehead, to his credit, turned himself into *Everyman*. That is, *Everyman* with tax shelters. Just don't kid yourself, Jill, Bonehead is the smartest person in the agency. The rest of the biggies are stuffed with sawdust."

"Chip, is this a cram course?"

"Mere openers. Lesson *Deux*: how to make it through one of Bonehead's Chinese fire drills without panic or paranoia."

Jill looked at Chip. "Chinese fire drills?"

"When Bonehead gets a big idea, and most of Bonehead's ideas are, he writes it down immediately. *Toute suite*. On toilet paper, his cuffs, margins of the *New York Times*. Then, his secretary makes Xerox copies of his notes and distributes them to several different creative groups. Whoever comes up with the most good ideas in the least amount of time, wins."

"Wins what?"

"Free drinks in the great man's office. Wait'll you see it. Art *directoire*."

Jill's heart sank. She'd never been able to work very fast. And now she was not only rusty but terrified. "How important are these... 'Chinese fire drills'?"

"How important is a fire extinguisher at a midnight fire at sea? We go to work like teams of paramedics."

The waiter plunked a salad in front of her and what looked like a mastadon graveyard in front of Chip.

"What's a 'CEO,' Chip?"

"Chief executive officer. Business-ese for grand vizier. And, love, one last thing before I forget. Eventually, you will be commanded to appear at a Bonehead agency-client gala, held at the Kincaids' penthouse."

"Ummm. What's his wife like, Chip?"

"Which one? Sassy Van Pelt? Bunny Longford? Sissy Maidstone Suzy Stanford Kincaid's the current one. She's great. Puts up with Bonehead's rotten kids. Actually, only one of them is rotten. The other one is a psychiatrist. Fighting back, I'd guess you'd call it."

"What's the matter with... Mr. Kincaid?" All the times she'd thought about running away from Ian! Bonehead had to be worse to drive three wives away.

"Combination male chauvinist-pip-spoiled-brat-marketing-genius-charmer. Clients really dig him. Plays squash with them and beats the shit out of them. They love him for it."

Jill chewed some lettuce. How in the world was she going

to cope with *this?* Maybe Pumpkin would take her back. With her hundred-ninety-thousand, she could afford to deliver lamp shades and still send Bethy to school.

"Know what else?" Chip gnawed at the ribs. "Bonehead sends clients the best presents on earth. And wait till you see the cards. Christ, they put fourteenth century monks to shame. Written by eighty-thousand-dollar copywriters. With Bonehead, it's real brush strokes. All the way."

Jill speared a cucumber. The Bills. The tired old clothes. They seemed like such good friends. Friendlier even than Pumpkin's decorating business.

If she let herself dwell on her precarious new position, she'd crack. What was she afraid of, anyway? Not Ian. Not the agency. Not even Charlie. Maybe she was afraid of herself.

All the new things she had to remember. All the new things she had to learn. And not just the important things. The not-so-important things.

The more she listened, the more afraid she became.

It seemed like she'd traded in one set of fears for another. And with this one the risks were greater.

Black cats and thunderstorms and getting her period in a white skirt paled in comparison to Charlie's, Pumpkin's, even Chip's expectations. And it was exhausting, having to hide all along how vulnerable she was.

What if she failed?

It hit her with the unexpected swiftness of a poisoned dart. With all the books she'd read about re-entering the job market, with all of Pumpkin's pep rallies, she was woefully ill-prepared for BDK&C.

How long could she bluff, before a Charlie or a Chip or one of those account management people stripped off her shell and left her naked in the marketplace?

"You know, Jill, you're the best thing that's happened to BDK&C since the bomb scare last summer...when we all left at two and went to a bar." He grinned. Barbecue sauce stained his front teeth.

"And Jill, Charlie will try to keep you away from Bonehead.

So, when he asks you to work on one of his so-called 'secret projects,' which he will because you're new and beautiful and have great legs, don't tell Charlie anything."

"Why not? She's bound to find out."

"Finding out is one thing. Confiding in her is another. You see, Charlie is after Bonehead. She considers herself the quintessential geriatric sex symbol.

"Rumor has it that S. S. Kincaid is fed up to the porcelain jackets with Bonehead. They've been married three years. A new world's record. The rotten kid is getting to her. He made a bomb in chemistry class and blew the door off the chemistry professor's house with it."

That sounded like the young Ian. Tomorrow, at lunchtime, she had an appointment with Ralston Rhodes, who'd handle the divorce. Tomorrow, at this very moment, she would be getting a full report on Helen and Juliet and whatever else Ralston had come up with on Ian. In an odd way, she was looking forward to it. Sometimes she still couldn't believe all this had happened to her. Now that she thought about it, she really wasn't jealous of Helen or Juliet. That surprised her. More than anything, she wanted revenge.

Emptying Ian's Visa and Mastercard accounts had helped a little. But not enough.

Chip studied Jill as she stared off into the smoky, red, pine-disinfected room. Had he bored her? Maybe he'd said too much.

"Look, Jill," he began gently, "I like Bonehead. I really do. I even like Nellie Nellie, in my own dumb way. But liking someone has nothing to do with the real world. When you work at BDK&C, the real world is situated on floors two-through-ten. If you should happen to have another life outside the agency—God forbid—don't mention it to anyone upstairs. Don't give them any problems unless you've already got the solutions."

Jill stared at a tomato in her salad.

"Jill, you're not angry or anything, are you? I mean, I know I'm jaded, but I'm just trying to help—"

Jill smiled. "Of course I'm not angry. I was just thinking about something that has to be resolved tomorrow. About my—husband." The old pain came flooding back.

Chip reached across the table and touched her hand. "I probably shouldn't tell you this, but last week, the cashier was bitten by a rat."

"But she's miles from the kitchen."

"Shows you what rats think of the cuisine here."

Chip had done wonders for her confidence. Now all she had was the rest of her life to get through, starting with this afternoon.

It all seemed so improbable. Alison Dollberg. Lamont Fredsmith. FiFi Woolverson. Bonehead. Nellie Nellie. They couldn't be real. Chip must have created them with a Magic Marker on a layout pad. Slick, fast and one-dimensional. Well, she'd find out soon enough.

At two-thirty, she met Chip in front of Nellie's office. Chip leaned close to her ear. "Just remember, Nellie's gone down on everything but the *Andrea Doria*."

The office door flew open and a wiry, little man with a crew cut told them to come in and sit down.

"Tea? Coffee?" he asked amiably. He was wearing a baggy Brooks Brothers suit, a faded blue shirt, and a narrow striped tie. Jill smiled. Ian Harrington reject store.

Jill and Chip declined tea and coffee, and started spreading Country Kitchens layouts on the cocktail table.

"No need to do that. I've seen that shit a million times," he growled. "Let's get to the point, shall we? Hate beating around the bush."

"Ellie never beat around a bush in his life," Chip whispered.

Jill smiled politely. It seemed she'd spent the entire day smiling. She didn't feel like smiling.

"What we have here, er, Miss Harrington, is an age-old advertising problem: How to give the client what he wants and still not compromise our integrity. Translation, how can we look good and still do it their way?"

Jill nodded and turned to Chip. Chip nodded.

Ellie continued. "I'm here to tell you how to do it. How to do it! We do exactly as we have in the past. No surprises." In his baronial leather swivel chair he lit a cigar and exhaled a cloud of smoke into the air.

"This client hates clever. *I* hate clever. Now, I want you two to get off on the right foot down the yellow brick road." He puffed more smoke into the air.

He leapt from his chair and began pacing, his head down. He looked like an angry bull, except he was wearing trousers that were only as long as Elizabeth Taylor's formals in the Fifties.

So, he'd gone down on everything but the *Andrea Doria*. Well, if he ever tried to intimidate her—which she was sure he was going to try to do—Jill would remember that. At least she didn't have to worry about sexual harassment. She fixated on the hem of his trousers.

"You see, guys, we've got certain funds heel-marked for ads and we've got to stay within that budget or we're dead in the water. Dead in the water."

Chip spoke up.

"I think I'll have that coffee now. And Jill will, too." The goddamn meeting was turning into the Potsdam Conference.

The door burst open and in strode Buster Niles, the account supervisor on Country Kitchens. Buster's chest had fallen somewhere north of his belt. His shiny black shoes were crafted entirely of mad-made materials. His eyes darted around the room. Should he smile first or get down to business first? Which power ploy should he use?

"Got the figures right here," Buster announced with caution.

"Good. Good." Ellie grabbed the manila folder from Buster's anxious fingers. "Which figures are these? Or are they just all-purpose figures? How do I know they don't belong to another account?"

Buster Niles didn't know whether he should laugh or leave

the room. "Those are the correct, most recent figures on the Kitchens."

Ellie sniggered. "And, Niles, what have we learned from these 'correct, most recent figures'?"

"That we really don't have enough money for new photography. Well, actually, we *do* have enough money for new photography, but if we spend it we won't have enough money to buy space."

Jill had never been in a meeting with top executives before. At Philpott Associates, she'd only met with the youngest account men, who'd always appeared with endless memos and due dates, and before she'd had a chance to learn their names, they'd quit and gone to other agencies.

Buster Niles was shaking. His putty upper lip was damp. Maybe no one will ask me a question, Jill prayed. If this job meant making any sense out of this mess, she might as well sign up for unemployment now.

"OK. OK. Got the picture? Understand where we're going?"

Where the hell *were* they going? Jill swallowed the urge to ask.

"Well," said Chip, stretching up to his full five-three, "it looks like everything we've discussed since Sears discovered Roebuck. Go with old art, old photographs and rearrange them with new headlines."

"Right. Right," Ellie nodded. "And we need it tomorrow. Eleven o'clock meeting. Nothing clever. No surprises. We don't want to make waves."

Panic gripped Jill. How could she go to an eleven o'clock meeting and still make her noon appointment with Ralston Rhodes?

"How about tomorrow at *four?* It may seem like the same old shit to *you,* but we have to pull it together," Chip said heartily. He marched to Ellie's desk to make the point. "Four."

"Four? Why not, La Doza? Why not? Now, take a hike." Ellie waved them toward the door and picked up the telephone.

Jill caught a sideways glance at Buster Niles. He was paler than his shirt. He looked at her. He shook his head, excavated a gray handkerchief from his hip pocket and mopped his face. He mouthed a "phew," and grabbed his manila folder.

Ellie was shouting at someone named Joe Chang. Then he began yapping about the cough syrup strategy. Apparently the meeting was over.

Jill had never been so confused in her life. She stumbled after Chip La Doza to the elevator.

"That was the meeting?"

"Yup."

"Well, he didn't lisp into action. And his clothes, while a bit rumpled, are fine. All he did was ramble on and try to give Buster Niles premature cardiac arrest. That's a captain of industry?" Christ, why had Ian had so much trouble?

"That's pretty perceptive, Jill. Keep up that thinking and you'll end up running this account." He rang for the elevator.

"You know Ellie isn't playing with a full deck. But he makes up for it in devotion to the company. Ah, the elevator. Now, we'll have some real coffee. In my office. After you."

"What happens now?"

"We go to my office. We have some coffee to clear away the negative ions in Ellie's office. Then, we do some ads. Lots of 'em. And along about four, some of Ellie's flunkies—Niles and Snarty—will meander up to 'look over our shoulders' as they like to say. Don't let it bother you. It makes them feel as though they're contributing."

As they got off the elevator, they almost decked an emaciated woman in a sable turban. "Hi, Chipper," she chirped, eyeing Jill suspiciously as she slipped into the elevator.

"Who is that, you ask? *That* is FiFi Woolverson. She is either going out to one of her fabled late lunches or she is leaving early, for the day. Perhaps she's going to Elizabeth Arden to have her behind sanded."

Jill glanced at her watch. Three-thirty-two.

"Or perhaps a late afternoon tryst with a romantic lover.

Or, a late afternoon fuck with a not-so-romantic lover. Who gives a *merde?*"

Chip's office. All the pencils were the same length; all the books were slipcovered in shiny white paper with gold hand-lettered titles. The walls, furniture, curtains were white. A hot pink neon sign spelling *Breathless* flashed on and off at two-second intervals.

"First, coffee. Then, work. Followed by derision. Cheer up, Jill, you and I'll have some fun. The writers and the art directors are the only ones who have any fun in an advertising agency. And if you don't believe me, do you think Buster Niles ever had any fun in his life?"

"Doesn't seem like Buster ever had any fun anywhere."

Chip handed Jill a steaming cup of espresso. "I drink only espresso. Those with Sanka-brand hang-ups need not apply."

Chip's espresso was delicious. Just as delicious as Jason Picker's had been backstage at the Community Theater. Until she'd wrapped her fingers around the delicate demitasse handle, she hadn't realized how cold she was.

"Now what?" The idea of actually sitting down and working terrified her.

"What's this 'now what' stuff? You and I are going to do some ads. We are not going to panic. We do not give it a second thought that very soon those maniacs will burst through the door like Nazi Storm Troopers on a panty raid. I will do squiggles indicating a benign kitchen scene. You will write some lines. It will be easy. Charlie says you're a kitchen expert."

"I guess you could put it that way."

"Need more strength?" Chip reached into a large file drawer and took out a bottle of cognac. He waved it at her. She shook her head no. He wasn't making her feel any better.

"You know, it's impossible to give them too many layouts. If it weren't for us, they wouldn't have any jobs because *without* us, there wouldn't be anything for them to sell to the clients. But they treat us like second class citizens anyhow."

In an hour, Chip and Jill had managed to do twenty different layouts. In less than two hours, they had almost fifty. There was an ominous banging on the door.

"Ludwig of Bavaria," Chip whispered, opening the door. It was Buster Niles. Alone.

"Just thought I'd look over your shoulder. Ellie... er, Mr. Nelson is too busy to pop up."

"I doubt that," Chip smirked.

Buster smelled faintly of a mildewed closet. "But, he does want to peek over your shoulders at eight tomorrow."

"Where *is* he, really, Buster? You can come clean with us. Bet he's putting himself on cruise control for the evening."

Buster scanned the layouts. They looked okay to him. But then, everything always looked okay to him. He wanted to pick up the layouts, read the headlines, but he was a little in awe of Chip. And this new woman. He hadn't been able to figure her out yet. She sure didn't come on like Old Leather Cunt.

"Seriously, gang, is that okay with you?"

"Seriously, Buster, it is not okay with us, but do you care? If you don't tell Ellie it's okay, he'll make chopped liver out of you."

Buster knew the truth when he heard it. "Great."

Chip went on. "Now remember, Buster, Charlie has first refusal. She may hate everything we've done. So don't you guys go sneaking it out of the agency before she sees it, or all hell will break loose."

"Well, Ellie *was* expecting..." Buster began.

"I don't care if he's expecting the Queen Mother."

"Can I ask you something, Chip?"

"Anything," Chip grinned. "Mrs. Harrington and I are at your disposal."

"Okay if I have some of that?" Buster pointed to the cognac which stood next to a can of rubber cement in the bookcase.

Chip handed Buster the rubber cement. "Take it with two cyanides and don't call us in the morning."

Buster had to laugh. No wonder those goddamn creatives got paid so much.

Jill staggered back to her cubicle. Eight-thirty. She didn't feel like an advertising whiz, she felt like a woman with the whitest wash on the block, the shiniest kitchen in town and the sweetest-smelling bathroom in America. She felt exhausted.

She'd written more ads in one day than she'd written in a year at Philpott Associates. She wouldn't have believed it herself, had the proof not been pinned all over Chip's virginal white walls.

The last thing on earth she needed was a drink with Chip. But he'd been so sweet. He'd saved her sanity, maybe her job. She looked at her feet spilling over the throats of her success-oriented black patent pumps. If she took them off, she'd have to walk home in her panty hose.

Someone had left a layout on her desk. No, not a layout, but some typewriter-type pasted on a thick piece of foamboard. She looked at it more closely:

> ex-ecu-tive, *n.* one who holds a position of administrative or managerial responsibility, divided into two groups:
> 1. male executive. *syn.* comer, turk, tiger.
> 2. female executive. *syn.* bitch, cunt, ball-breaker.

Attached to it was a little pink note "Dear Jill, Welcome to BDK&C. Let's have lunch and dish. FiFi Woolverson."

At least FiFi Woolverson had a sense of humor. Chip hadn't mentioned that.

Jill wondered which of the three synonyms best described FiFi? Which of the three would ultimately describe *her?*

There was a single red rose in a cut-plastic bud vase on her desk. The card had obviously been taken out of its envelope and then resealed. Who would have done that? She tore it open. "If you ever get out of your meeting, let's have that drink. Keefe."

When? Tonight? All she wanted to do was go to bed so she could face the... what had Chip called them? Account bennies?

There were two telephone messages. One from Pumpkin. Not important. Probably true. One from Brodhead Kincaid. He'd like to see her in his office as soon as her meeting was concluded. Jill's heart pounded. It was so late. Would he still be there? She dialed the number on the little pink slip. Halfway through the first ring, "Mr. Kincaid's office," steamed from the telephone.

"This is Jill Harrington returning Mr. Kincaid's call."

"Come right down. Seventh floor." The dial tone came on.

Jill called Chip. "I'm in a total panic. Mr. Kincaid wants me to go to his office. What does that mean?"

"That we'll have a drink some other time," said Chip, "and that you'd better remember everything I told you." The dial tone again. People in advertising certainly didn't believe in hanging on the phone.

As Jill fluffed her hair, the phone rang. "Kincaid is a major leg man, in case I forgot to mention it. So show yours off. And put on plenty of what you were wearing at lunch today. It's dynamite."

"It's Breathless. Didn't you recognize it?"

"I'm aroma blind. Get off at the seventh floor. You can't miss Bonehead's office. Nothing like it since DeWitt Clinton was vice-president."

Head up. Shoulders back. Everything suspended from invisible wires. She tried to remember how Pumpkin had taught her to walk. What did Brodhead Kincaid want with her? How did he even know she existed?

And what was on Pumpkin's mind? And what would Charlie say when she found out that Jill had been asked to Bonehead's office? At least now she didn't have to worry about Beth in the bosom of Laurel Hall.

Jill inched her way through the carpet toward an enormous pair of rosewood doors obviously designed to dwarf mere mortals. "BDK&C" glowed in the mellow light of a pair of old gas street lamps.

Someone was playing the piano. *Haydn's Piano Sonata in D.* Strange. For an advertising agency. Whoever it was played beautifully.

Claret wallpaper. (Or was it silk?) A pair of black leather sphinx chairs guarded the doors. There didn't seem to be anyone around. "Mr. Kincaid?" Jill called. No answer. She looked around more carefully.

What did his office remind her of? All purples, clarets, blacks. A mahogany table with a luster that could only have been achieved through a hundred-fifty years or more of beeswax, mayonnaise and tireless, devoted hands.

Then she noticed the life-size oil portrait above the onyx mantel. It *had* to be Grayson Palmer Kincaid.

But it could just as easily have been Ian.

Brodhead Kincaid moved smartly along the corridor toward his office. He looked ten years younger than his fifty-three.

He worked out every morning at Alex & Walter's Physical Fitness Studio. At noon, he played squash at the University Club. He was limber and taut and his custom-made Turnbull & Asser shirts and suits hugged him like they loved him.

At six-three, one-sixty-eight, with neatly-clipped blond hair, which he permitted to go subtly lighter in summer, Brodhead was, indeed, close to perfection. He reveled in it almost as much as he reveled in his advertising agency.

Let the poor and socially inept be scapegoated. Let those who deluded themselves that there was a middle class in America—and that they were part of it—bitch and moan about the shrinking dollar. Brodhead sure as hell knew the difference between those who could afford to enjoy life and those who lived vicariously.

Among his plastic Country Kitchens floors and air-inflated chocolate bars, Brodhead had only two ultra nouveau riche-appeal products: Breathless, at three hundred per ounce, and

Tzarina Blue Diamond Vodka, made in Hoboken and sold at thirty dollars per litre. Both of them were Charlene Whitrock's doing. He'd let her talk him into it. He was glad, he supposed. But what did women really know about marketing?

What was that new copywriter like? Pumpkin Osborne's friend. If Pumpkin's taste in friends was anything like her taste in decorating, the girl had to be spectacular. But what had Charlie said at lunch? Smart-but-not-smartass. Plain-but-honest. Doesn't know how talented she is. No self-image, but Charlie could fix all that. Was she married? Yes! It came back to him. About to divorce some creep of a husband. A child killed in the street. Too many Puerto Rican drivers. Teddy Roosevelt should never have ridden up San Juan Hill. A second child in some second-rate school in Westchester.

God, how Brodhead hated Westchester and the idiots who lived there. Half of them seemed to work for him. Nincompoops, swiveting around in half-paid-for station wagons. Their estates consisted of their income tax refunds.

He marched into his office. "Ahhh, Mrs. Harrington ... may I call you Jill? I'm so glad you're here. I didn't keep you waiting, did I?"

Jill smiled. One more time. "Just got here, Mr. Kincaid."

"Brodhead. I was trying out the piano in the audition room. Do you play?"

"Yes, I ..." she stopped before she told him how they had to sell the Steinway to pay for the girls' braces.

"Welcome to BDK&C." He grasped both her small hands between his strong, tanned ones.

"I've been admiring your office, Brodhead. It certainly is unique." Her eyes swept the room. The dark mahogany walls sprouted large and menacing trophies. Elephant. Eland. Ibex. Entire alligators. A stuffed Irish setter. Disgusting.

"I don't think there is another room quite like this. It was my father's office. Scotch all right? The long distance drink, I call it."

Brodhead Kincaid poured two long distance drinks the color of varnish. "Cheers, Jill!" He lapped his drink. "I have a special project I'd like to discuss with you. I know it's late, but I've found that there's nothing like a fresh point of view. But before we get to that, how do you like the Country Kitchens account? Beautiful products. Beautiful."

"I have a Country Kitchen," Jill beamed.

"Well, that's the kind of enthusiasm I like to see here at BDK&C." Suzy refused to have a Country Kitchen installed in their penthouse. She said it would make her cats leave home.

Brodhead raised his glass. "I'm told that you are the most talented copywriter we've hired in quite a while. That's something we can always use: Talent! Wish I had more myself."

Jill studied Brodhead's face and then turned to the portrait. "Your father?"

"Indeed. Indeed. Handsome devil, wasn't he?"

"Actually, I was thinking how much you resemble him." It was uncanny how much he resembled Ian. *If* Ian had had on a perfectly cut English hacking jacket, a good haircut and had ever bothered to shave.

"I'd like you to work on a little project with me. Just you and me and maybe La Doza. What do you think of La Doza?"

Jill sensed a trap. She took a deep breath. "We did a lot of work today. We lunched. He seems to understand the account very well." God! She'd only been here eleven hours. She smiled. It was getting easier and easier to smile.

"Great! I have an idea for Ida-Ho Fluffy Mashed Potatoes that'll bring homemakers to their knees!"

"Yes?" Jill sat up straighter.

"I want to tell women just how delicious these potatoes are. I bet you've tried Ida-Ho Fluffy Mashed Potatoes, haven't you?"

Say delicious, dummy. "Delicious...Brodhead. Yes."

"So—and listen carefully—my idea has never been done on TV before. There's this presenter only he's inside a potato sack—an Idaho potato sack. He extolls the virtues of instant potatoes over fresh ones. In fact, my presenter tells women that our potatoes are *better* than fresh. What do you think, Jill? Think that'll give us more bang for the buck?"

"I have a question."

"Shoot."

"Why is the presenter hiding inside the sack?" An escaped convict? A member of the Klan?

"He's inside the sack because he doesn't want to make Idaho potato growers angry—the men who grow and sell the fresh potatoes. Get it?"

"Sort of the masked crusader for the greatest potato taste?"

"Exactly!"

"And this talking potato sack...what does he say? Do we have a strategy statement? Some facts?"

"Just to convince women in every village, hamlet, town, city and mobile home park that Ida-Ho Fluffys are the answer to their prayers. I want mouths watering!" Brodhead took two giant steps to the bar. "I always find that I'm more creative when the brain is oiled. Jill?"

She had to go home. She was on the verge of passing out smack in the middle of Bonehead's Duncan Phyfe settee. Why should women listen to a talking potato sack? Whatever made men think they knew how to sell women's products to women?

"Okay, Jill? I know it's late. But I'd like you to get back to me with your thoughts around seven-thirty. From what Charlie says, I feel confident that you can do it."

Did he mean seven-thirty tomorrow morning? Jill stood in shock, riveted to the floor. She had no choice. She remembered what Chip had told her about the paramedics. "Sure. No problem. How many commercials did you have in mind?" Did her voice sound weak or was it her imagination?

"Just as many as your pretty head can come up with."

Jill tried to be philosophical. If she had to work all night, she had to work all night. But for a brief moment, she wished she were going home to a Barry Pozner instead of to Pumpkin and her favorite dancing partners. Pumpkin would die when she heard about the man in the potato sack. "How shall I present the work, Brodhead?"

"Just jot down everything that comes into your mind. You

don't even have to type anything. I can read anyone's handwriting. Pride myself on it."

Jill rose to leave even though she hadn't been dismissed. "I really must go so that I can get started on the potatoes."

"One for the road?" asked Brodhead, snatching her glass. "After all, Jill, you haven't told me a thing about yourself."

Now what? Jill was tired of talking. Sitting there in her ragged bathrobe. No makeup. Old slippers. Hair Medusa wouldn't be caught dead in.

Her fingers sought the reassurance of her charcoal flannel skirt. What was she suppoed to tell this handsome, dynamic, CEO who was responsible for her very livelihood? This brilliant, successful Ian who stood over her waiting, expecting, encouraging?

"I've always dreamed of working at BDK&C," Jill began.

Brodhead nodded encouragingly, eyes blazing.

"I think I could come up with lots of ideas to help the company."

"Glad to hear it. I'd like those ideas on my desk in, say, one week from today. A week should be enough time for you to get a pretty clear picture of how we do things around here."

CHAPTER NINE

Trepidation. Facing the sympathy cards was like facing The Bills, only worse.

Jill had ignored them for weeks, half afraid that reading them would force her to re-live the whole thing. Roosevelt Hospital. Wendy. Smashing Ian with the water pitcher. Sodium pentathol. Rose-Delia. The bottles and glasses. The letters. Helen. Juliet.

How had she gotten through it? It still seemed like it had all happened to someone else.

How had she survived her first month at BDK&C?

This was life? This was style?

She slid a paring knife along the top of the first envelope. Carefully. The only way.

From the meat man at Gristede Brothers. Color photograph of buttercups and daisies. Much dew. No message. Just a name: Dino.

A textured picture of dogs and pheasants from the liquor store.

A cross, radiating gooey golden light from the Clarkes in Badger Hollow. Maybe it was just a sunset. A long poem about meeting on some distant shore. No shore was too distant when it came to the Clarkes. She'd tried not to think about them. They'd written her a nasty note about the state of her lawn.

Several painstakingly written letters from Wendy's classmates, many dictated, or so it seemed, by caring parents.

A miniature of Wendy done by Noël St. Martin. No message. "Love," written on the tissue that enclosed the portrait.

The usual. The boring. The silver roses and silver type. One that proclaimed "So sorry to learn of the death of your aunt." It was agony.

From Keefe, a card dated weeks before, asking her to call him when she felt like dinner. Eerie. They were having dinner in an hour.

From Rose-Delia: "My dear Jill," flowed the spidery script, "keep a hold on yourself. This might help. Remember, without money, there are *no choices*. Lovingly, R. D. Harrington."

A check for fifty thousand dollars and a poem. It was typewritten in purple, on onionskin, much creased and splitting in the creases. *No title*, by Edgar Guest.

> "I'll lend you a little child of mine,"
>   he said
> "For you to love while he lives and
>   mourn when he's dead.
> It may be for six or seven years or
>   twenty-two or three,
> But will you, 'till I call him back,
>   take care of him for Me?
>
> "I cannot promise he will stay,
>   since all from earth return,
> But there are lessons taught down
>   there I want this child to learn.
> I've looked the wide world over in
>   my search for teachers true
> And from the throngs that crowd
>   life's lanes, I have selected you.

119

> "I fancied that I heard you say,
>   Dear Lord, Thy will be done.
> For all the joy Thy child shall
>   bring, the risk of grief we'll run.
> We'll shelter him with tenderness;
>   we'll love him while we may.
> And for the happiness we've
>   known, forever grateful stay."

Fading at the bottom was written "Roxanne, December 25, 1936." Who was Roxanne? Ian had always said he was an only child.

Jill's throat tightened. She looked around vaguely for a Kleenex. It seemed like she was always looking for a Kleenex. Now she had Rose-Delia to add to her list of people to be grateful for. She wanted to do something for somebody else for a change. God, she was so much older than Chip and yet he had become her mentor; she and Pumpkin were within months of each other and yet Pumpkin had turned herself into surrogate mother. And Keefe. Where, exactly, did he fit in?

She'd had drinks with him, coffee with him, lunch with him. Light, humorous conversation. She might have been talking with Tansy, if Tansy didn't constantly erupt with advice. Or Bethy, if Bethy didn't invert every sentence to suit her own devices. Or, with Chip, if he hadn't been constantly on the *qui vive* for plotters, schemers, thieves and creative whores.

Tonight, dinner with Keefe. Just the two of them. Noël was in Palm Beach, hanging some of his newest paintings in an icing-pink beach house. The Lord was back in London, scouting a paneled dining room for one of Pumpkin's clients. And Pumpkin was in bed, trying to recover from culture shock brought on by a trip to California.

Jill tucked the cards into a manila envelope, rinsed her teacup and put it back into the cupboard. On her way back to her room, Pumpkin called out.

"Are you going out tonight, Jill?"

Probably wants me to have dinner with her. She owed Pumpkin, certainly.

"Yes. Can I get you anything?"

"I guess not."

Pumpkin's sanctum was overly-Pumpkined. Red and green Art Deco tulips grew in stylized rows on the walls. A gold pleated silk half-moon headboard. Pillows and a gold handled phone. Pumpkin had an ice bag on her head. "I'm dying, Egypt. Find my asp," she moaned.

"Pumpkin, give me some advice. About Keefe Neuman. You've known him forever, haven't you?"

Pumpkin stuck her nose above the sheet.

"You know everything about men. What are they really interested in?"

"Sports, business and younger women, not necessarily in that order," Pumpkin said matter-of-factly. "Once you understand that, Jill, you'll have a much happier life. You'll be able to go and do whatever it is *you* want to do—without worrying about what *he* wants to do."

"Ian was never interested in sports. And you know how excited he was about business. Younger women? Helen is superannuated, even by my standards. Juliet is fairly young. Twenty-eight, I think Ralston Rhodes said. He's having her tailed. But she's a Peruvian twenty-eight. A bit wizened. Maybe it's dirt. She doesn't know hippies are finished."

"Oh? You saw her?" Pumpkin sat up, suddenly alert.

"Pictures of her. Ralston had lots of photographs of her. And of Helen, the last time I met with him. It's all true, Pumpkin. Some swell mess," Jill sighed.

Pumpkin squinted at Jill. Her head ached from jet lag. How could people live in Beverly Hills? Mud slides. Freeways. Aging chorus boys with frosted hair. Nowhere else on earth did the clichés thunder louder. She reached for a Valium. The bottle was empty. She tossed it, missing the wastebasket by several feet.

"Ian isn't like most men, Jill. Ian isn't like any man you're ever likely to meet in business. Ian will never be a client, a brand manager or an account man. Speaking of which, give my love to Keefe. Seen much of him lately?"

"I've been too busy to see anyone. Tonight'll be the first time we've had dinner."

"Don't be defensive," Pumpkin chided.

"I'm not being defensive," Jill said, her composure spray-paint thin. "I'm just so goddamn tired. It's not the work; it's the stress. Everyone seems to spend so much time stirring things up. Just when you think you've got something solved, wham-bam, back to Go. The potato thing is getting to me."

"What's the potato thing?" Pumpkin asked tiredly. As much as she adored Jill, she couldn't bear to think about potatoes right now. She felt as boneless and hollow as a hundred-ten-pound chicken Kiev. Maybe Jill would leave for dinner soon.

"Bonehead—I mean Brodhead—Kincaid has an idea for a mashed potato commercial. It's a lousy idea but everyone is afraid to tell him. He thinks it's a major breakthrough in television advertising. He doesn't want to show the product... you know, the potatoes all fluffy, with melting butter cascading into pools. Appetite-appeal? Got the picture?"

"Even *petite moi* knows that you have to sell the sizzle first. So the great one doesn't want appetite-appeal? What else? You should see the look on your face!"

Jill started to giggle. "Well, you see, the spokesman for the product—Fluffy Ida-Ho—is wearing a potato sack, with the ends tied into sort of little ears."

"And he talks through the sack?"

"Right."

"I thought things like that only happened in California."

"Bonehead told Chip La Doza to design an *attractive* potato sack. Something women would relate to. Ever try putting words into the mouth of a talking potato sack?"

"What's *really* wrong, Jill?" Jill looked fragile. Maybe she was working too hard. But how could anyone take potato sacks seriously?

"I'm exhausted. Dead. Besides, I guess all of this is taking its toll on me. I mean I still can't believe it—Ian. Wendy."

"Why don't you just get on with the divorce? What does

Ralston Rhodes say?" Pumpkin felt herself fading. Not even Robert Redford could keep her awake at this point. And talking about Ian wasn't exactly stimulating.

Jill rose to go.

"All right," Pumpkin sighed, resigned. "Ian will never be the husband you wanted or the man you thought you married. How do you feel about him now...now that it's all out in the open about Helen and Juliet and the child?"

"I'm not exactly sure. Kind of like people in newscasts. You know, when the TV interviewer smiles and asks the father how it feels now that his wife and nine children have been burned to death in their tenement."

"Sounds like you're still in shock."

"Pumpkin, this may sound crazy; maybe I've already gotten what I was meant to get out of life. Maybe I just haven't recognized it."

Pumpkin sat up with a jerk. The ice bag flew to the bottle green carpet. "What is that supposed to mean? You've made your own life, Jill. So have I. I mean, was I meant to have married Stephen and spend the rest of my life having my hair teased? Was I born to decorate stretch limos? No. I made my own life mainly because I had to eat."

"I thought you loved your work, Pumpkin." Jill sat upright, perched on the edge of Pumpkin's bed.

"Some days I love it less than others. But listen, Jill: No one with any sense would have married Ian." There! I've said it, thought Pumpkin. She'll probably never speak to me again. But it's the truth.

Jill looked hard at Pumpkin. "You're right. I guess it took me a long time to realize it."

"Well, you can't stand still now. Are you going ahead with the divorce or not?"

"I am. Ian hasn't responded to any of Ralston Rhodes' communiques. He's up in New Hampshire, or so Ralston thinks. No one's seen or heard from him since he got out of the hospital two weeks ago. He hasn't been in touch with Helen or Juliet."

"What do you care?"

"I don't. It's just habit, I guess. Like picking up those empty bottles and cans and throwing them into the trash. Sometimes I think habit motivates me more than anything else."

"Know what I think, Jill?"

"About what?"

"Men, idiot."

"Think I'd better get ready," Jill said, standing up.

"When are you going to get it through your head that no one man can ever give you everything you want?"

"I don't think I ever asked for that much, Pumpkin."

"You expected a *life*, silly. And a life is a great many things. That's my next point. And that's why I have such a fragmented life: Opera dates who love music and don't talk during the performance. Cocktail dates who love to quack about nothing. I have conversation dates, for dinner parties. They're my favorites, actually. Especially if they don't try to compete with me."

"But Pumpkin, I can never be like you."

"If you can find someone who can do *all* those things I just mentioned, grab him, Jill, because he's the only one on earth. Frankly, I don't think such a person exists."

"I guess, a long time ago, Ian was like that. And I thought he loved me, too, Pumpkin, in his own way. Until we found those letters from Helen."

"Those letters meant that Helen was interested in Ian. And maybe not even that. People do lots of things when they're bored. And the Badger Hollow public library couldn't have been all *that* riveting. Maybe she was just interested in a fling."

"Maybe. I don't think I care about Helen. And Juliet is even duller. But what made Ian gravitate toward *them?* What's wrong with *me?*"

Pumpkin reached for the Excedrin P.M. "I don't know. Mid-life crisis, maybe. It certainly wasn't you. And now, good night. I know it's only seven o'clock, but my poor middle-aged body thinks it's yesterday or midnight or something."

Pumpkin turned out the light. "Jill, forget Ian. Have fun with Keefe. By the way, did Ralston Rhodes have any insights about the cash machine withdrawals?"

"Didn't mention a thing."

"Sooner or later, something will happen," Pumpkin yawned.

Quickly, Jill slipped out of her navy suit and green silk shirt and into her new sequin dinner suit.

She really didn't feel like dinner. She was too goddamned tired. But she'd promised Keefe. She'd also promised herself. She owed herself for a change. Tonight, she was going to have fun. She grabbed her sable jacket, purchased from Pumpkin with some of the credit card money, and the first extravagance in years that hadn't made her feel guilty.

If only Pumpkin would stop chipping away at her, telling her to sell her house, divorce Ian, blot out her past. There, she'd thought about it. Maybe Pumpkin's influence on her was fading now that she was building her own life. Maybe, now that she was finally a success in her own right and had a career, she felt like she didn't need Pumpkin. And maybe Pumpkin felt left out. How did everything get so complicated? Sometimes even The Bills seemed easier than all this.

Charlene kept after her with "accidents steer our lives." Chip told her daily that "life was one big crap shoot." Each of them had a philosophy and was trying his damndest to stamp it onto her life. Why? She didn't seem to have time to think about it all. And she still couldn't get over the fact that overnight—or so it seemed—she'd gone from moping in one kitchen to writing commercials addressed to other kitchen mopers. *A CAREER IN THE KITCHEN, the autobiography of Jill Harrington.* Who'd read *that?*

The bell. Keefe. He kissed her cheek, shook her hand and held her for an instant longer than a social hug. She leaned against him briefly. He smelled of fresh wind.

"Helping Bonehead create a better mousetrap?" Everyone on Madison Avenue called him "Bonehead."

"God knows, I've been trying. We've all been trying. I think tomorrow we're going to re-invent the wheel."

"Shall we mooch some of Pumpkin's scotch or shall we just silently drift away?"

"Let's drift. After L.A., Pumpkin is ready for a week in a padded cell."

"It's snowing, you know. I thought we should go somewhere in the neighborhood but then I got a better idea. Feel like an adventure?"

Even his light kiss was an adventure. "Why not?"

Keefe's Jaguar danced through the thick, wet snow and onto FDR Drive. Traffic was thin and soon they pulled into the circular entrance of the River Café, tucked beneath the Brooklyn Bridge.

It was an old barge, permanently anchored across from the glittering Manhattan skyline. But to Jill it looked like Atlantis glowing in a shower of show.

"Pumpkin would kill for that lamp," Jill whispered as they waited for the maître d'. The lamp was a bronze monkey holding a frosted glass umbrella. Under the umbrella, a tiny lightbulb cast a balmy glow across the keys of the baby grand.

They were seated next to a large window. The snow, driven by a stiff wind off the ocean, lay in drifts on the window ledge. Jill felt like a snow princess inside one of those glass balls.

"I think I like adventures," she said.

"More fun than a hamburger at Melon's, sitting there watching them pile garbage on East Seventy-fourth Street, eh?"

"It's sticking. Think we'll get home?"

"Hope not." Keefe smiled. His top teeth were very straight and his bottom ones very crooked. Maybe his family had run out of money somewhere in the middle. She studied his face. There were tiny wrinkles around his crisp blue eyes, and he had a thin scar that ran around one nostril and down to his upper lip. Plastic surgery? But he was beautiful, nonetheless. She could almost see the musculature beneath the gunmetal chalk-striped suit. She wanted to dive across the table. She smiled demurely.

The waiter recited the specialties, but she barely listened.

Who cared? The field salad cost more than her lunch. Stop thinking about what things cost, a voice told her. But she couldn't. Pumpkin wouldn't have cared if the field salad cost fifty dollars and the field hands had had to swim across the East River in the snow to get it there in time for dinner. But that was Pumpkin. Anyway, all that really interested her were those crinkly blue eyes.

"I guess I had this longing to return to the scenes of my childhood," Keefe's voice brought Jill back from her daydreaming.

"You're from Brooklyn? I didn't know that."

He was sure he'd told her that. But she had been through an awful lot lately; maybe she forgot. "Right off Flatbush Avenue. It used to look a lot better when I was a kid."

"I grew up in Badger Hollow and then I escaped for a few years. College. And Manhattan. Philpott Associates. Ever hear of them?"

"Almost went there to work once."

"We probably just missed each other."

"Probably."

Had there ever been a duller conversation? They were doing everything but yelling "my turn."

Jill lifted her scotch. "Here's to an adventure in the snow. What a lovely idea! Who says account men aren't creative?"

"Charlie Whitrock, for one," Keefe laughed. "What do you think of BDK&C?"

"Did you almost go there, too?"

"Of course. But I would have had to work with Charlie. I didn't think my hormones could stand it. Here's to the loveliest copywriter—" he hesitated—"on earth."

"I can't live up to *that*, Keefe."

"Try. Just for me. But what do you think of that madhouse? Bonehead give you any special assignments?"

"Please." Jill stifled a giggle. How could she tell Keefe about the talking potato sack that was supposed to bring homemakers to their knees?

"Tell me something, Keefe. Why do they always put men

on the bra or bone china or tampon account?"

"I've been on the bra account and the girdle account and the feminine hygiene account. I've been on the sanitary protection account and the underarm deodorant account. I've also been on the boxer shorts account, the cigar account and the automotive account. So I can't draw any conclusions. Only that back then there weren't any women account executives. Now, there are. It used to be that most of the women on Madison Avenue were only copywriters."

"You have just described BDK&C. There's a woman, a girl, art director. But all she does is paste-ups. And the account women are scattered rather thinly. They never seem to go to any of the meetings."

"Charlie doesn't let anyone go to meetings. Haven't you noticed that?"

"She asks me to go. And Chip La Doza. He's my art director. Terribly good. But I think he still sleeps with the lights on." That was a cruel thing to say about Chip. She never would have said that in Badger Hollow. What was happening to her?

By the time they'd gotten to the wine, Keefe and Jill were sitting as close as possible across the table. Their knees touched. The heads were bowed. They spoke into their plates. His hands covered hers. The field salad danced alone.

"You know, Jill, I didn't romp on the beaches of East Hampton or Bay Head when I was a kid. With me, it was right off the end of a pier. Even now, when I'm swimming in the pool at the Beverly Hills Hotel, I still find myself on the lookout for used rubbers." He raised his head. He looked into her eyes.

Jill smiled. Was it too dark for him to see how closely she was listening? "More, Keefe." She squeezed his hand.

"Well, when I was very young, I wanted to be a cantor, but my mother wouldn't hear of it."

"She didn't want you to be a priest, did she?" Jill asked.

"My father wouldn't hear of it! No, she felt that it was a

step too far. Remember, I told you that my mother was *Abie's Irish Rose?*"

Of course she'd remembered it. She'd remembered everything about Keefe, especially the way he folded his handkerchiefs in his breast pocket into three precise snowy Alps. She'd read in "*W*" that peaked handkerchiefs were out, but if Keefe wore them, they had to be in.

It was hard not to compare him to Ian. Keefe won on all counts. He didn't put her down or try to outwit her. He didn't insult her or tell her how to order in a restaurant. He didn't challenge her knowledge of the Brooklyn waterfront or goad her into discussing the effect of melting ice in the East River or the velocity of the wind that drove the snow against the glass. Keefe seemed to be enjoying himself. And enjoying her.

"Mummy married again after Daddy died," Jill said. "A nerd. Five years older than I," Jill said. "A falsetto flatterer with a sneer for every occasion. I had no brothers or sisters to protect me."

Keefe reached for a breadstick. "I have one brother. Three years older. He plays piano in a bar in Delray Beach, Florida. With nice Jewish boys, the older brother takes violin lessons from the most prestigious violinist money and talent can come by, and the younger brother studies piano with the accompanist. Garson Kanin talked about it once on the radio. All *he* wanted was saxophone lessons. All my brother wanted was to play the piano."

"I used to play," Jill said haltingly. "That is..." she tried to continue. The past hit her in the face.

"You did?"

"Yes. Until something happened. It's not important."

"Sure it is. Tell me."

"I had to sell the piano to pay for my daughters' braces," Jill blurted. Why did she have to tell him that, of all things? Would she ever get over the need to confess when she met a willing ear? He wasn't interested in her problems.

"See? That wasn't so bad," Keefe said, grinning.

"Christ, Keefe, there are so many things we do because we don't have any choice. I hope I don't have to go through anything like that again. I want so many things. Maybe too many. But not just for me, for Beth, too. She's suffered so."

"I want everything I can get, Jill. I want to wring life dry before the Boneheads of this world decide to terminate me."

"But you already have everything, Keefe. Everyone knows you—you're a—well, a celebrity. Chip La Doza...he's my art director, almost had a double coronary when he spotted a phone message from you on my desk this afternoon. He couldn't help himself. He absolutely *had* to read it."

"I suppose I can't complain," Keefe laughed. "Cognac?"

"Love one." Jill knew she shouldn't. More calories. What the hell. And tomorrow there was some sort of gang-bang meeting for the entire creative department with someone named Tige Barnett. Oh, well. She'd skip lunch in favor of two Tabs.

Keefe was reassuring. He seemed so kind, in the same way Tansy was kind, like he'd come the long, hard way to compassion. She reached across the table and held his hand.

"Were you ever married?" she asked. Screw what Pumpkin had always said about being coy.

Pumpkin had told Jill that if you never asked a direct question people would eventually tell you everything. It was human nature. Jill held her breath. Would this turn out to be the perfect rotten end to a perfect evening?

Keefe toyed with a bread stick. "Weren't most people?"

"I guess so," Jill answered in a little voice.

"Are you still married, Jill?" Pumpkin had told him Jill was either in the process of getting a divorce or she had gotten a divorce. He couldn't remember. It didn't matter. He would have liked to have changed the subject. Back to Madison Avenue? But they'd gone too far for that.

"Almost not...married, that is. My lawyer is working out the details. It's a little complicated. At the moment." How could she tell him about Helen and Juliet and little Ian? It was just too tacky. Keefe may have been brought up swimming off a pier but he wouldn't understand this mess.

"Jill, please look at me."

She looked up into his eyes. The candlelight twinkled on the red highlights in her hair but she didn't know that. All she knew was that she was in love with Keefe Neuman and she would kiss the hem of his robe if it would make him love her back.

"When I look at you, Jill, I know I'm somebody."

Not just a kid from Brooklyn who learned to speak English from going to *Thin Man* movies, but somebody, he thought. God, it sounded so corny. But the way she looked back at him did something to him. Her eyes. Her smile. Her animated little laugh.

"You're magnificent, Jill."

She didn't know whether to believe him.

He leaned across the table and kissed her. Her body tensed from her neck to the tops of her legs.

"Cognac?" Keefe asked.

Jill nodded. Her arms were covered with goose pimples. Her nipples were hard as coral under the loose sequin blouse.

"There is something I should tell you, Jill. We're falling in love. And we can't. It's just no good."

Christ. Did he have some kind of disease? And if they weren't supposed to fall in love, why had he brought her here?

Keefe was dissolving into Ian before her eyes. "All right." What could she say? You can't do this to me? It was a *fait accompli*—as final as selling the house. Getting the divorce. Wendy.

She was a mother, anyway. What the hell was she doing sitting here—no matter how romantic it was—sipping Rèmy Martin, idolizing a man she knew practically nothing about?

She hadn't felt like this since the summer she'd turned seventeen and had fallen in love with a law student home from Harvard for summer vacation.

They'd spent the summer writing rotten poems and drinking a lot of gin and tonic and sour white wine. The night before he'd left for law school and she for her freshman year, they'd slept together. Mostly, it had frightened her. They'd rolled around in his parents' king-size bed for hours, mouthing things they'd read in bad novels. Right now Jill felt exactly the same way. Terrified. Vulnerable. Not able to handle whatever it was that Keefe was trying to dish out. And she hadn't read any bad novels in ages. Suddenly she felt sick. She excused herself and went to the bathroom.

When she'd returned, Keefe had paid the check and was waiting for her by the door.

"Shall we?" he asked pleasantly, as though they'd spent the evening discussing the shelf life of instant mashed potatoes.

The drive back to Manhattan took a lifetime. Neither said much. The snow attacked. The Jaguar behaved. When they got to Pumpkin's, Jill decided to take a chance.

"I think you've earned a scotch. All that heroic driving."

To her amazement, he accepted.

Tansy had left a fire, now reduced to embers. Keefe poked it and threw on two big logs.

"That should do it for a couple of hours." He went right to the bar. "Incidentally, what made you marry Ian?"

Jill paused, not sure how to answer.

"I was bored and he was amusing." That's how Bette Davis would handle that. But it sounded too cold. She went on hurriedly. "He knew all the answers. He was the only one who could beat me at the Sunday *Times* crossword puzzle. I guess it was a kind of challenge."

"Were you in love with him?"

"I think so...thought so."

"Did he make you happy?"

"You mean did he take out the garbage?" Jill laughed. "He did. Sometimes." His questions were coming at her too fast, like bullets. It scared her. Maybe she wasn't ready to share all of this.

"I guess that's the criterion, huh? Garbage. The universal symbol of married life. I never took out the garbage. It was a major source of pique. Didi claimed it was my one giveaway." He sipped his scotch and draped his arm along the back of Pumpkin's puce suede Chesterfield.

The fire filled the room with friendly shadows.

"Giveaway?"

"That I was raised in a slum."

"But you weren't," Jill protested.

"Her view from Fifty-eighth and Park didn't include Brooklyn."

"Were you in love with Didi, Keefe?"

"Yes. Only I'm not so sure she was in love with me. She only showed it once."

Poor Keefe. How could anyone not be in love with him? As he spoke, she looked deep into his eyes. Her heart pounded. Please, Keefe, keep talking to me so that I don't have to say anything. I don't want to answer any questions.

The only thing she felt like saying was "I love you," and she knew she couldn't. Not after what he'd said at the restaurant.

She felt like she was nine years old. The teacher was calling on her. "What is the chief export of Bolivia, Jill?"

She'd opened her mouth and nothing came out.

"Jill? I asked if you thought Ian was in love with you." Keefe repeated softly.

"I guess so... maybe not." Maybe *not?*

So why had she lain on the altar, waiting for Ian to cut her heart out?

"Ian is a strange person, Keefe. There is no one else like him."

"Is that good or bad?"

"Mostly bad. He thinks he's a hangover from the eighteenth century. I think he's a hangover from Nero's Rome. Whatever it is, he's never felt comfortable in his current incarnation."

"Ah, Ian. Complex. Devious. Full of intrigue."

"You don't know how right you are, Keefe."

She knew she shouldn't, but she wanted another scotch. The first one *had* taken the edge off.

Keefe seemed to want to talk. Why shouldn't she? For the moment, at least, she was caught up with everything at the office. Her first meeting, New Products taste testing, wasn't until ten. She settled back in her chair. But to really talk—it still terrified her.

Keefe looked at their glasses and mixed some drinks.

"What was Didi like, Keefe?"

"Didi suffered from agoraphobia. You know, when you're paralyzed by the thought of leaving the house? She'd been to Europe several times. She'd had a job with the Metropolitan Museum. She used to love to walk. Gradually, she began staying home. More and more until finally she'd only go out to the hairdresser or the opera."

Jill nodded encouragement. His words came out in a rush.

"Then the hairdresser began to come to the house and she started watching the opera on television. Finally she got to the point where she refused to get out of bed."

"What did you do?"

"Well, I talked to her. That was futile. I talked to her doctor. He came to the house. She wouldn't see him. He waited for hours, until she went into the kitchen for something to eat. When he'd caught her there, she pretended that she'd asked him to lunch. She made elaborate shrimp omelettes. Opened champagne."

"Is that consistent with...agoraphobia?" Jill asked, fascinated. She'd only read about the disease.

"I don't know. It seems they talked about the ballet and the opera. New acquisitions at the Metropolitan Museum. She agreed to see a therapist. A friend of his. But only if he'd take her. And he did. Took her by the hand, like she was a little girl."

Jill listened intently. She'd always known she wasn't the only woman on earth with problems. But hearing about Didi didn't make her feel any better.

"Did the therapy do her any good?"

"Little by little. She started going back to the hairdresser. Then to Bloomingdale's. One night, she went to the ballet with a woman friend. Some kids grabbed their purses."

"Oh, Christ, Keefe."

"Hold on. I thought that would set her back into the Dark

Ages. But it didn't. She came slugging back. She seemed to be determined to beat this thing. And, in a way, she did."

"Determined to beat this thing." That's what one of the patients in Jill's therapy group had said. She wondered if she should tell Keefe about it.

It had been so hard to call and arrange to attend the meeting—sort of a group therapy for parents who had lost their children. Without any drinks, without any of Pumpkin's Valiums, Jill had forced herself into a cab, given the driver the address and tried not to bite her nails until she arrived.

The group hadn't been very large, only about fifteen or sixteen people. Some came in couples, some alone, because their husband or wife couldn't face it.

The nice doctor from Roosevelt Hospital had been there. He'd nodded to her across the room. She'd smiled back weakly. In his checked shirt and tweed sport jacket, he looked a lot older than he had at the hospital.

No one had wanted to start. They just sat there, looking at their feet. Finally, the nice doctor spoke up, but he was barely audible. His son had been killed instantly. Riding a dirt bike in a forbidden area. All trespassing had been banned because of high tension wires. But the several acres of unobstructed flat turf lured bikers in droves. The owners had installed criss-crossed wires at intervals to deter the bikers.

The nice doctor's son hadn't known about the wires, one of which decapitated him when he'd hit it at sixty miles an hour.

The nice doctor kept saying that somehow he and his wife "were going to beat this thing."

Jill had quietly left the room and been sick in a trash basket on the corner. She'd known then that she could never "beat this thing." She didn't want to.

"Didi was so happy to be back in charge. She was like her old self. Even better. Then I got my pilot's license."

"I didn't know you flew, Keefe." Was there anything he couldn't do?

"I knew Didi was terrified of flying but I wanted to impress her. She thought advertising was a business for the assholes of the world. Her father didn't even consider it a legitimate business. God knows, he didn't consider me a legitimate businessman. He was the kind of guy who got home from the office at four-thirty, took out the garbage and still managed to make two million dollars by the time he was forty."

Jill laughed.

"Anyway, I asked her to fly up to Nantucket for a lobster lunch. I never thought she'd take me up on it. I was all set to take a guy from the office, another pilot. Christ, Didi couldn't get into a 747 without a herd of martinis."

He drained his scotch. "We had a Piper Cherokee 180. You know... with four seats. I thought Didi might want to sit in the back but she climbed in front, fastened her seat belt and got out her binoculars. She seemed thrilled. I couldn't believe it. I know it sounds corny, but it really felt like a kind of miracle."

Jill kicked off her shoes and curled her feet under her. The heat from the fire was making her drowsy. She propped herself against the back of the sofa. God forbid Keefe should think he was putting her to sleep.

Jill thought flying was boring; a necessity, of course, if one had to go to Europe or the Coast, but to do it just for fun? All those hours taking off, landing, wasting gallons of gasoline flying from one dinky airport to another. God, she was beginning to sound like Rose-Delia!

"We had our lobsters. Didi had lots of champagne. She was beginning to relax. Over-relax, actually. I had plenty of black coffee. After lunch, we headed back. It was a crystal day. You would have loved it, Jill, you could see a couple of hundred miles in every direction. Then, I got the weather for Westchester Airport. A storm was on the way but we had time. We could beat it."

Keefe slipped out of his jacket and loosened his tie.

"All of a sudden, Didi began to scream. We were somewhere over northern Connecticut. We hit an air pocket. Didi was uncontrollable. She just went berserk. I'd never seen her like that before."

He lurched from the sofa, grabbed their glasses and crossed to the bar.

"We were about four hundred feet off the ground, going about sixty-five miles per hour, when Didi opened the door."

Jill inhaled sharply. Dear God. He'd killed his wife.

"She was trying to get out onto the wing. She wanted to escape. Poor Didi couldn't stand being out, and yet she couldn't tolerate being cooped up either. It was hell, Jill."

Jill leaned toward him. Was this what he was leading up to in the restaurant? Is this why he'd shifted the conversation so abruptly?

"There was no reasoning with her," he continued. "She was panicked. Christ, Jill." His eyes met hers.

"Keefe," Jill said softly, "It wasn't your fault." Jill put her arms around him, the way she used to put her arms around Wendy. It seemed like the only thing to do.

He pressed his head against her breasts.

"I didn't make sure that Didi's seat belt was fastened. She'd drunk a bottle of champagne. I guess it made her irrational."

Jill held Keefe tighter. He put his arms around her.

"Jill, Didi hated planes. *I* got her into the goddamn thing. I was so impressed with my new skill, my new toy. Christ."

He straightened up, and fumbled for a handkerchief.

"I was trying to grab her and land the plane at the same time. It was impossible. The storm had begun to move in. The thunder scared the shit out of Didi. We hit the ground. I was trying to stop. I had to pull the plane around to avoid some trees. For a split second, I let go of Didi. She got out onto the wing. She fell off. The wing came around and clipped her. Oh God, Jill."

Keefe buried his head in his hands.

She smoothed her hand over his soft hair. What could she do?

"Keefe, get it all out."

That's what they'd all told her, over and over. Noël. Pumpkin. Tansy. Well, she'd gotten it all out. But there was still plenty left over.

"Jill, I've been to shrinks. Nothing helped. You're the first person I've been able to talk to about it. I guess I sensed it the first time I met you. Right here in this room." His voice was husky with feeling. He was sweating. The fire. The scotch. The memory.

Jill kissed his hair. What was she going to do with him? He was in no condition to go home. It was after three. Snow stung the windowpanes. Wind howled up the elevator shaft.

She lifted herself away from him and dropped another log on the fire. Then she snuggled next to him on Pumpkin's *petit point* hearth rug. It exuded the comforting smells of camphor and cedar. She pressed her face closer to his.

"Keefe, stop torturing yourself. You didn't kill Didi."

"No, Jill, I didn't." He spoke in a monotone.

What did he mean? Didn't Didi die on the tarmac at Westchester airport?

"It was an accident, Keefe. A dreadful accident."

"Didi is alive, Jill."

She looked at him, uncomprehending. "But, Keefe—" Jill stopped. She froze. His pupils were dilated.

"You can't believe that anyone could fall out of a moving plane, be knocked unconscious by the wing and live. No one can. But Didi is alive. She can't talk. She can't feed herself. But she's alive."

Jill touched his hand. It was wet. His arms were wet. She felt his forehead. Burning.

"She sits and stares. The doctors say that physically there's no reason she can't talk. But she doesn't want to. At first, right after the accident, we took turns trying to get through to her. Even Pumpkin went to the hospital and read to her. We tried everything. The way they do with coma victims. But Didi wasn't in a coma; she just didn't want to respond. She's alive, but I guess she doesn't want to be."

Jill was glad Keefe couldn't see her face. So this was why

Pumpkin had warned her not to fall in love with Keefe Neuman.

Jill kissed his forehead.

She kissed his salty lashes. He slipped his arms under her. She fit her body against his and clung to him.

Why wasn't she allowed to love him?

Didi and Ian could go to hell. She wanted Keefe and she was going to have him.

Keefe slid his arm out from under her and stood up. He pulled Jill to her feet and kissed her softly. Then, he took her hand and led her silently down the little hall to her room.

He closed the door and began to undress her.

"I didn't know we were going to make love," Jill murmured.

"Neither did I. Until about two minutes ago."

Her small hands explored his body. He did have the body of Adonis, Brooklyn or not. She wasn't Aphrodite but she could pretend. For a few hours, anyway.

He kissed her breasts, one at a time, until a shower of spasms shook her.

Ian had always made love as if he were running a race. They'd each have their orgasms and then they'd fall asleep. Keefe's lovemaking was different. It grew in intensity with each caress—each kiss. Jill wished she'd spent more time in bed and less in the kitchen. Who needed cooking lessons?

Keefe's body was poetry. Lyrical. Singing. Thrilling.

Jill had never known such pleasure. Over and over. She had told Pumpkin Ian was sexy. That's why she stayed with him. How had she convinced herself of that?

Jill gave way completely to the uninhibited desire Keefe ignited in her. And after the comforting rhythm erupted in a shower of meteors, Jill couldn't move, couldn't speak. It had been a celebration of body and soul.

Jill pressed against him. His natural smell mingled with the tart cypress of his cologne.

Jill closed her eyes. Damn the risks. She would let herself love this man. She had to.

Keefe's fingers stroked her damp curls, moved down her

neck, between her breasts. Her legs parted of their own volition. Helpless waves of pleasure coursed through her body. She savored the taste of him lingering on her tongue.

There was a blinding flash and a thud.

Ian stood at the foot of the bed, holding high a Polaroid camera. "A performance like that deserves an Oscar. At least a nomination." He bowed. "Bravo! Brava!"

Keefe, momentarily blinded by the light, pulled a sheet around his waist. Jill groped for her robe, and remembered that it was hanging on the back of the bathroom door.

"How did you get in here, you cobra?"

"By inserting a key into the lock of the front door. It's a simple operation. Most people have mastered it by the age of five." He held up his key and swung it in the air, as though to hypnotize them. Then he patted his camera. "Now that I have my evidence, think I'll wriggle back to the Plaza."

"Evidence?" Jill asked, still numb.

"Surely you can't be so naive as to think—no matter what that cud-chewing Ralston Rhodes says—that I intend to pay you alimony? Let this fellow help keep you in groceries, Jill." He nodded toward Keefe. "He seems to be able to keep you amused."

Jill tried to collect her thoughts. As usual, he's doing his best to ruin everything. But Keefe isn't saying anything. He knows it isn't your fault. Christ! It had all been so perfect. So uncomplicated. So right. Dinner seemed a million light years away.

"I thought you were in Vermont, with your opera."

"I've been in Vermont. I've been in Palm Beach. I've even been in Paris. I'm trying to recover from my traumatizing accident. Or have you forgotten?"

Forgotten? She wished she had the plastic water pitcher. Or a block of stone from the Great Pyramid. Or a neutron bomb. She bit the inside of her lip and started counting. So, he'd been traveling. That meant he'd been using his credit cards. The cash deficiencies had not yet turned up. But soon they would.

"I also have been having you two tailed. Week after week, *Nada*. Then tonight, a jackpot. You were so enraptured, you didn't notice the two well-dressed, very tanned men in sunglasses sitting across the room in the River Cafe. My private eye and me. We followed you back uptown and I bid him good night. I wanted to be in on the moment of truth all by myself."

"But..." Jill sputtered.

"I merely walked into the building, said 'good evening' to Franklin, got into the elevator, let myself in, poured myself a scotch and waited."

"But the key. Whose is it?"

"Mine, naturally. Do you think I purloined it from the august Mrs. Endicott-Osborne? The afternoon of that noisome cocktail party, I borrowed Bethy's key and had a copy made."

Using his own daughter. What would he stoop to next?

"Did you reimburse Pumpkin for all those broken things? Those antiques?"

"Certainly not. They were probably all copies. She made a killing from the insurance company, I'm sure. *They* don't care how atrocious Pumpkin's taste is. Almost as horrible as yours, my love." Ian shot Keefe a withering look.

"I should probably do something nasty and physical to you, Harrington, but I don't think it's worth the effort." Draped in Pumpkin's Porthault sheets, Keefe looked curiously like the last of the twelve Caesars.

"No one here has the least interest in violence. Words are so much more potent, don't you think? Good night."

Ian went out, closing the door quietly. Once again, they were in total darkness. Jill reached for Keefe's hand.

As Ian walked down the little hall to the living room, they heard him singing: "Heigh-ho, heigh-ho, to Fotomat we'll go..."

Keefe started to laugh. He laughed until the bed shook.

"Jill, darling, you never told me that the dreaded Ian had a sense of humor."

"And the Marquis de Sade is your favorite stand-up comic,

right?" Jill stared at Keefe. Why wasn't he outraged?

Keefe wrapped Jill in his arms. "Somehow, I don't think we were destined to get any sleep tonight."

"Who could? After our appearance on *Candid Camera?* Listen, Keefe, what am I going to do about those photographs?"

"Absolutely nothing."

"Absolutely nothing?"

"Think about it for a minute. You certainly don't want to stay married to Ian."

"Christ, what a statement."

"And you never even considered alimony, right?"

"Right."

"Okay. Pictures or not, Ian will have to pay support for Beth. Unless, of course, he wants custody, which I doubt, or alimony for himself, which I don't doubt."

"I wouldn't put anything past Ian, Keefe." Should she tell Keefe about Helen and Juliet and little Ian? Not now. Maybe someday.

It was getting light. The snow had stopped. Pink and gold tinted the sky.

"Shall we watch the sunrise?" Jill asked. In two hours, she would have to leave for the office.

"Even for an account man, I have a much more creative idea," Keefe said, kissing the nape of her neck.

After he'd fallen into a deep sleep, Jill slithered out from under his leg, found her robe, and went to her typewriter in the library.

Quickly, she reassembled her notes and began to whip them into some sort of shape. She'd promised Bonehead some ideas on how to run the agency.

No matter what Keefe had said about working on both the bra account and the boxer shorts account, the way things worked at BDK&C had been bothering her. She'd decided— despite what she'd been told—that women should work on the products that women bought—and that included eighty percent of the goods and services advertised by BDK&C. It was beyond women's lib, equality and what was fair; it just made good business sense. And Jill had discovered that if there was anything Brodhead liked, it was a strong pont of view with facts to back it up. It didn't necessarily matter if the facts were real, as long as they could be supported by statistics. Brodhead loved statistics.

Last week, when Bonehead had started one of their meetings with "Jill, you must understand that facts prove...", Jill had graciously interrupted him with "Brodhead, what you're really saying is: 'A job well done is a job done two ways.'"

"I love it!" he'd exclaimed, jumping up. "A job proved two ways, a job shot two ways, an ad rendered two ways! Christ, Jill, you've added a new dimension to advertising."

Every day she'd realized that presentation was the greater part of winning on Madison Avenue.

She stared into her typewriter. Noël St. Martin had said something interesting to her on the telephone. "Never mind nature, art imitates art. That's why they're all copying me."

How could she use that?

Maybe, unconsciously, she'd already used it. On herself. She'd sifted through Pumpkin's advice. Charlie's. Chip's probably had been the best because he was a man. Gay, yes. But a man. He wasn't as competitive with her as the other women. She sighed.

The day stretched ahead like the Baja Run. Rife with unknown twists and turns. Ruts. Poisonous snakes. The danger of losing one's way. The danger of running out of gas. And of course, there were the vultures.

Jill hung onto the closet door, swaying slightly as she peered into its depths.

Was there a color, a shade, that would make her look a little less like something out of *Night of the Living Dead?*

Certainly not black. Or white. Yellow was bad news most of the time and green was how she felt.

Contrary to what steamy novels say, a night of love does not make one glow in the morning. At least, not after thirty-five. Jill was exhausted. Her eyes were puffy. Her tongue was wearing a thrift-shop mink coat. It hurt to stand up. It hurt to sit down.

Her fingers parted the hangers. There! A pale coral silk Valentino blouse. Perfect with the Calvin Klein gray tweed. she just had time to put it on and call for a cab. Makeup could go on in the cab with a quick once-over in the bathroom when she got there.

When would she see Keefe again?

Was he falling in love with her? He'd said so. And at their ages, you did not have to say that to get someone into bed. Probably not at any age, these days. God, she felt out of touch. But she shouldn't. Had Mrs. Clarke of Badger Hollow spent the night in the arms of a fabulous lover? Had Pumpkin? Had Charlie? Had Bammie Pomino?

Jill smiled smugly. Of course they hadn't. She straightened up, took a deep breath and sprayed her naked shoulders with a cloud of Fracas.

"You smell like my pillow," Keefe said from the depths of the bed.

"You scared me. I thought you'd fled like a thief in the night when I went to the library."

"Well, I didn't. I thought someone might make me some hot coffee. And maybe some juice."

"Someone has."

Jill handed Keefe her glass of chilled fresh juice, dutifully squeezed by Tansy, and her cup of steaming black coffee.

"I have to run. I promised to get this stuff into Brodhead before eight o'clock."

"Call a messenger."

"Call a messenger? Just like that?"

Keefe picked up the phone and dialed. Jill watched him in wonder. Was there anything he didn't know? He said something in a low voice and hung up.

"The messenger will be here in ten minutes and your priceless 'stuff' will be in the hands of the great one by eight. Simple as that."

"Do you think he'll mind?"

"Mind what? He asked for the work. He's getting it. Why should he mind? You're not the handmaiden, you know."

Keefe was right. And it was probably better to let Bonehead read and digest it before she saw him.

"Now that I've solved your most pressing problem, madame, will you solve mine?" Keefe held out his arms.

She'd have liked nothing more than to tear off her clothes and jump back into bed with Keefe. For the morning. Or the day.

"I can't. I'm ready to meet my public. And you, my darling, had better get ready to meet yours."

"What time is it? I can't read Pumpkin's gilded clock from ten paces. I have a terrible feeling it's getting late." He finished her coffee.

"What time is your first meeting?"

"Nine-thirty."

Jill wrenched the covers off Keefe with the dramatic swoop of a matador. "This is it," she said scanning his lean muscled body.

"I suppose we should have dinner," he said.

"I suppose we should," she said, smiling.

CHAPTER TEN

*S*ome guys worked out at the University Club every night to keep in shape. Let those idiots chase their little rubber balls around until they dropped. Since he'd been living at the Plaza, Ian had found a new way to restore his vitality.

Club Sam-oah, open twenty-four hours.

What Sam-oah lacked in old world charm and old school ties, it more than made up for in good, clean fun. And it said so, in 18-point hot pink italics on the cover of the official *Club Sam-oah Brochure and House Rules:* "Bet you'll have more fun in our rec room than in yours."

And Sam-oah lived up to its promise. Not that they'd ever had a rec room in the Badger Hollow house. Ian abhorred the word. It brought to mind subterranean lairs paneled in weathered railroad ties and hung with vintage license plates.

"Jesus H. Fuck," Ian gasped, his lean, stubbled face half-hidden in the girl's frosted pubic hair. "That's got to be the greatest taste in the world."

He came up for the third time. "Missy, let me see your flip side."

Missy was Ian's favorite fantasy. She embodied the three B's: busty, bawdy, barbaric. She required no conversation.

In one graceful, nonchalant move, the girl turned over and stuffed a pillow under her stomach.

"Ohh," Ian yelled, thrusting into her and quivering as she tightened on him.

How long could he control it? Five minutes? Ten? He'd drunk too much. Plus those hours at the River Cafe, spying. Not to mention the workouts with Helen and Juliet. He was glad Jill was off his payroll. But at least she could cook. Sometimes he missed that. The other two wanted to talk. And screw. Sip wine. And screw. Listen to Mozart. And screw. He was whacked.

But there was little else he needed. Except to sing *Don Giovanni*. And, of course, Rose-Delia's money.

Not that he wished her dead. He kind of admired the mean old bitch. She didn't understand him, of course. She and Hogwood, her doddering legal adviser, had been bombarding him with letters—threatening, cajoling letters rife with ultimatums, redundant with Jill and Beth. Rose-Delia had never given a figwort about Jill—and God knows he hadn't wanted to disabuse her of that—until they'd had their ladies' lunch. Now, Old Ironsides cared about Beth and Jill and the golden boy was the dog in the manger.

He was overjoyed that Jill had stumbled into Keefe Ad Man. They could discuss marketing together. She was so fucking dull. She thought she could write. She was illiterate. She thought she could act. The only place she could enter stage left and say "Dinner is served," was her own kitchen.

Shades of Jason Picker. Ian had heard that Picker was teaching in a trendy boys' school on the East Side.

But Jill wasn't as boring as Juliet. Juliet had been his only mistake. Juliet and little Ian. He was about as closely related to little Ian as he was to Warren Gamaliel Harding. How the hell could he have let her name that child "Ian"?

And the fair Helen. She certainly did not have the face that launched a thousand ships—more like the mouth that demanded to be taken out to dinner at the stroke of eight.

Well, tonight, they were going out. For the last supper.

Ralston Rhodes was on his ass. Bigamy. Who cared? His marriage to Juliet probably wasn't legal anyway. The ceremony had been performed by her guru in the Church of Astrologers of Scientific Hope.

Sam-oah gave him the courage to face it all. Sam-oah gave him Mai Tais, free champagne and a free hour in the Jacuzzi. Sam-oah gave him needle showers, rubdowns, lickoffs and a communal sauna. Sam-oah gave him plush, over-sized pillow beds in mirrored rooms scented with simulated jasmine blossoms. Sam-oah gave him topless dancers, bottomless hostesses and the famous all-over toothbrush scrub.

What had Badger Hollow ever given him except a lot of tiresome nattering from Jill?

The Bills! Jesus, he was sick of it all.

What bliss to escape to this paradise and let Missy kiss it and make it better.

Best of all, he could charge it on his American Express or other major credit card. He silently congratulated himself on how brilliantly he'd kept his credit card collection a secret from Jill. The bitch would surely have bankrupted him if she'd known about it.

"Missy, where did you learn to fuck like this?"

"Not at Smith," she replied, lightly biting his scrotum.

"You know, Missy, I'm crazy about oral sex."

"You gotta pay to play, Mr. Harrington."

"I wasn't thinking of anything too wild."

"I'm not kidding, Mr. Harrington. Any extras will cost you twenty bucks."

"All I want is a little tongue-in-cheek, Missy," Ian drawled. Did she get the double entendre? Probably not.

"Twenty bucks more."

Suddenly he remembered that Juliet was waiting for him. His prick went limp and crawled out shriveling before his eyes.

"Sorry," Ian said lamely, "something weird is going on here. I think I need a little mouth-to-cock resuscitation."

"An additional ten," chirped Missy.

At eight-thirty, Ian lurched out of the giant pillow bed and into the shower. If he hurried, he might be able to grab a cab going the wrong way for business people and make it to Juliet's in time for breakfast. He'd better take her out today.

There would be hell to pay. Ralston Rhodes, who couldn't spring a Buick from the car pound, had written to Juliet, asking her to have her lawyer contact him. Juliet wanted *him*, Ian, to act as their attorney. Christ.

He toweled off with one of the Club Sam-oah's thirsty giant bath sheets, so stated in purple embroidery at both ends. Missy handed him the bill. It was nicely itemized. He glanced over it.

1. Rear entry
2. Running jump
3. Between-the-breasts
4. Toothbrush-off
5. Fellatio while having blood pressure taken
6. Fellatio solo
7. Mai tais (3)
8. Service charge plus gratuity...$ 267

Ian handed Missy one of his Mastercards.

"On anything over your basic twenty, Mr. Harrington, we have to call up." Missy's words rang with the enthusiasm of an airline hostess explaining the oxygen mask.

"Yeah. I have a Mastercard charge here for two-sixty-seven. Right. The number is five-two-six-three-zero-zero-zero-zero-nine-one-zero-zero-two-five, expiration date, seven-eighty-three," she purred into the telephone. "What? Say that again? Oh, okay. If you say so. You've got the computer." Missy hung up.

"I don't know how to break this to you, Mr. Harrington, but they said you're over your credit limit or something. They won't accept the charge. I guess your credit's been stopped."

"Over my limit? Terminated? I've never been over my limit with this card. In fact, I've barely used it. Here," he said, handing Missy a Visa card, "try this one."

Phone call after phone call. All his credit cards. All over the limit. Ian simply had no credit with any of his Visa cards or Mastercards. He had some more cards back at the Plaza. But what if they were over the limit too? How the hell was he going to pay the bill?

"Call TRW. Run a credit check on me, Missy. *They'll* tell you what a great credit risk I am. I'm the best. THE BEST, do you hear?"

"I hear you, Mr. Harrington. All my senses work."

How dare those bureaucrats tie his hands behind him. His face went from pink to fuschia. His hands shook. He was hot. He was cold.

"Missy, gotta tell you, no one has a better credit rating than I do. Forget American Express. That doesn't count. What counts are the bank cards. *That's* who makes or breaks your credit rating. Not even Rose-Delia Harrington has a better credit rating than I. Not even the president of fucking Mastercard!" He wiped his hand across his forehead.

"Who do they think they're dealing with? Some yo-yo with a thousand dollar line of credit? He sunk into the giant pillow bed and mopped his steaming face with a thirsty giant bath sheet.

"Read them the expiration dates. You know as well as I do when they expire. And it isn't today."

It had to be computer error. That was it! Ian almost wept in relief. Good old computer error. Computer error could happen to anyone. Even David Rockefeller.

His credit couldn't have run out. It just couldn't have.

"Missy, can you get Mastercard on the phone for me?"

"Okay, Mr. Harrington, but don't talk too long." Adroitly, she punched the phone buttons. "Hello? I have a question." She read the numbers and the expiration date and asked them to re-check. She waited.

Ian snatched the phone from her. "What's all this about my Mastercard's being cut off? What? I have *what?* I have to go to the nearest branch and discuss this with an officer? What the fuck is going on? The cock-sucking banks don't open until nine." The line went dead.

Missy stared at him. Her eyes had all the sparkle of a trout's, ready for the pan.

Ian had four dollars and two subway tokens. What was he supposed to do now? It wasn't like he'd charged a pair of socks at Bloomingdale's.

"Missy, sweetheart, put the charge through. Put it through for three-hundred-sixty-seven. You keep the extra hundred for your trouble. I'll fix the whole thing up later. Promise."

"Gee, Mr. Harrington, I could really get my ass in a sling or something."

"Make it four-sixty-seven, Missy. Christmas is coming. I'll fix it. I'm a man of my word."

Ian had been reading about credit card cutbacks, but he hadn't believed it. Not a word. Any more than he'd ever really believed that there had been a gas shortage.

"I just can't do it, Mr. Harrington. I could ask Mr. Sydney, but he won't be in until noon. And I'm sure he'd say no anyway. Mr. Sydney always says no. Mr. Sydney even said no to me. Something, huh?" She fixed on him with the trout stare.

"I don't know what I'm going to do, Missy. I don't have any money. I don't even have a check."

"Cheer up, Mr. Harrington, we don't accept checks."

How was he going to pay for *any*thing? The Plaza? Helen's dinner? How was he going to explain what had happened to some pillar of bureaucracy at the Chemical Bank?

How could the country that had produced George Washington cut off his credit?

Stay calm. Get dressed. He pulled on his dissolute green boxer shorts. No one exuded authority facing the world with a pimply bare ass. He had to call someone. Who?

By the time he had shaved and put on all of his clothes,

Ian still hadn't come up with anyone. Rose-Delia would melt the telephone lines. Jill might have him arrested. Pumpkin would have him committed.

None of his former business associates would speak to him. He certainly had burnt his bridges.

What about Helen? Forget it, she'd only make things worse. Juliet? She was probably scouting the back alleys of Greenwich Village for dead bodies, hoping one was his.

Hogwood! That was it. No, Hogwood was in Palm Beach. He needed someone who could get him the money by lunchtime. Bethy! Brilliant! He'd call the headmistress. Explain that he was calling from Florida. Rose-Delia was sinking fast. She was calling for Beth. All she had to do was to put Beth on the train with five hundred in travelers' checks and an overnight bag. Beth would be met and taken to Kennedy. It was foolproof.

"Missy, I have to make a phone call. I'll pay. Cash." Ian held up the four singles.

"I guess so, Mr. Harrington. Local, right?"

"Right." Ian's heart raced as he dialed Laurel Hall. In fifteen minutes, it was all set. Bethy would arrive in Grand Central at eleven-forty.

"Okay, Missy, I'll be back after lunch, with the money."

"Ya know something, Mr. Harrington? I think I'd better keep your camera as security—like, you know, collateral. Otherwise, Mr. Sydney will have my ass, if you know what I mean." She winked.

"Fine. Fine," Ian agreed. In ten minutes, the banks would be open. He'd straighten everything out.

As he loped down the stairs to Third Avenue, it hit him. Jill. That bitch.

It had to be her. She must have found his stash of credit cards. Money-grubbing gold digger. Probably egged on by the queen B-for-bitch herself, Pumpkin Endicott-Osborne. He probably didn't have a nickel's worth of credit left. Rose-Delia would have to give him another advance on his inheritance.

He'd move to Palm Beach. It was getting colder and colder

in New York anyways. He'd butter up Rose-Delia. She loved it when he came to visit her.

He'd really reform. No more backgammon at fifty dollars a point. Coats and ties to breakfast, if necessary. Pay Jill alimony. Pay her almost anything. With eight million, it would be worth it to get her out of his life. Good-bye, Jill. But he didn't have the eight million. Yet.

He stepped into a phone booth. The smell of stale urine caught in his throat.

"Hello? Jill? Harrington here. Listen, Jill. I don't want a divorce. I never wanted a divorce. I see no sense in it. Pumpkin has filled your head with a lot of silly ideas about me."

"Pumpkin has nothing to do with anything, Ian. Ralston Rhodes and I have had several discussions. I'm not permitted to talk to you about anything unless it's in his presence."

"Ralston Rhodes, and his ass-holier-than-thou claptrap. It surprises me that he isn't still wearing boiled collars and a pince-nez. If you think I'll roll over, Jill, you'd better call Edward Bennett Williams or maybe Marvin Mitchelson. Ralston Rhodes..."

The operator asked for another dime. Ian didn't have one. Could he reverse the charges?

Jill hung up and then took the phone off the hook. She poured herself another cup of black coffee. Not good for a stomach already in knots. Oh, for a nice, soothing, hot rum toddy. Maybe she should reverse the charges on those credit cards. Who needed more of Ian's rampant insanity? More of Brodhead's obsessive ego trips? More of Bethy's cryptic letters, chock full of veiled references to "Daddy's other wives"? Now she was sorry she'd let Keefe call a messenger. Brodhead liked his vassals to enter the throne room and wait, respectfully, until he deigned to speak to them. At least she'd gotten the work to him on time. At least she was dressed. That had been a monumental effort. Keefe was sloshing around in her shower. Maybe she should get him more coffee. Forget it. She was too tired. How much longer was it going to take Ralston Rhodes to get his act together? But Ian wouldn't pay attention to anything legal anyway. How much longer was she going to dwell on Ian? Idly, she stirred her coffee. The doorbell rang.

Franklin, the eternal watchdog from the lobby, handed her a telegram. She thanked him. What had Ian done now?

It was from Hogwood, Rose-Delia's attorney in Palm Beach:

> Rose-Delia drowned in Lake Worth during a dinner cruise last night. Possible suicide. Cannot locate Ian. Disregard recent check; no longer valid. Accounts are closed. Contact me earliest. Regards and sympathy, Hogwood Worth.

Rose-Delia. It wasn't possible. Jill sank into an uncomfortable Regency chair and buried her face in her hands. "Cannot locate Ian." If Ian knew, he'd hitchhike to Florida. His more than forty years of scheming, cajoling and wheedling had finally come to an end.

Pumpkin's Joseph Mulliken tall case clock pinged out eight. Get cracking, a little voice told her. That's what Rose-Delia would have done. She wouldn't have sat around in tears when there was work to be done. Jill dried her eyes.

Damn! She'd planned on stopping by the bank to deposit Rose-Delia's check. *Why* hadn't she opened those sympathy cards sooner? She reached into her closet and pulled out a black gabardine suit and blazing red shirt. That just about said it all this morning.

CHAPTER ELEVEN

Bammie sat hunched at her desk, immersed in *How to Dress Like Nancy Reagan for Under $50*. She was depressed. Big meetings always depressed her. She was the only one who had to stay at her desk. Why couldn't Charlie at least ask her to serve coffee or sharpen pencils? She'd do anything to see and hear what *really* went on in the boardroom.

Charlie was struggling with her makeup. The lights in the boardroom were all wrong for her usual daytime outdoorsy look. Never mind. She was busy inventing nasty questions and arranging to be interrupted at least twice with important long distance calls, preferably from London or Paris.

Why was she bothering? It was just a new products meeting. Nobody important. No clients. A couple of research and development creeps from Jersey who sashayed around in lab coats like the Curies.

Tige Barnett came in for a landing beside Bammie's desk.

"Are Ms. Whitrock and her group attending this morning's new products session in the conference room? *Hers* was the one and only group not heard from." Tige bared his teeth in what was supposed to be a smile. "What's the good news?"

"The good news is, Tiger, that Ms. Whitrock *and* her group will be in attendance. We RSVP'd last week. Your girl must have lost it in the shredder."

They might have been having a telephone conversation. Bammie would not dignify his presence by looking at him.

Goddamn drip-dry suit. Nosing around. Sucking up to her to get to Charlie. Trying to make his impact felt on the creative floor. He'd been with BDK&C for three whole weeks. What was he expecting? A gold watch?

"This is a landmark meeting, Bammie. Maybe you'd like to sit in on it? Take some notes?"

"I've already been invited to sit in on it. By an executive vice-president. And I don't take notes. I record."

Unabashed, Tige flashed three or four smiles in rapid succession. "Better tell Ms. Whitrock to get in there as fast as possible. Five minutes till countdown."

"Right." Bammie turned a page.

Tige Barnett stole a glance at his watch. "Time is of the utmost. That is, if she wants a good seat for the performance. Got it?"

"Ms. Whitrock always has the same seat, Tiger boy. She sitteth on the right hand of Mr. Kincaid, God the Father." She closed her magazine and handed it to Tige with a wink. "Better take this. It can get pretty dull in there."

Charlie sailed out of her office. "I'm going to some half-assed new products meeting in the conference room. They think they've topped all-natural-ingredient shoe polish. I'll be about an hour, if that. Transfer any important trans-Atlantic calls. Find Jill. Tell her I want her next to me."

Charlie looked right through Tige Barnett. He flashed his teeth.

"I'm so sorry," Charlie said, "do you have an appointment? I'm running late. You'll have to forgive me."

"As you were saying, Tiger?" Bammie asked sweetly.

Fifty art directors and writers milled around the board room, drinking coffee and grinding crumbs of stale prune Danish into the gray industrial carpet.

Jill was bone tired, yet exhilarated. She slid behind a noisy group near the coffee urn and into the chair second from Bonehead's. Lately, Charlene had asked that she sit next to her. What did it mean? Probably nothing.

Jill put her attaché case on the chair to her right. Might as well save Chip a seat. Where was he, anyhow? Mary-Sue Cratchitt was angling for his seat. She sure as hell didn't need Mary-Sue Cratchitt, a.k.a. Hairy-Sue Cat Shit, nattering at her throughout the meeting.

The huge double doors at the far end of the conference room swung open. Ellie and Buster, models of obsequity, showed the research and development team in.

Chip slipped in the back door and into his seat a second before Bonehead's earthquaking "Good Morning" reverberated across Madison Avenue.

"Ladies and gentlemen," he boomed, "this morning we have a rare double-barreled treat for you all. Dr. Holly Webster and her assistant, Professor Morgan de Blatz have consented to let us in on some of their little secrets—little secrets, which, in the marketplace of tomorrow, will mean big bucks and big business."

"It's docudrama time," Chip scribbled on the yellow lined legal pad in front of him.

Jill clamped her mouth shut.

"And now to present our good friends from research and development, the new management supervisor on the South Forty Home-taste Foods account, Traphaggan Barnett, otherwise known as Tige. Tige will be taking over from Nils Nelson and Buster Niles."

All eyes shifted to Ellie and Buster. While it was a surprise to everyone in the room, it was a shock to them. Surprises were Bonehead's trademark.

"And now, a warm welcome for Tige Barnett, from Princeton, Harvard Business School and the Bates Agency via SSC&B. Tige!"

Tige shook Bonehead's hand. Bonehead slammed Tige in the arm. They shook hands some more. Bonehead sat down, pushed his chair back two feet and crossed one leg over the other. Tige cleared his throat.

"Well, now, let's get down to business, shall we?"

"For those of you who question the impact of R&D—research and development—ask yourself this: has war changed the world? No! Have politicians changed the world? No! Has religion changed the world? No! Who or what *has* changed the world?"

"This could bring tears to a hyena's eyes," Chip scratched on his yellow pad.

Jill bit her lip.

"Anybody? Don't be afraid to speak up. We're all family here."

Jill looked at Ellie and Buster. She was glad they didn't have a nail gun.

"Advertising?" suggested Mary-Sue Cratchitt, batting her eyes.

"A-ha! Advertising! Close. *Ve*-ry close. But a better answer would have been 'R&D'! The men and women in white coats. They've controlled static cling. They've decaffeinated coffee. They've baked bread with real wood fiber. They've created instant powdered orange juice so that our brave astronauts could enjoy a little bit of home on the moon."

Tige Barnett took a sip of water. It gave him a chance to check up on the impact of his words on the room.

"R&D has made instant tea with a deep-rich color achieved with half a dozen chemicals unknown six months ago. They've fought cavities, rushed into the fray against bad breath in dogs, cats, and humans. They blasted dulling soap film into outer space, and practically single-handedly wiped irregularity from the face of the civilized earth."

"Wrong part of the anatomy," Chip scrawled.

"They conquered the ravages of aspirin-caused stomach upset, eased the heartbreak of psoriasis. They've gotten down to where the rubber meets the road in the face of icky toilet bowls, legs with razor stubble and marching armies of roaches."

Tige exhaled. Flashed his teeth. Pretended to ruffle notes that Jill could see were really only sheets of blank paper.

"And who, I ask you, *who*, needs cheese from the caves of France when R&D has deduced a way to put it in aerosol cans?

"And that is just the beginning, ladies and gentlemen. R&D has worked long and hard figuring out how to inflate chocolate with air and so induce one to believe that a new chocolate bar twice the size of the old one and at the old price, is a modern-day miracle of Lourdes.

"Ladies and gentlemen, Dr. Webster and Professor de Blatz, and men and women like them all across the country, working day in and day out, have given America its split-screen personality!" Tige Barnett paused dramatically.

"And now," continued Tige, "I'm going to prevail upon these fine people to open up their big bag of tricks!" Tiger turned toward them and bowed.

Four women from the test kitchen marched forward, starched uniforms holding them upright as they lifted platter after heavy platter and placed them on the long rosewood table.

Everyone strained forward to see.

When the women had finished, Dr. Webster and Professor de Blatz stepped forward.

"Ladies and gentlemen," Dr. Webster began, "we have several new and exciting items to show you this morning. In the field of fast food, actually. But these new products are the fastest foods you've ever seen."

She began whipping sheets of aluminum foil from the big platters and bowls.

"Here, we have a real miracle. You spoke of a miracle, Mr. Barnett, yes? Well, what do you think of coleslaw that makes its own dressing in ten seconds?"

There was a murmur followed by a buzz. People stood, trying to get a better look.

In a large glass bowl was a mound of sticky white shreds.

"And on this platter, griddle cakes. They look just like any other griddle cakes, don't they? That's right, look closer. Watch them."

Everybody watched. Slowly, a thin, pale liquid began to seep out from between the layers of pancakes, down over the edge of the plate and onto the table. Professor de Blatz grabbed a handful of paper napkins from the coffee table. The liquid kept coming. It seemed unstaunchable. What *was* it?

"What you are witnessing ladies and gentlemen," said Tige Barnett, "is not unlike that fateful night when Thomas Alva Edison, in his laboratory in Menlo Park, New Jersey, said 'I see the light.' This, my friends, is a stack of new Griddle Fakes making its own syrup. It doesn't matter that they've made a bit too much... you are witnessing history!

"And Griddle Fakes are made from soy beans. No cholesterol!"

Jill and Chip grabbed all the paper napkins from the coffee table. FiFi Woolverson returned from the ladies' room with a box of sanitary napkins, tossing them into the gunk like roses to a matador.

"Brodhead, what's going on?" Charlie whispered.

"Don't make any judgments yet, Charlie. This guy's a real comer. Bright, talented people are hard to handle. You want more of those mediocrities skulking around? We're getting it together, Charlie. Ellie and Buster have an appointment in the Sahara."

Jesus. As brilliant, articulate, successful as Brodhead was, he clearly had never read John O'Hara. Jill sighed. She felt like *she* had an appointment in the Sahara, to be staked out for the red ants.

Once the syrup had finally been conquered, the noise level rose.

"Ladies and gentlemen. Ladies and gentlemen," Tige barked,

"please. What you've seen is only the beginning! And best of all, we're going to have a taste test. Now, Dr. Webster, what is your next enticing entrée? I see mouths watering all around me."

Dr. Holly Webster and Professor Morgan de Blatz pushed a large soup tureen in front of Tige Barnett. "We think you should be the first to taste it, Mr. Barnett," said Morgan de Blatz. "We think this particular soup product could have major implications in the Third World."

"A-*ha*. Thinking ahead. That's the byword here at BDK&C. And what is this delicious-smelling concoction, Doctor?"

"We'd like you to taste it and then ladle some out into these plastic cups. We'll pass them around. I have here an evaluation sheet for taste, texture, appetite appeal, what you think it costs per serving and what you think we could charge. That isn't too hard, is it?"

De Blatz passed out the questionnaires. Webster ladled. Everyone began tasting, swishing, chewing.

"What do you think it tastes like, Chip?" Jill asked.

"The only thing they don't have at Chez Venezia."

"I think it tastes like *ragout der osterhasen*," said Mary-Sue Cratchitt.

"I wonder what Pumpkin would call this?" Jill said to no one in particular.

Dutifully, they filled out their questionnaires and returned them to Dr. Webster, who glanced at the answers on the top sheet.

"Ahhh, let me read at random: 'Texture: hearty. Taste: ambrosial. Cost to make: $3/10$ cent. Cost to sell: 89¢ per can, undiluted. Repeat purchase: Are you kidding.' Well, well, well, whoever we owe those kudos to, *merci*."

"Dr. Webster," Chip raised his hand, "I'd like to ask a question, if I may."

"Please."

"Did you study at the Culinary Institute?"

"No, Cordon Bleu." Her face fell. Caught. *Merde*.

"Ahh, that explains the finesse, the delicacy of touch." Chip smiled his ecstatic, angelic smile. "Mademoiselle, the minute I tasted this...*potage*...I knew I was in the hands of an...*ange*."

"Okay. The results are *in*, ladies and gentlemen. And I'm going to say, right off the top of my head, that I think we've got some real winners here. The coleslaw that makes its own dressing is unique. New Griddle Fakes will have Aunt Jemima getting her pacemaker recharged. And this soup. Well, *if* we can use it to solve Third World problems, help to stamp out hunger where the pangs stab deepest, amen."

"All right, I'll bite," said Bonehead, suddenly assertive. "What's in the soup?"

Morgan de Blatz smiled with confidence. "Since I developed it, I'll try to explain. All over the world, people eat different things. In Italy, for example, they love pasta. In India, they eat rice, a good deal of it curried. And here, we like French fries and burgers. Do I make myself clear?" He pushed his glasses back up on his nose.

No, thought Jill. Not in the least. Christ.

"And so," de Blatz continued, "there would be really no point in trying to feed the Indians pasta and the Italians curry. In order to feed people one must take into consideration not only nutrition but taste appeal. So, in order to prick the appetites of the starving Asians, we had to strive to find a taste that was universally acceptable."

"Birth of a nation," Chip wrote, "reel one."

"And so, this nourishing soup...with five thousand calories per cup..."

General unrest spread through the room like liquid margarine. Jill searched for something, anything, in her bag.

"This nourishing dish is made entirely from soy. One more time that the universal bean triumphs. But, just imagine soy with the unmistakable flavor of...dog!"

FiFi Woolverson left the room, Mary-Sue Cratchitt on her heels.

"Dog, as I'm sure you know, is considered to be a great delicacy in many of your Asian countries. I'm sure that many of you have seen dogs yelping in their cages, waiting to be chosen for dinner. Very Asian. Much as lobsters in tanks are seen in many of your better seafood restaurants here."

Charlie shot Bonehead a scathing glare and left. Jill and Chip leaned toward Morgan de Blatz, hanging on every word.

"And so, ladies and gentlemen, modern science goes to the dogs!" His eyes raked the small group that remained around the conference room table. He smiled broadly and finished his cup of soup.

"Well," said Tige Barnett, "I guess we owe you a great big hand, Professor de Blatz. That is what *I* call a real breakthrough. Does anyone have anything to add?"

Morgan de Blatz was once again on his feet. "I just want to add one thing. You may have noticed the little stringy pieces of 'meat' in the soup?"

Several heads nodded.

"Dog tails. Made completely from soy protein. Only the taste is authentic!"

"Chip, get me out of here," Jill whispered.

"Well," Tige Barnett began, "I guess that about wraps it up, right guys?"

"Couldn't have put it better myself," commented Brodhead. "Jill, I'd like to see you in my office when you're free."

Jill smiled. "Okay, Chip. I think we can walk out of here with our heads held high."

"I feel the need of some bottled poetry, Jill. Would you care to join me below after your meeting?"

Tige Barnett was moving toward her, all teeth. "Sure, Chip. The instant I'm free."

"Ms. Harrington, how'd you like to join me at table eighty-nine at the Four Seasons? Around twelve-forty-five? I think we need some follow-up work on this session."

"Yes. But I'd like Chip La Doza to join us."

"Mr. Kincaid said specifically that I should work things out with you alone."

"Meet you there," said Jill as she floated out the door.

It was becoming easier and easier for her to go along with things without questioning them. But then, she always had, hadn't she? Only now the things made her feel good about herself. God, it was all so complicated, but in a funny way, so simple, too.

CHAPTER TWELVE

"*It's about* the worst thing I've ever overheard of," said Chip, referring to the din coming from Charlie's office. "Just listen. You don't even need your ear to the wall." Jill sat down.

Chip was right. Charlene's voice registered twelve on the Beaufort scale.

"My back is turned for five minutes and you go for the jugular, you scheming little...little...rat."

"Who's she reaming over?"

"Beats me. Whoever it is, he or she is retaliating in very low tones."

"I let that moron, FiFi Woolverson, steal you out of my group. You promised you'd do some discreet and articulate spying for me. Fine. Twice you came through. But now! This! Do you know what this means?"

Mumbles.

"It means that unless we're very careful, Mr. Kincaid is going to be on to us.

"I told you, you ass, that I wanted her exact campaign so that we could do spin-offs, other versions. But no, you have to give me the *other* versions. Do you realize that I was just about to present Mr. Kincaid with her exact campaign?"

Stomping around the room. Door slamming.

"You silly nitwit. If Jill Harrington hadn't seen those storyboards in Bonehead's office this morning, you'd be on the beach. And so would I. And don't tell me a miss is as good as a mile."

"Oh my God," Chip exclaimed, "it's Hairy-Sue Cat Shit. Getting the old riot act read to her. Is it true, Jill? Did you see the storyboards in Bonehead's office?"

"Yes," said Jill. "I did. They looked so familiar, I took a closer look. It wasn't *déjà vu;* it was almost as if the storyboards had been run through the Xerox machine."

"What campaign was it?"

"Crack-A Pack-A Snack-A Chocolate Corn Chips."

"Guaranteed to rot teeth in minutes. Programmed to send *Crest* toothpaste R&D back to the drawing board."

"Don't ever mention R&D to me again. Ever." Jill exhaled. "I wish I were having lunch with you instead of Tige Barnett. Even his name makes me gag."

"Listen, listen, Charlie's at it again."

"As far as I'm concerned, you can stay in FiFi Woolverson's group and if you get a raise before you're eighty years old, I'll roll over in my grave."

Inside Charlie's office, Mary-Sue smiled broadly. FiFi had already given her a raise. A handsome one. Ten thousand dollars just for setting Charlene up. It had been fun. Mary-Sue hated Charlene. She hated FiFi, too. She didn't want to work for either of them; she wanted a group of her own. It had all seemed so easy. Until that bitch Jill Harrington came on the scene.

"I told you that when you get appropriate information, you've got to do it with finesse." Charlene threw the storyboards at Mary-Sue. "Maybe I should just let it drop to FiFi that you pirated her ideas and passed them off as your own to Brodhead."

"Okay by me," answered Mary-Sue. "But who's going to

believe it? Face it, Charlie, everyone in the agency knows that FiFi Woolverson couldn't write her way out of a literacy test."

"So who did write Crack-A Pack-A Snack-A?"

"You did, Charlie."

"What?"

"At the preliminary meeting, when we first got the business, you were throwing out examples of how to think of the products, and you said 'Crack-A Pack-A Snack-A, put some music under it and we're on our way.'"

Charlie couldn't believe her ears. "Bammie, get me the tapes on file."

"This is getting serious," said Jill. "Wish I could hear the rest but it's time to fold my tent."

"Where did you get that ridiculous expression, anyhow?" Chip asked. "You never folded a tent in your life." He was definitely not his usual sweet self.

"It's from a poem," Jill said curtly.

"Oh."

"Cheer up, Chip. This afternoon we can work on dog soup."

"Have fun with Jaws."

Jill left and Chip drew his chair closer to the wall. Such ripe opportunities rarely presented themselves during business hours. Most of the good dirt happened at lunch or cocktails.

Charlie's voice had lowered a few decibels. "Mary-Sue, who wrote 'a tingle of tantalizing temptation in every mouthwatering morsel' for Pizza Raisin Bagels?"

"My mother, Mrs. Amory Barlow Cratchitt. She's always wanted to be in advertising."

"Mary-Sue, we are not amused. We are going to sit here until midnight if that's what it takes to get to the bottom of this."

"Charlie, I appeal to your sense of reason," Mary-Sue went on. "Who would ever admit to writing that piece of shit—much less stealing it? I mean, it's like stealing from FiFi's wastebasket. I'll tell you what I think we should do: let's get Chip La Doza in here, order a sandwich and do a new campaign over lunch. I happen to know that Mr. Kincaid has gone to Le Cirque. Ms. Harrington is off to the Four Seasons with that new Barnett guy and Mrs. Woolverson is having her hair done in preparation for the three o'clock meeting on Crack-A. We've got almost three hours. I'll get someone to get some food up here."

Chip groaned as the knock resounded on his door.

Charlene didn't look in the least upset.

"What's a mother to do?" she smiled, her arm around his shoulder as they sauntered into her office. "Chip what do *you* think? I know you've heard it all."

"It is written that art directors are paid not to think."

"Chip-per, you are not helping. We're in a bind here."

"What do you want from me? A shoulder to lean on?"

"Wrists, Chip. Agile wrists. Get some Magic Markers and everything you've ever thought of, written about, or drawn on those obscene chocolate-covered corn snacks."

Charlene pushed the intercom. "Bammie, sanitation duty!" Charlene turned to Chip. "First, we put all of our stuff into the shredder. No one will ever know that both groups were going to hand in the same campaign."

"Only that Irrawadi swamp viper, Mary-Sue Cratchitt."

"At the end of the week, Mary-Sue is getting her walking papers. That's just between you and me."

"Charlie, be reasonable. You can't fire her. She's not even in your group any more. And second, she's one of the best copywriters here. How are you going to explain *that* to Bonehead?"

"Chip, I don't need any more problems. Now, here's the strategy statement, written by none other than Mr. Nelson and I quote: 'This is a brand new snack food made from real corn and real chocolate. It tastes good. It is geared to today's high-energy men and women eighteen to thirty-four years of age who like chocolate and corn. Note: no sense in trying to go after users who don't like chocolate *or* corn. It's possible to go after *chocolate* lovers or *corn* lovers. This product is salt-free, cholesterol-free, caffeine-free. It contains no artificial colorings or preservatives. This last has proved to be a double-edged sword of Damocles: the shelf life is about two weeks. The prime prospect is very broad.'"

"I thought he said it was geared to high-energy eighteen to thirty-four year olds?"

"Maybe he means *fat* eighteen to thirty-four year olds?"

"Chip, what would I do without you? Now, there's advertising with vitality!"

"Right, Charlene. It jumps off the screen and into their laps." Chip looked at Charlene. "Did you try any of that stuff this morning?"

"An experience."

"I think I hear Mary-Sue with lunch. Don't say anything."

"Anything about what?"

"Just anything."

Unbeknownst to Chip and Charlie, Mary-Sue had made several Xerox copies of everything.

Table eighty-nine at the Four Seasons is unique. It occupies the northwest corner of the pool room. It is the only corner table in the room. It is a table for two, and it commands an uncluttered view of everyone who enters. One can observe what the patrons are wearing and who they're with and discuss it without fear of being overheard. It was Brodhead's favorite table, in his favorite restaurant in New York.

Tige Barnett was already seated when Jill arrived. Many people noticed what she was wearing: a black fitted Calvin Klein suit with broad shoulders and petal skirt. They wondered who she was for a brief moment between sips and bites.

Jill knew she was on time. She did not look at her watch. She did not apologize for being late.

"What shall it be?" asked Tige Barnett, all smiles.

Jill looked closer to see if his teeth were capped. They weren't. "Glass of champagne, please."

"Ya know, Jill, I may call you Jill?"

She nodded absently. What was with the gallantry stuff?

"I thought we could use this opportunity to get to know each other better."

"Un-huh. And chose Mr. Kincaid's favorite table for a *tête-à-tête*. I'll bet I'm really Dr. Holly Webster or Mr. Morgan de Blatz of R&D, so far as accounting is concerned."

"*Touché*. Now that we have that out of the way, I'd like to know your thoughts on the new products meeting."

Jill stared at him. "I've never seen anything like that. I think it was absurd. Dog-flavored soup. Who do they think they're kidding?"

"Not you, clearly. Actually, it was beef broth with little strands of top round slivered in it."

"No soy? No puppy dog's tails?" So it was a hoax. But *why?*

"It was an exercise in perception. Mr. Kincaid feels that many of his creative people aren't perceptive enough. *Sooo*, we cooked up the whole thing. You see, Jill, I'm not really an account man. I'm a behavioral psychologist."

"I loved the way Nelson and Niles behaved when you were announced as the new management supervisor on their accounts."

"All part of it, Jill. Kincaid wants them to resign."

"So the agency doesn't have to pay them severance and all those goodies, right?"

So! Bonehead *was* playing God. There was something frightening about it all. As much as she didn't like Ellie or Buster, she certainly didn't appreciate Barnett's *Gaslight* tactics.

"Ever notice that elaborate gold leaf Baroque mirror in the conference room? The one reputed to have come from the Schoenbrun Palace?" Tige Barnett asked.

"Who hasn't? Every man, woman and child who's ever been in the boardroom has admired himself in it."

"It's a two-way mirror, Jill. Brodhead and I watch every meeting that goes on in there."

"You mean he monitors us when he's not actually in the room?"

"You got it."

"And you probably have it all on videotape, too, right?"

"Ditto. We liked your reactions right across the board, Jill. That's why we're having lunch today."

And Jill used to think that Pumpkin had picked up her 'how to diet' techniques from the KGB.

"We wanted to discover just how much the staff would buy—on several levels, so to speak. For example, would they believe that the products were as presented? That they had eaten soy soup with authentic dog taste?"

He sipped his martini. "Would they believe that the products would perform for the consumers—that those pancakes would really make their own syrup? And finally, would they believe that consumers really *needed* these products to enhance their daily lives?"

"Since when was that a factor in marketing?" laughed Jill. "Nobody *ever* needed any of those products you ticked off in the meeting this morning. Charlie Whitrock's favorite was the 'All-natural ingredient shoe polish'—the quintessential unnecessary product." She glanced at her watch. At least another hour of Dr. Caligari.

Tige Barnett laughed heartily. "All a big game, Jill. And we're the big game hunters. Just let's make sure our elephant guns are loaded around BDK&C. Cheers."

A real pro, thought Jill. A knack with words. Christ.

Slowly, Jill was beginning to trust her instincts again. The years with Ian had shaken to the foundations her confidence in her intuition, but that was changing. Every time she did something particularly good—even something as simple as having the right reaction and expressing it, she felt just great. There was something in that.

Barnett seemed nice. What was he doing in such a Machiavellian enterprise?

To hell with her diet. Jill ate two tiny croissants with butter. She ordered the littlenecks first, followed by the pheasant-stuffed cabbage and a glass of champagne.

She was feeling pretty confident. After the so-called "new products" meeting, she'd gone to Brodhead's office. He'd asked her about suggestions for improving the agency. Jill had told him exactly what she thought. Nicely. Politely. And firmly. Even without Rose-Delia's check, she could survive with the credit card money. And as soon as she sold the Badger Hollow house, her money worries would be over. She had nothing to lose. By now she knew that Brodhead Kincaid loathed the fawners and the cringers.

She'd suggested he put more women on the staff, though not necessarily permanent additions. New thinking from people other than the regular staff. Uncanny that she had been thinking along the same lines as he. Or so he said.

When Brodhead had described FiFi and Mary-Sue as innovative thinkers, she'd dodged him. After all, she didn't know them.

But everything she heard about both of them made her warier and warier.

When Brodhead had asked her what she thought of the new products meeting, she'd answered that she was surprised that so many people had left the meeting early. Period. Pumpkin would have been proud of her. She hoped.

"Brodhead is very interested in you, Jill, in case you haven't figured that out by now," Tige said.

"Oh?"

"He feels that you represent the new breed of women."

"Sounds like I'm running in the Kentucky Derby or something."

"He feels that you represent the *type* of woman who is taking over more and more of the business, the management, the general running of things in America. The woman who copes with money! He feels that the time is ripe for women to feel capable of thinking about it: how to earn it, how to manage it. Because of what you've recently been through, he feels that your first-hand knowledge is critical to the agency."

"Oh?" Good Christ, if Bonehead and Tige Barnett had only seen her sitting alone in the kitchen in her old bathrobe, fumbling with The Bills!

Jill speared a littleneck and dunked it into the red vinegar sauce in the little glass cup—so much better than even the Four Seasons' cocktail sauce.

Say something, idiot. *Anything*. But preferably something Tige has set you up to say.

"Well, Tige, I *have* had a lot of experience in home budgeting." That was as good as anything. "Twelve years' worth. But I can't believe that it qualifies me as an expert. Plenty of women have had the same experiences." Lucky them.

"That's what we're counting on, Jill. For you to strike the empathy chords of America."

"What about the other women at the agency?" Better tiptoe in and out of this one.

"Brodhead doesn't feel that Mrs. Whitrock exactly has her fingertips on the pulse of America, Jill. Ditto, Mrs. Woolverson and Ms. Cratchitt."

"But I do because I have practical experience as well as agency experience? Sort of a high school equivalency test... and I've passed with flying colors?"

"Couldn't put it better myself."

"Since you know everything, Tige," Jill smiled sweetly, "I suggested to Brodhead that we get some new thinking into the agency. Right after the new products meeting this morning, in fact."

"Good. I didn't hear about it."

"*And* I suggested that we start right here in the agency... with wives of the account men, art directors, and writers. *Wives*. Lord knows, they have practical experience. And they already live a vicarious agency life. We'll get *their* opinions on new products. Bet you anything, Tige, if you pull the dog soup trick on them, you'll risk multiple injuries."

"Look, Jill, I think it's a great idea. Maybe Brodhead can get some publicity... some good publicity, for a change."

"Know what he wants to call the project?"

"Bad taste, right? Male chauvinist pig to the tenth power?"

"Wife Swappers Week."

"Typical Bonehead."

"Oh? You know about 'Bonehead'?"

"Bonehead and I went to Lawrenceville together."

There it was, the Old Boy Network again. It was time for a little Old Girl Network action, Jill thought. She tried to keep from giggling at the idea and shifted into frozen smile. Of course Tige Barnett was so busy beaming he didn't notice.

"I agree with you about publicity. I'll give Phil Dougherty at the *Times* a call. We'll get our clients to do it at their companies. I can see the scene at Country Kitchens now! The biggest breakthrough of the twentieth century: Women in the Kitchen!"

CHAPTER THIRTEEN

"*Don't sit* on toilet seats. Don't drink martinis. And if your roommate tries anything, go straight to the dean."

Armed with such motherly advice and a trunk full of cashmere sweaters, Suzy Stanford set out for Smith College in the autumn of 1950. In the spring of 1954, she appeared on Madison Avenue and was promptly hired by Young & Rubicam. Six months later she was married to a commodities broker and forgot all about advertising until she met Brodhead Kincaid on the Queen Elizabeth II. He was divorced; she was about to be.

Suzy yawned and patted a stray wisp of carefully tinted blonde hair. Only three hours before Brodhead's client dinner. Carefully, she parted the louvered doors of her closet. Here was every gown, dress, suit and blouse she'd bought during the past twenty years. Bagged and boxed. Stuffed with tissue and classified under a code system that would have given Dewey Decimal experts pause.

Why was she so nervous? She'd given hundreds of client

dinners. They were easy enough. Always serve beef. Avoid artichokes. It never failed.

Suzy pawed through the array. A black silk suit and pink organza blouse. Obvious, but ladylike. Perfect for the Bronkhorst Drug account. Whenever she dressed for a Bronkhorst party, she always took off two pieces of jewelry and changed into lower heels.

And then, before joining them for cocktails, she'd repeat to herself the rule about conversation. No discussion of religion, politics, servants or illness. The last was particularly difficult, since Bronkhorst produced some of the leading pain relievers, cold remedies and hemorrhoid preparations.

Of course, there'd been that one evening when the rules went to hell. One of Brodhead's young account executives, a woman of thirty, had appeared in a black lace top and silver stretch satin jeans. Suzy had taken one look at the expressions on the faces of the Bronkhorst chairman and executive vice-president and, snatching a tray of champagne and martinis from the waiter, had plowed her way into the group. The new account woman was chatting with a grim Carstairs Bronkhorst.

"I adore Fire Island," she was saying, "it makes the Hamptons look tame."

Suzy had begged Brodhead to fire the woman, but he'd refused. It was the beginning of his campaign for new blood.

Suzy retreated to her bathroom and slathered on some more foundation. Then, she picked up a blue-gray eye pencil and went to work, humming to herself.

"Lizzie Arden took some whacks/ to compensate for nature's lacks/ And at last when she was done/ she knew she wasn't twenty-one."

Suzy sighed. Tonight, a dozen from Bronkhorst. On Thursday, two dozen from Country Kitchens. "God, grant me strength and watch over my liver."

No wonder she wasn't happier. But other women—wives mostly (who else did she meet)—were invariably commenting on how much they envied her charmed life. Entertaining.

Going to the theater. The opera. Planning menus and never cooking any of it herself. It all sounded like bliss to them.

Once, a tipsy office wife had confessed that she'd love to steal Brodhead away from her.

"Steal away," Suzy had replied. "It might last for two days. If you're lucky."

Suzy had been kidding. But lately Brodhead had been talking about another woman. A lot more than any woman he'd mentioned since she'd known him. Someone new at the agency. Jill something. Waddington? No. Jill Harrington.

It seemed this Harrington woman could do no wrong. She was the smartest, the brightest, the prettiest, the most incisive. She'd suffered and survived.

Brodhead had never suffered, but apparently he had recently developed an ocean of sympathy for those who had.

Anyway, on Thursday night Suzy would find out what was so wonderful about Jill Harrington.

She gave her hair a few more random sprays. Not bad for someone on the brink of senility.

Until now, Suzy had envied no one, and no one else's life. All she wanted—at least thought she wanted—was for Brodhead to distinguish between her and his fucking advertising agency.

Every time he said he was too busy to make love, she told him to go screw some storyboards. As usual, her humor was lost on him.

He was one of life's over-achievers. Nothing touched him, unless it was directly related to his business.

Suzy felt around in her vanity drawer for some Q-tips. Gone! Christ, why couldn't Brodhead use his own Q-Tips, in his own bathroom?

And why did he insist on leaving his crap in *her* bathroom? His medicated dandruff shampoo, sticky blue oozing down the side of the bottle, towered over her bottles of expensive scent. Suzy had never had dandruff. She hadn't washed her own hair for years. Brodhead's foot medicine stood next to the shampoo. Suzy had never had athlete's foot, either.

His shaving cream. His deodorant. His razor.

He used her razor to scrape the dead skin off the bottoms of his feet, leaving the unsavory residue in her bathtub. Why? When he had a perfectly marvelous bathroom of his own?

If she ever took a lover, which was doubtful but she thought of it at times like this, she wouldn't let him use her bathroom. Not even to piss.

She'd considered leaving Brodhead. But neither of them had time to talk about it, and besides, where would she go?

Women who divorced at her age had someone else waiting in the wings. The way she had had Brodhead. But now she was older, if not wiser. And the next stepping stone had to be nearby.

So she stayed with Brodhead even though he dominated her just as her first husband, Wainwright MacBain, had.

Brodhead was tall, trim, handsome and brilliant. He had plenty of money and plenty of power. Overall, it wasn't exactly an unattractive package.

The front door slammed. God approacheth.

"Suzy? You there?"

No, I'm out with my Peruvian gigolo. "In here, darling. Waiting."

"Are you ready for Bronkhorst?"

"Of course." She was always ready for Bronkhorst. Waiting for the riveting tales of over-the-counter pain relievers and how at last America was on the march, headache-free.

Suzy leapt from the chaise lounge to check her makeup. She felt an argument coming on. And arguing with Brodhead always made her mascara melt. It really wasn't worth the bother.

She watched him slip out of his Turnbull & Asser pinstripe suit and carefully hang it up.

"Make sure this is pressed for Thursday. I have a biggie lunch. I want a blue shirt with white collar and cuffs, the gold knot cufflinks and that dark blue silk tie. The one I got at the Beverly Hills Hotel. On second thought, better make it the red silk one I got at the Greenbrier."

"Brodhead, about dinner tonight..."

"Tonight? You're supposed to be ready for tonight. Instead, you're sitting around. You're not even dressed. I have a car waiting downstairs. I'll be ready in exactly"—he checked his watch—"nine-and-a-half minutes."

"Brodhead, dinner is *here* tonight. At home. Everything's ready. Smoked trout with whipped cream horseradish sauce. Filet de boeuf. Braised endive, baby carrots and asparagus tips. Cold lemon soufflé. Four kinds of hors d'oeuvres. Espresso. Chateau Palmer '75. Perrier-Jouet '75 with dessert. Plus..."

"You've got to be kidding," he roared. "My secretary booked one of the upstairs rooms at '21'."

"But who ordered the dinner?"

"I don't know. I guess she did. Or one of the account executives. June Metcalf, I think."

"June Metcalf? I wouldn't trust her to organize a fast-food orgy. Don't you remember the time I'd spent four hours with the banquet manager at '21'? And she changed the entree! Without even asking me! I asked you to fire her, Brodhead. Of course you wouldn't. But I'll tell you something, darling, if *you* had ordered the dinner and she'd pulled that kind of crap on you, you would have fired her."

"That's why I love you, Suzy. You know how to deal with these things. Now, let's figure out how to handle this situation."

"We'll keep the food for Thursday. Have cocktails here. I *did* send everyone a hand-written invitation. I can't understand how all this happened."

Suzy was on the edge of tears. It isn't worth it, she told herself. She told herself the same thing several times a day.

"Oh, Suzy, don't take it that way. Most of the people who work for me—us—are assholes. They think that not getting fired means you're a success."

"You pay everyone too much. Especially women. Maggie

Harlow is thirty-three years old and she makes sixty thousand dollars a year—and she thinks she's underpaid. How do I know, you ask? It pays to stay sober at company parties."

"I know, Suzy, I know. Sometimes, I think, though, that the guys are worse than the women. The women are competent. But, the men, especially the suburbanites"—he said the word as if it denoted some sort of cursed Biblical tribe—"are a bunch of card-carrying, banner-waving members of the marching, militant middle class. If Papa were alive, heads would roll."

"I thought you were trying to chic-up BDK&C."

"Chic-up is hardly the way I'd express it. I'm trying to get rid of the dead wood."

Christ. All those commercials that sang and cheered "Stand up, America; Come Home, America; Sit down, America." Suzy dialed Brodhead's private secretary, Dorothea Stand-in-Awe-Of.

Dorothea answered on the first ring.

"Good evening, Dorothea, this is Mrs. Kincaid. Dorothea, *where* are the Bronkhorst people having cocktails this evening?"

"Why, at your apartment, Mrs. Kincaid."

"Got it. I was a bit concerned about cocktails. I've been out of town," Suzy said coolly. "Wanted to make sure."

"Isn't *Mr.* Kincaid there yet?" Dorothea squeaked. "I'd booked at '21' but I canceled it when I found out you were doing the dinner."

"Well, Dorothea, things couldn't be better. Good night."

It wasn't like Brodhead to forget something that had to do with the clients. He must have something else on his mind.

"Well, love, I see why they call you 'Bonehead.' Dorothea canceled the '21' when she found out we were having the dinner here."

"Bonehead? That's just a *joke*. Got it? A *joke*."

"Sometimes you come home with a very large chip on your well-tailored shoulder, darling."

"Suzy, I come home tired. Exhausted. Dying for a drink

with my beautiful wife. A respite from the rigors of my harrowing day. And what do I get? Shit. A hard time. From you. From my secretary. From everyone at the agency. I'm sorry about '21.'"

"Brodhead, I don't care about '21.' I have a fabulous dinner ready. The tables are set. All I have to do is light the candles."

"Let's take a trip." That was the magic word. That always shut her up. "We don't spend enough time together."

"Brodhead, we spend every evening together. We even spend out-of-town evenings together. But you've never noticed that, have you? An evening's not a success unless you have a court jester, six fools, and ten dancing girls. And of course, the meandering simp, *moi!*" Suzy executed a perfect curtsy.

"As I was saying, Suzy, I come home wiped out, longing to enjoy one perfect martini before lurching back into the fray. Where, pray tell, is my perfect martini?"

"Right here, in its perfect silver thermos, perfectly mixed, perfectly chilled, with a choice of onion, olive or twist." Suzy waved a hand frosted with diamonds toward a small eighteenth-century hunt board at the far end of their bed-sitting room.

"Well, I'm happy that there are still a few things one can depend on these days. Today was a killer. An absolute killer. We had a new products meeting. Wait'll I tell you about it. You'll laugh your pants off." He poured two martinis and handed the one with the twist to Suzy.

"Tomorrow, it's Chicago. Seven A.M. flight. I'll be home in time for the International Truck, Tire and Chassis dinner. On to St. Louis Thursday, back in plenty of time for your Country Kitchens gala. You'll finally get to meet Jill Harrington."

"But Brodhead," Suzy cried, "tomorrow is *La Traviata!*"

"I know that. I have it all worked out."

"But International Truck..."

"Listen: I take you to the opera. Eight o'clock curtain. We arrive in plenty of time for champagne before the curtain. I stay with you for the first act. We have more champagne, just so that you won't feel deprived, and I take you back to your seat for the second act.

"I then go to Doubles and have a cocktail and first course with the International people. I return to the Met and join you for the third act. Then, we both go to Doubles and have our main course with International. Dessert. Coffee. Dancing. Backgammon, if anyone feels like it."

"I always feel like it."

"I call that a brilliant plan. What do you think?"

"It may be brilliant. But it's impossible."

"Haven't you learned by now that nothing is impossible for Brodhead Kincaid? Read this." He held a small card toward Suzy.

Suzy read aloud. "'La Traviata. Second act ends at 10:10. There is a twenty minute intermission. Third act begins at 10:30. The opera ends at 11:06.' I suppose it *could* work..."

"Of course it can work. And will. I promise I'll be on time for the third act. I *do* love you, Suzy. Do you honestly think that the great Brodhead Kincaid could function without his devoted wife?"

Christ! Here lies the devoted wife. Suzy poured what was left in the thermos into her glass.

Brodhead Kincaid could not function without his two secretaries and his chauffeur. Or his office full of people, hanging on every word. Or the housekeeper who'd worked for him since the day he'd graduated from Princeton. Or the cleaning woman. Or the laundress.

Brodhead didn't need a wife. All Brodhead needed was a dictating machine and a pen and pad.

"Well, Suzy, what shall we do? The vultures aren't due to descend on us for a half hour. Backgammon? Watch the news? Gin?"

"Why don't we just sit and talk?"

"Great! What do you want to talk about?"

Suzy sighed softly. "Well, here it is: I own two hundred name tags."

He eyed her quizzically. Where was this leading?

"Two hundred name tags with my name 'Mrs. Brodhead Kincaid,' and 'BDK&C' printed, painted or silk-screened on them. Two hundred divided among 'Host,' 'Hostess,' 'Hello,' and, God bless us every one, 'Have a Nice Day.'"

Brodhead waited.

"Two hundred holes in my beautiful clothes. And they're *my* clothes, goddamn it, not corporate clothes."

"Buy some new ones."

"That's *not* the point," Suzy sobbed. Then she remembered her makeup. Quickly, expertly, she blotted her eyes.

"I'm sorry our lives are so wrapped up in the business. But that's the nature of things. Perhaps you'd be happier if you could get more involved with BDK&C."

More involved? As it was, she ate, drank, breathed, slept and woke up to BDK&C. But she had no power.

"I adore *our* advertising agency, Brodhead. And you're right. Maybe I should get more involved."

If only he'd put her on the board, she'd fire June Metcalf, the scourge of Fire Island. And FiFi Woolverson. What was with her? Those yellow teeth and fingers. Smoking. Those dresses. *Where* did one go with clothes like hers? All too short, showing off fatted calves.

"I've got a terrific new idea, Suzy. You know how much I value your opinion on new products."

"You do?" Put it on the six o'clock news.

"What would you think if I asked all the wives to come in to the office and do their husbands jobs for say, a week?"

"And what do the husbands do?"

"They do their wives' jobs."

"Brilliant, Brodhead. When do I start?"

"Next week. Just as soon as we can line up the wives. Do you think they'll flip for it?"

"They'll do handstands, Brodhead. Remember I mentioned how important it is to stay sober at agency parties? How much you can learn just by meandering around the room, sipping a glass of water on the rocks with a twist?"

"Right. Got it."

"Well, wives love to kiss and tell. And especially tell each other. From what I've heard, there aren't too many BDK&C wives who are happy their husbands work there."

"I've heard that. Honestly, Suzy, I've been trying to *do* something about it, too."

"Is this idea really *yours*, Brodhead?"

"Well, actually..."

"Who would have thought of it? Not Charlene Whitrock. She'd feel threatened. And those younger account women. Never. They're the biggest bunch of misogynists I've ever met. It must be that Jill Harrington."

"What makes you think that?"

"She's new. The devil you don't know is always better than the devil you do know."

"Suzy, I always knew you were smarter than anyone at BDK&C."

She kissed him. It was the first time in months that Brodhead had actually acted as though he relied on her.

"Know what you can organize for the first day of 'Wife Swapper's Week'?"

"Wife Swapper's Week?"

"That's what I want to call it... when the wives come in to do their husbands' jobs."

"Typical," murmured Suzy.

"What do *you* want to call it?"

"Gosh, Brodhead, I don't know. How about something as obvious as 'Role Reversal'?"

"Why not?" That sounded like something Jill would go for in a big way. Every day, he was getting more and more fond of Jill Harrington. "Now, Suzy, about the ladies' lunch. I want you to have creative freedom."

"Great!" Something not too fattening. No cocktails. Just white Burgundy. Diet drinks. A luscious salad. Shrimp. Lobster. Maybe Green Goddess dressing, diet of course. What fun. She hadn't done a ladies' lunch in ages.

"I'd like you to use only products we advertise, Suzy. Nothing too fancy, but have fun with it. Bring Mabelle into the test kitchen. You two can have a ball with the home economists."

Mabelle was French. She had studied at the Cordon Bleu. She did not know the meaning of the words "frozen, fast, instant or convenience." "Darling, I don't think Mabelle is a very good idea for this experiment."

"Well, I do, Suzy. Mabelle is on our payroll. Therefore, she must be loyal. Put it to her like it's a challenge. Let her have her head. Go crazy with the products."

"Gee, darling. I've got it." Suzy jumped up. "I'll tell her that we'll use her recipes in a book. 'Cooking with Mme. Mabelle Montaigne.' She might not buy it, though."

"Don't kid yourself. If there's one thing people love, it's their name in print."

"Okay, Brodhead. What foodstuffs (I hate that word) are we talking about?"

"Mamma Mia Pizzeria, Deviled Chili Doggies, Pizza Raisin Bagels and Mocha Dessert Bagels. Those are from Happy Hills. Now, we also have a line of pancakes and waffles from Moody Valley Enterprises. The prime chicken parts from Arcadia Acres, instant coleslaw, re-hydrated baked beans, freeze-dried sour cream, and Rice Jambalaya Creole Cuisine."

Mabelle will go straight back to Paris, Suzy thought. I may join her. Je-sus. No wonder grocery bills were so high. How much did it cost to de-humanize food?

"Tell you what I think, Suzy. I'll have Dorothea prepare a list of all the food products we have at the agency. There are more than two hundred, so you can be just as creative as you like.

"We'll send over everything we have in the test kitchen and you can shop for the rest. That way, you and Mabelle can work with the raw materials in the privacy of your own kitchen. And you mustn't forget the potatoes."

"Potatoes?"

"Su-*zy*, you've been resisting me on these potatoes for three years," Brodhead exhaled. "I've been begging you to serve them at a client dinner."

"Ohh, you mean those steam-blasted, salt-infused, chemically-peeled, real-potato-flavor-added blobs that are dried like adobe brick and then pulverized into deadly white powder? Fluffy Ida-Ho Instant Potatoes? *Those* potatoes?"

"Those potatoes."

"No, darling, I won't forget."

CHAPTER FOURTEEN

he wives reported for work.

Twenty-three women, ranging in age from twenty-eight to fifty-two. Ranging in dress size from six to sixteen. Ranging in household income from forty-one thousand dollars to five-hundred-sixty thousand dollars.

Suzy had screwed up the mean. "But what the hell," she'd told Brodhead, "we're not talking about statistics, we're talking about real people."

They *were* talking about statistics, but she didn't have to know that.

They filled out their questionnaires, created by Jill and Charlene. They took tests. Were photographed, measured and everything but fingerprinted.

They loved it. At last they felt important.

In answer to the question, "What do you, as a wife of a BDK&C employee, dislike most about the agency?" the tie that bound them emerged:

"BDK&C takes too much time from my family."

"BDK&C has taken over my life."

"My husband works all weekend. I never see him except for when he's snoring."

"Who did I marry? Ronald Bandman or the hemorrhoid account?"

Not once, in any answer to the hundred questions, was Brodhead's name mentioned. He was hurt.

"But Brodhead," Suzy said seductively, "they don't relate to you in terms of what's happening in their lives."

"What?" Brodhead's handsome face grew stormy. "I'm their leader, Suzy."

"I think they think they're directed by a higher voice."

"What the fuck is that supposed to mean?"

"The Puritan Ethic. You've heard of it? If I'd had to fill out that questionnaire, I think I would have answered in exactly the same way. I'm on the side of the wives, Brodhead, even though I'm Mrs. Kincaid. Since men went out in their bearskins to club the dinner, wives have complained that they never see enough of their husbands. Now, they are going to understand *why*."

"Okay, I'll bite. *Why?*"

"It makes the guys happy to work at BDK&C. And it's going to make the wives happy, too."

"I seriously doubt that. Believe me, at the end of the week, they're all going to be happy as pigs in shit to get back to their kitchens." His head hurt. His sinuses hurt.

"Brodhead, they're saying 'let me play with you, let *me* be a part of it all.' The way pioneer wives were. They were right out there, blowing heads off Indians, defending home and hearth. Surely you can understand that?"

"Suzy, I never knew you had such an aggressive streak. Christ, will I be glad when this week is over. How did I ever let Jill Harrington and Charlene Whitrock talk me into this?"

"Promise not to forget just one thing, Brodhead."

How many years had he been promising not to forget just one thing? "Okay, Suzy. What?"

"As terrific as Fred Astaire was, Ginger Rogers did everything *he* did. Backwards. *And* in high heels."

Suzy decided to view the ladies' lunch from behind the magic mirror which lined one wall of the small conference room.

With the magic mirror, one could watch and listen to everything that went on in the small conference room, but the people in the small conference room could not see or hear *anything* that went on in the room behind the magic mirror.

The room was used mostly for "focused group sessions"— interviews with selected groups of men or women to determine their reactions to new products and advertisements. It was a mini opinion poll that the agency used as a barometer to discover if their thinking was in the right direction or the wrong direction. People in the small conference room quite naturally presuming that this was a regular mirror, hiked up their bra straps and girdles, applied fresh lipstick, picked their teeth, and scratched their balls. And why not? It was as safe as Bloomingdale's ladies' room or the men's room at the Oyster Bar. Or so they thought.

Lunch was spectacular. Suzy and Mabelle had managed to use almost half of the products with mercifully no help from the dour home economists. They had created hot mashed potato salad, baby pizza hors d'oeuvres, *coq au vin*, instant steaks stuffed with frozen cabbage, and chocolate mousse. The mousse was made from Chocolate Dream Creme to which Suzy had added a dozen eggs and a pint of rum. Just for the hell of it, she'd thought of adding a cup of Lax-A-Fixit, the new chocolate laxative. After all, it *was* a BDK&C product. What a vicious idea, giving everyone the trots so they could blame Happy Acres and Arcadia Farms or whatever all those companies were called. Brodhead had probably named them all. But it *would* be fun. In the end, she decided to stick to her wonderful cooking.

The wives approached the buffet with caution. Animals circling a kill. Who took the first bite? Where was the poison taster? What did the agency really want with them?

When a waiter appeared with a tray of champagne in Suzy's very own crystal flutes, everyone began to relax.

Jane, the wife of Jonas Kratz, senior art director, breathed a sigh of relief. The other "focused groups" she'd been to had served only Coke and Diet Pepsi, corn chips and dip made from toothpaste and chives. This was terrific. Jonas told her he usually ate in and worked through lunch. Now she knew why.

Peggy Crump, wife of the senior money man, loved champagne. It was on her diet. In fact, that's how she stayed on her diet—by including everything beyond everyday reach. Caviar, quail eggs, Irish smoked salmon filets and white truffles were the mainstays of her regimen. Cheeseburgers were *not* on her diet. Once she'd seen a photograph of Elvis Presley at the end of his life, bloated on drugs and cheeseburgers. That had been what had gotten her on this kick in the first place.

One by one, the women seemed to relax, introduce themselves, and talk freely to their neighbors. The champagne blotted out their initial suspicions. If they'd only known that every gesture, every nuance, every word was being recorded on videotape.

Suzy hadn't been this happy in years. She'd actually helped create something for the agency, something for Brodhead.

After lunch, Charlene Whitrock appeared, introduced herself as the creator of the "Breathless" and "La Francais Frozen Gateau de Fromage" campaigns, and led a spirited discussion on what women don't want.

After lunch, a waiter passed espresso, Brie and pears, and a third round of champagne. Charlene pried more secrets from the women. What did they want?

They *didn't* want cockroaches in the kitchen, ring around the collar, or boredom in the bedroom.

So far a big yawn, thought Suzy.

They didn't want their kids on drugs and they all hated and despised dogs. Man's best friend! Charlene Whitrock was shocked.

Brodhead appeared and introduced himself. Asked about

the lunch. Better than lunch at home? Most definitely. Better than lunch at a restaurant? Yes from New Jersey and Westchester. No from Connecticut and not sure from everywhere else.

Jill Harrington appeared.

Buzzing suspicion. Rampant buzzing suspicion. Who was this good-looking "kid"? No wonder their husbands worked late. How many more Jill Harringtons were around? Charlene Whitrock hadn't bothered them at all. She looked like everybody's seventh grade gym teacher in an expensive dress.

But what did Harrington know about life? Wandering husbands? Bills? Broken plumbing? Screaming babies? Dirty dogs? Stinking in-laws? Lousy neighbors? Diets? Constipation? Self-doubt? Lack of sex? And all the other wonderful pieces and parts that constituted a happy marriage?

Jill smiled for the ten zillionth time since she'd joined BDK&C. "I know you're going to tell me that you enjoyed your lunch because I fixed it for you and you're all too polite to hurt my feelings." The wives laughed nervously.

Clearly one of Bonehead's dumb speeches. But, rationalized Suzy, if Brodhead thought so much of her, Jill must have something. Suzy studied her closely. Petite. Well, *almost* petite. Red curls. Sensational legs. And her voice. Jean Arthur, reincarnated. *That's* what had gotten to Brodhead. He was in love with Jill Harrington!

And all along she had thought it was for the Cause...to improve relations at BDK&C...to make good publicity for *their* advertising agency. Hot potato salad be damned. Now she wished she *had* put the Lax-A-Fixit chocolate laxative into the mousse.

"Dorothea, please get me a bottle of champagne," Suzy whispered, "and a glass with ice in it." It was her champagne. Why the hell shouldn't she drink some? She brushed away a tear.

Dorothea, who had never taken an order from another woman in her thirty-eight year career at BDK&C, groaned to her feet and went in search of a chilled bottle of Perrier-Jouët. She knew the tone of fighting words. Bonehead had trained her well.

Suzy didn't even mention Jill Harrington's name to Brodhead when he called from out of town the next night. What was the use? She knew the signs. Tonight, she had to get through the Country Kitchens buffet dinner. Then, Bonehead *had* promised to take her to London. At this rate, maybe she'd go by herself. The trip, so far as he was concerned, would probably fall through anyway.

Jill Harrington.

Jill Harrington was one of the most beautiful women Suzy had ever seen. She glowed. She had an air of delicacy about her that made even Suzy want to protect her. It was positively disgusting.

A conversation she'd had several years ago with one of the wives came crashing back to her. Pauline Johns had been sobbing drunk in Suzy's bathroom. Her marriage was in shreds.

"How do you know Howard is screwing his secretary?" Suzy tried to be helpful.

"*I* used to be his secretary," Pauline sniffled.

Somehow, Suzy would rather not know. Was Brodhead sleeping with Jill Harrington? She almost couldn't blame him if he were, human nature—especially his—being what it was.

Suzy surveyed her gourmet kitchen. The sun rising over the East River poured through the window and twinkled on her vast collection of copper pots, each big enough to cook a dog.

An evening of Charlene Whitrock. That voice like acid rain and hair of a shade found only in nylon bathroom carpet.

Maybe she shouldn't be so hard on poor old Charlene. Soon, they might be saying "poor old Suzy Stanford Kincaid." Christ.

Once, when Suzy had asked Charlene what she did at BDK&C, Charlie had told her, down to the last excruciating detail. It had taken three hours and had been one of the dullest experiences of her life and for a wife of Brodhead that was pretty damn dull. Was this the independence all those women were clamoring for? Getting to the office or an airport at six o'clock in the morning, returning home at midnight, with barely a minute to find the ladies' room? Phone calls all day, all evening, all weekend?

Your body bound by call reports, strategy statements, meetings? Your soul owned by the corporation?

Suzy's respite came when Brodhead went out of town. She could skip lunch, skip the hairdresser, turn off the telephone and eat diet cottage cheese.

But Brodhead would always return, shattering her solitude with his enormous, energetic presence. And his bags. And his laundry. And his wadded handkerchiefs. All reeking of airplane fuel and cigar smoke.

Suzy flipped through her menu book. Had they really eaten that much gazpacho? Curried turkey breast in cantaloupe halves? Baked potatoes with sour cream and caviar? How much filet de boeuf, how many pink lamb chops had crept down their throats?

She read on. The Bantams from San Francisco. Gorff Drugs. Mrs. Bantam had thrown up in Suzy's elevator all over two minks and a poodle. The Kingsleys from Chicago. Yummy Treats for dogs and cats. The Martinsons from St. Paul. She was a Hubbell. The Hubbells could buy and sell ten sheiks.

She'd put Jill Harrington at her table. La Doza, too.

Suzy could not get Jill out of her mind. What was someone like who'd gone back to work in her forties? Suzy assumed Jill was in her forties. Maybe she was younger. She looked about thirty.

Why had she done it? Women's lib, probably. Suzy hated Women's lib. She *liked* male chauvinist pigs. They were easy to handle.

At seven-thirty tonight her curiosity would be satisfied. They were all so in awe of Brodhead, they wouldn't dare be late. It was warm and sunny. The too-early snow had melted.

A few roses clung tenaciously to the vine that spilled over the trellis on the terrace. No dripping umbrellas and soggy boots to ruin her parquet floors.

Her life had come down to that. Worrying about the floors. Somewhere, people were having fun, making love, having babies, eating pot roast. But not here.

Tonight, there was to be *lobster fricasse primavera au beurre blanc*, tossed green salad with Suzy's special dressing (tequila and olive oil; no vinegar) and for dessert, Suzy's chocolate pie made with Lindt chocolate bars.

Dinner parties were Suzy's forte. The food-and-drink part of dinners was a snap. It was the conversation that got to her. So many people had nothing to say. She encouraged them to talk about themselves. That usually worked.

Suzy longed to be like Emerald Cunard during the years when she'd entertained the Duke and Duchess of Windsor at her spectacular London home. *She'd* known how to whip the conversation into shape. Once, Suzy had read, Emerald bridged an awkward silence with "I think Christ had quite an unpleasant face, don't you agree?" London had talked of nothing else for days. Now, there was a hostess!

If things dragged too badly tonight, she just might say the same thing. La Doza was the only person who might recognize it. And she knew her secret was safe with him.

Suzy called the fish market to check on the lobsters. Then, she removed three quarts of stock from the refrigerator and poured them into her professional chef's soup kettle. Cooking always soothed her ragged nerves.

Last week, she and Brodhead had had a terrible fight as he was about to leave at six-thirty in the morning.

"I don't know why you have to spend three hours a week screaming at your psychiatrist when you could spend an extra three hours with me. In bed."

"Oh, for Crissakes, Suzy," he'd snarled, "I'm under a lot of pressure at the office. It makes me feel better when I yell at Dr. Burke. I told her that she was like a paid prostitute. Paid to be yelled at."

"Why *don't* you go to a prostitute and yell? It would be a lot cheaper."

"Because she might try to talk back. I'm a busy man, Suzy. But no one seems to understand that." With that, he'd stormed out. An hour later, he was on the telephone. "Suzy, lover, this is the last company dinner. Country Kitchens. Next month, we're going to London. Christmas in London! You'll have a wonderful time."

"Can't wait, darling."

Suzy had been happy. At least she always knew what to expect on a trip with Brodhead.

They'd arrive at Claridge's, check into the Art Deco suite—her favorite, with its curvy natural wood walls, torchère lamps, Thurberesque sofas and chairs and a bathtub big enough for the Australian crawl.

Before the bags were unpacked, thirty people would be assembled in the living room, eating, drinking, smoking. At least they all had lovely British accents. Even the most mundane remarks sounded better in British.

At four o'clock Suzy had finally filled one hundred pink and green balloons with helium. She opened the French doors and stepped out onto the terrace. The balloons and hurricane lamps would make the terrace so much more festive. And tonight was the last night anyone would be able to go outside for a drink until spring. Thank God, in another week she could call room service. See her pals. Go to the theater without being afraid of being mugged. Listen to the string quartet, dressed in eighteenth century livery, in Claridge's cocktail room.

Suzy loved Claridge's. So many of their friends preferred the Connaught's Dickensian charm and magnificent grill room. But Claridge's, with its pink Thirties madness housed in Victorian brick, was more fun. And it had a hairdresser. Dammit, she couldn't quite reach the top of the awning to tie up these last two balloons. Why had she ordered so many? Fifty would have been enough. And what a pain in the ass that helium tank had been.

What she really needed was a drink. A nice scotch and not too many rocks. Something to relax her and let her sparkle for the dunderheads. And Jill Harrington.

Suzy didn't intend to give up without a fight. Maybe she didn't intend to give up at all.

She put her empty glass in a clump of azaleas, so that it wouldn't blow over and smash. Then she climbed up on a ladder. As she reached for the top bar of the awning, her foot, squeezed into a high-heeled maribou-trimmed satin bedroom slipper, edged off the top step of the small kitchen ladder.

She arced out over the terrace and soared, like an exotic Chinese dragon, the gay balloons caught around her wrist, plummeting downward in the fading autumn light. She came to rest in the middle of East Seventy-fourth Street.

It was the first time in her adult life that Suzy Stanford Kincaid had ever gone out without first checking her lipstick.

The superintendent was off duty. The new doorman had just come on that afternoon the first time. The police thought it was a hit-and-run, and took Suzy to the morgue.

The Country Kitchens clients and the agency people arrived promptly at seven.

Charlene Whitrock, her large mouth turned down, confided to Jill, "We'll have to wait a few more minutes for the zany Suzy. She loves to make an entrance. I swear, she'll be late for her own funeral."

After Suzy's death, Brodhead seemed smaller, sadder. His wrinkles were no longer laugh lines. His crisp hair, lightly shot with silver, turned battleship gray. His body seemed to be inhabiting someone else's too-large suit.

More and more, he looked to Jill for help. In the office and after hours at cocktails.

They worked out marketing plans, copy strategies and television commercials. No longer did Brodhead jot his ideas in the margins of the *New York Times*. No longer did he villify account men publicly.

In a funny way, Jill admired Bonehead. She knew he was in love with her. And even though she knew she couldn't return the feeling, some crazy desire made her want him to try to take her to bed. She wanted power—some power beyond her work. Funny, the very thought of power used to make her weak in the knees.

What was happening to her?

CHAPTER FIFTEEN

The Neptune Society scattered Rose-Delia Harrington's ashes across the North Atlantic, south of Newfoundland, at the exact moment that Jill, Ian, Juliet, Beth and Ian, junior, stood with Hope Hogwood Worth in his Henry Morrison Flagler office in Palm Beach. The setting was more turn-of-the-century gothic romance than nineteen-eighties resort. The only sounds in the room came from the air conditioner and an occasional hiss from the gas logs in the Grinling Gibbons fireplace.

Mr. Worth, Harvard Law '28, stood erect, all six foot six of him, his blue eyes watery. He had loved Rose-Delia for fifty years and now she had, as she so enjoyed saying, gone for a last walk in the valley of the chateau of death.

He studied the faces of the bereaved. Ian certainly had the Harrington features and Beth could have been the young Rose-Delia. Juliet Harrington left him opinionless.

After a moment of silence, Hogwood asked them to be seated. Then, he sat down behind the colossal renaissance refectory table that served as his desk.

"As you know," he began, his voice strong, "Rose-Delia

wanted no funeral, no fanfare of any kind. She felt she'd had enough in life. Her last wish was to be returned to the waters that had spared her so many years ago."

Juliet started to cry. Jill scowled. Juliet had never even seen Rose-Delia. Who was she to cry?

"It was indeed a shock to lose Rose-Delia. But it may have been a blessing of sorts. Rose-Delia was diagnosed as having cancer last summer." He paused and looked around the room. Ian stared ahead. "As you know, Rose-Delia did not believe in crying." Hogwood took out a large white handkerchief and dried his eyes. "Rose-Delia always believed in doing her best."

Jill watched Ian. He shifted in his high-backed velvet chair. He crossed his legs and uncrossed them. He pushed his cuticles back with his thumb nails.

"And now to Rose-Delia's final thoughts." He handed the three adults copies of the will. "It was her desire to have all of you together in the same room to hear this."

He cleared his throat. "Mrs. Jill Harrington, you shall have Frog's Leap—her Palm Beach home—and her two automobiles. In addition, you are to receive her townhouse at Thirty-One Sutton Place in New York City, along with all of its furnishings, antiques, works of art, and including her clothes and jewelry. You are to promise to keep the servants at both places. Provisions have been made for pensions when the time comes."

Jill, her throat dry, kept her gaze fixed on Ian. He sat up, his hands white-knuckled, clenched the arms of the chair. God, how he must feel. He'd been waiting for this all of his life. In a funny way, she almost pitied him. But why should she feel sorry for Ian? He'd almost ruined her life. He'd killed one of her children.

What was wrong with her? How could she even stand to be in the same room with him? He had to be the most selfish creature in the world.

All those psychiatrists who preached that selfishness was desirable should spend an hour with Ian Woodside Harrington. They'd turn in their shingles.

Of course he's miserable. He deserves to be miserable. But he'd try to find ways to get out of it. First, he'd sweat and squirm and curse. Then he'd switch into high gear charm, using every wheedling, childish bit of cajolery he could conjure up.

Well, it was time he danced to the tune of a different dancing master.

No one moved. Hogwood continued.

"On the death of Mrs. Harrington, the principal is to be divided equally between Elizabeth Woodside Harrington and Ian Woodside Harrington, junior. During your lifetime, Mrs. Harrington, Jill, you are to receive the income on the principal from the estate which shall come to, after certain duties and taxes, about six hundred fifty-thousand dollars per annum."

She heard the words but she still couldn't believe it. The income from Rose-Delia's estate. The Rolls. Two houses. What could she do with the houses? The clothes? The jewelry? Clearly it was what Rose-Delia had wanted. She'd come back from Wendy's funeral, after seeing Ian in Roosevelt Hospital, and changed her will.

"In addition, Mrs. Jill Harrington is to provide an income for Ian Woodside Harrington, senior and Ian Woodside Harrington, junior, of not less than fifty thousand dollars per year, and payable only in the event that Ian Woodside Harrington, senior, has gainful employment."

Hogwood paused, giving everyone time to mull over his words. "There are certain small bequests to servants and to myself. MacDougall Harrington's watch is to go to Ian Woodside Harrington, junior, along with gold cufflinks and a coin collection which is to be kept in the vault at Citibank, where it now reposes, until Ian Woodside Harrington, junior, is thirty years of age. That is about everything."

Ian jumped to his feet, his face pale, his eyes blazing. "Mr. Worth, Jill is divorcing me. Won't that affect anything?"

"Not in the least. And she can remarry anyone, and as often as she likes. The terms of the will are firm."

They'd ganged up on him again, those two bitches. Well,

he wasn't going to take this lying down. Imagine at his age, getting an allowance!

He walked across to Jill's chair. "You think you're pretty smart, don't you, Jill?"

She looked up at him, not moving, not speaking.

"Well, I'm here to tell you that you're not. You're the same dumb broad you always were."

"Mr. Harrington, please," Hogwood interrupted. "There are little ones present. I'm sure you're upset. But there's no contesting the will."

"I *will* contest it, Hogwood. You and Jill and that flaming asshole, Ralston Rhodes are not going to get away with this."

"*Mr.* Harrington, Ralston Rhodes is a most distinguished member of the bar. And I'm afraid any accusations at this point are totally irrelevent. Perhaps you would like someone to escort you home?—" Hogwood glanced at Juliet, who shook her head "No" furiously.

"I'm going to sue the shit out of you, Hogwood."

"Mr. Harrington, I doubt you can afford it."

Jill sighed. Maybe that would shut him up. Ian couldn't leave anything alone. Once he got hold of something, he'd shake it until it was limp, like a dog with a smelly old bone. It wasn't a pretty sight.

She was rich. It still didn't register. Mr. Worth had just said so. It was impossible to grasp what having so much money meant.

How did those lottery winners handle it? How much was it all worth? The house? The cars? The jewelry? That pink diamond pendant on the two-hundred carat necklace? Ian had been champing at the bit to send it to auction. Too bad, Ian.

Jill never had to put up with anything from anybody ever again. She remembered Rose-Delia's words: "Without money, there are no choices, Jill."

She had so many choices, she didn't know where to start.

And it couldn't have happened at a better time.

Her newly-raised-to-$35,000-a-year salary from BDK&C might seem like a fortune to other women but once she was paying for an apartment of her own, it would barely leave her surviving. And there were the Laurel Hall expenses.

Without this inheritance, she would have been forced to stay in the Badger Hollow house and commute to BDK&C.

Tears started to film her eyes. But she'd loved Rose-Delia. She'd give it all up to have her back.

"Mr. Harrington," Hogwood said sternly, "may I point out that you have spent the better part of your life living as though you were alone in the world? You've always thought you could do things your way and then put the pieces together afterwards. Well, my boy, I'm afraid that's not the way it works. Your grandmother and I have had many conversations about you, Ian. You were a great concern to her."

Ian moved toward Hogwood. "You know how I hate violence, Hogwood, but nothing would give me greater pleasure than to bash in your face."

Juliet rose, took Ian, junior by the hand, and left the room.

"Now that Ian, junior has left the room, Ian, would you please tell me the status of his mother?" Hogwood Worth tossed Ian his most forbidding look.

"Why should I tell you anything, old boy, when clearly you already know? She's my concubine."

Beth poked Jill in the ribs. "What's a concubine, Mother?"

"In certain polygamous societies, a secondary wife of inferior social and legal status," Jill whispered.

"Oh."

"Do you intend to marry her, Ian?"

"I don't think that that is any of your business!"

"Ian Woodside Harrington, junior *is* my business, sir."

"Put it this way, Hogwood, it's better to be a rich bastard than a poor-but-legitimate employee any day."

"Your grandmother worried that your sense of reality was warped, Ian."

"She was absolutely right, Hogwood. I suffered through an overprivileged childhood. Down the Inland Waterway, up the Inland Waterway. Every known lesson the old girl could think of. Shall I tap dance for you? How about a tune on the lute? I know you have MacDougall's old lute here somewhere." Ian pretended to poke into the bookcases.

"Ian," Jill said, hesitating, "it's getting late."

"Christ, Jill, I wish I had a dollar for every time you've said that to me. I'd be richer than you."

"It's getting late," Jill continued, undaunted, "and I think we should all have the courtesy to leave Mr. Worth alone."

Since she'd started working again, Jill had found it easier and easier to handle things. Stores no longer upset her. Nasty letters from her former neighbors no longer bothered her. Even Beth's tantrums left her unmoved. As crazy as it was, BDK&C *had* changed her life. She couldn't wait to get out of Palm Beach and back to her new window office. But she never had to go back to work if she didn't want to.

"I'd be delighted to get out of here. Jill, my sweet, where are we staying?"

"Mrs. Joyner and her husband are expecting you at Frog's Leap. They have dinner prepared, rooms ready. I should think you'd like to see your new home, Jill," Hogwood said, smiling for the first time that day.

"I would," she stammered, "I just didn't want to ask..."

Ian turned and spoke, "Ah, the reluctant heiress. Bull shit. In spades."

"*Please*, Ian." She glanced at Beth, who immediately chimed in.

"I think I want a ride in the Rolls Corniche. Wait'll they catch that at Laurel Hall."

"Mr. Worth, won't you join us for dinner?" Jill asked. It was one way to keep the peace.

"Yes, indeed, I should like that very much."

"And maybe Ian, junior could be put to bed. I think it's getting very late for him."

"Mother, it's six o'clock. Is there a TV at Rose-Delia's house, Mr. Worth?"

"Yes, indeed. Several. And a grand piano. And a pool and a small movie theater."

"All just waiting for a visit from the loving family," sneered

Ian. "Hope they have stone crab, what do you say, Bethy?"

"I wish we could go to a Japanese restaurant. You promised, Daddy, and you still haven't taken me to one."

"Okay, you're on, Bethy. We'll go to a Japanese restaurant and Mommy and Aunt Juliet and little Ian will go back to the house with Uncle Hogwood. What a splendid idea!"

"Ian..." Jill stopped, realizing that it was futile to go any further. How could she ever have married this man?

When they arrived at Frog's Leap, Mrs. Joyner showed Jill immediately to Rose-Delia's room. "This is where Mrs. Harrington said I was to bring you first," she announced.

The room was done in several shades of yellow. Dozens of red roses stood in a huge cut crystal vase on a large marble console to the right of the fireplace. There was a card. "Arriving nine o'clock. Love, Keefe."

That's all she needed. Both of them in the same house. But why not? Ian had *his* concubine.

Jill had barely hung her jacket in one of Rose-Delia's vast closets when the phone rang, cutting into her reverie. She'd never seen such an opulent wardrobe.

It was Brodhead, his voice taut.

"Jill, I know this is a hell of a time to call you, but I need you back in New York for a meeting tomorrow."

"Meeting? Tomorrow?" What *was* he talking about? There hadn't been any meeting scheduled when she'd left the office last night.

"Jill, I really need you on this. It's Breathless. It's in trouble."

"Trouble? But where is Charlene?"

"Charlene *is* the trouble."

"What are you talking about?"

"They don't think her ideas are young enough."

"Oh?"

"They didn't like the last two campaigns. Did you see them? Do you remember anything about them?"

"Vaguely. A couple on a yacht, drinking champagne with linked arms and, let me see, the other one was a couple in front of a blazing fireplace, right? I can't remember the lines, though."

"Unfortunately, I can. The champagne one was 'Seems like gold times,' and the fireplace one was 'Turns the heat on.' Chuckie Blum almost threw up."

"Who's Chuckie Blum?"

"The wunderkind over at Aromateria. He says lines like that are for two dollar pop wine."

"Aside from that, Mrs. Lincoln, how did you enjoy the play?"

"The wives are taking over, Jill. You wouldn't believe this place."

"Can't some of them help you out?"

"No." Dead silence.

"Uh, Brodhead, suppose I try a few lines and call back to bounce them off you?"

"Jill, I'd like you to get on the next plane back."

"Of course, Brodhead." Her voice was all business.

"We're stuck with the existing footage. There is no way on God's earth that we can re-shoot. We're over our budget and the damn turkeys are going on the air in a week."

"So we'll have to put words in their mouths... words that fit. If it's out of sync, the commercials'll look like those spaghetti Westerns with the bad dubs."

"Jill, you haven't been studying at the feet of the master for naught. How's everything going down there?" He sounded sympathetic.

"How are *you*?" she countered, her voice edged with tears.

"Everything will be a lot better when I see you walking into my office with a notebook full of greatness."

"Okay. I guess I have no options. But you said you'd reserved me *a* seat. What about my daughter, Beth?"

"Isn't she home from school for Thanksgiving?"

"Yes."

"Well, then, can't she stay in Palm Beach? Isn't her father there?" Children and their endless needs had always irritated Brodhead. Maybe that's why his only daughter was a psychiatrist and his only son a crusader for Gay Rights. But he didn't have time to think about that now. Cool down, Bonehead, he told himself, Jill's just trying to understand you.

"Yes, Brodhead, I think she'd probably like to stay here. But I would like to have dinner with her."

"Fine. The limo is going to bring you right to the office, no matter when you land. Got it?"

"Right. Now, let's discuss the commercials for a second. You've told me everything but what you have in mind." His experience on the talking potato sack had taught her one very important lesson: find out what's going on in Bonehead's head first.

"Well, you know the problems. Too dated, too corny, too obvious. Chuckie Blum wants bedazzle, bewitchment."

"Brodhead, I'll do my best. But I'm really low on both at the moment. What's this Chuckie Blum like?"

"You'd knock him off his pins in minutes."

"How so?"

"He's the kind of good-looking, smart Jewish guy who loves WASPs. And you, Jill, fit that bill."

"Most people think I'm Irish, Brodhead. I hate to throw a wrench in your engine or whatever that expression is. I'll work on this. How about 'makes waves,' for the yacht commercial and 'fire power' for the blazing inferno?"

"I like blazing inferno. And that's what we're all going to be in if we can't pull this one off. Got it?"

"I'll see you later." Jill was tired. Her neck was beginning to hurt. She needed twenty-four hours' sleep.

"By the way, Jill, how are things?" He actually sounded concerned.

"Things? Okay. Want to sell me your advertising agency?" She hung up.

First, there was Beth. And Keefe, who'd probably be landing as she was taking off. She had to leave him a note. Oh, God, help. She'd never felt so alone in her life.

All that money. All that responsibility. All those people.

Little Ian. She didn't even know him. There was lots more in the will about him. Hogwood had only gone over the main points. The will was forty-two pages long, each page initialed by Rose-Delia two weeks ago. Rose-Delia.

Why couldn't Rose-Delia have been *her* mother or grandmother? Ian didn't deserve her. He didn't appreciate her. He didn't appreciate anything.

She had to find Bethy. Explain why she had to go back to New York. But first, she'd wash her face and put on some perfume. Rose-Delia had a vat of Fracas. Tuberoses damp under a new moon. But no Breathless. She hadn't asked who the prime prospect was for Breathless. Clearly, it was no one rich, chic, or well-dressed. It was a vicarious scent. *That* gave her an idea.

Jill grabbed her little notebook. Time for a little private brainstorming.

"Breathless," she scribbled. "Vicarious appeal. Illusion of upscale living. Veiled sexual allusion. Veils not too heavy." Shit. Breathless was not a romantic scent. It smelled like it could kill flies at twenty paces.

She splashed cold water on her face. Then she looked around the bathroom. *Her* bathroom. Everything was pink, even the lace negligée on the pink padded hanger on the back of the door. She longed to explore her new home. Why hadn't she quit right then on the phone with Brodhead? A nasty thing to do, but she could have done it. She could call him back. No, she couldn't call him back.

What if she'd gotten all of this without her new-found backbone? Ian would move right in. Ian was probably on his way there right now. It *was* his grandparents' home. Correction, now it was his almost-ex-wife's home.

She'd pay back all the money from the credit card scam. That had been bothering her. It had been kind of fun, and she *had* needed the money. But it was wrong. Not that Ian wouldn't have done exactly the same thing to her, if he'd had the chance. But then, thank God, she wasn't Ian.

Now she was talking to herself. She had a plane to catch. A job to do. Brodhead was depending on her. Beth was depending on her. Keefe was depending on her.

There were no happy endings. When something was over, it was infinitely, irrefutably sad.

She fixed her makeup and, before starting down the stairs, splashed Fracas all over her arms and neck.

The steps were gray marble with gray carpet, held down by gleaming brass carpet rods. The ancient Waterford chandeliers rained icy sparkle from the foyer ceiling. Bethy was sitting in a pale pink silk hall chair, talking to an enormous beige and chocolate cat. The cat lay on his back, purring, relishing every devoted stroke of Bethy's little hands.

"I see you've found a friend," Jill smiled down at her.

"This is Lamby, he always sleeps on his back. Have you ever met a cat who sleeps on his back?"

"I don't think so. Listen, Bethy, that phone call a few minutes ago..."

"I didn't hear any phone call. Lamby purrs too loud. He's a Himalayan. It's a Persian-Siamese cross. See? He has a long coat, like a Persian and the coloring of a Siamese seal point. Lamby, kiss me," Bethy said, burying her face in the cat's fat tummy. Lamby purred away.

"I have to go back to New York."

"We all do. I want to take Lamby with me. Mrs. Joyner said he was mine. Great-grandmother wanted me to have him."

"Of course Lamby can come. When you come. But *I* have to go back tonight. *Now.* I have to go to the office."

"Mother, really! People don't go to their offices on Thanksgiving."

"People who work at BDK&C go to their offices on Thanksgiving or Christmas or New Year's if Mr. Kincaid asks them to, Bethy. That's the way it is."

"Why do you want to work, Mother? It's such a pain in the ass."

"Bethy!"

"Mother, don't tell me you've never said stuff like that before."

"Be that as it may, Beth, I wish you could find other ways to express yourself. Is that what you learn at Laurel Hall?"

"Oh, can't I leave Laurel Hall? I want to live in Palm Beach. Mr. Worth says they have schools down here. And I could learn to sail and improve my swimming and have a tan all winter. Don't you just love Palm Beach?"

"Where's Daddy, Beth? Didn't he take you to the Japanese restaurant?"

"Of course not. He's somewhere with his concubine. Why doesn't she talk?"

"She's probably shy. Now, what are we going to do about dinner, Bethy?"

"I've already had dinner. Lamb chops with watercress. A baked potato. Chocolate milk. Salad with blue cheese dressing and a baked apple."

"I thought you hated all those things."

"Not when Mrs. Joyner or Tansy makes them; only when it's prison food at Olde Laurel Hall. Barf."

Jill patted Bethy's hair. It was so soft, just like her own. How could they share so little? "Bethy, darling, are you going to be all right here? What do you think? I'll be back in a day or two."

"Of *course* I'll be all right here. Mr. and Mrs. Joyner are here. She's my new best friend. And Uncle Hogwood is here. He lives here, Mother. Bet you didn't know that. He has this really great room and a bedroom and a bath and a bar and a private door to outside, so he can go skinny-dipping in the pool when no one's around."

The sight of Hope Hogwood Worth skinny-dipping was not something to be taken lightly.

"And Daddy's here. I guess," she said airly.

"What's that supposed to mean?"

"Oh, forget it." She toyed with the cat's paw.

"Hi there." Keefe Neuman walked into the foyer.

He looked tired, but his suit was perfectly pressed and his handkerchief still stood in snowy Alps. He squeezed Jill until she could hardly breathe. Then he hugged Beth. "Who's that, Beth?"

"Lamby. He's mine. Listen to him purr. Did you ever see anyone so beautiful in your whole life?"

Keefe said he hadn't. Jill asked him if he'd like a drink. Then she'd tell him about having to go back to New York.

They went into the living room. Fifty feet of spectacle. She'd suggest to Bonehead that they shoot the next Breathless commercial in the living room. All it needed was Margaret Dumont in ten strands of eight millimeter pearls and a Groucho lurking behind the potted palms.

Keefe whistled. "I shouldn't whistle. Too vulgar. That's what my wife always said. But this is a room to whistle about."

"Something, isn't it?" Just for a moment she wished the Clarkes of Badger Hollow could walk into her living room and trip over the rug and fall right to the old parquet.

"And now for a refreshing adult beverage?" he said, putting his arm around her. "What are the plans for Thanksgiving?"

"I was just getting to that, love. I...my plans...are first, the airport, then BDK&C. Bonehead called about an hour ago. Seems as though they're in some sort of trouble with the fragrance. He asked me to come back. Work on plans. Have an emergency meeting tomorrow."

Keefe was very quiet. He bit his lip, studied the floor. "Okay," he said brightly, "we go. But first, my scotch."

"*We?*"

"Certainly. I came down here to see you. If you're going back and I still want to see you, which I do, it looks like I go back, too."

"All that time. You could have flown to London or Paris or someplace fun."

"I thought I did fly to someplace fun. Turns out otherwise."

"Fix me a scotch, too. I have to talk to the Joyners. And Mr. Worth."

The Joyners were eating in the kitchen. When they heard Jill, they jumped up.

"Please," she said gently. "I must go back to New York for a day or so, Mrs. Joyner. And I'd like to leave Beth with you. Would that be all right? School is closed for Thanksgiving..."

"Mrs. Harrington, we have Thanksgiving dinner all ready." She opened one of the four glass-doored ovens. An enormous turkey sat browning inside. "All the trimmings. That's the way the Missus would have wanted it. Bless her. She left the holidays to us. She said she hated them. The holidays. We trimmed the tree. Bought the presents. Everything. After the Mister died, she was a changed person. The joy went out of her life. Same when her granddaughter drowned. Missus was cursed by water, she always said."

Jill touched Mrs. Joyner's hand. "You have the telephone numbers in New York? My office? And Mrs. Osborne's apartment?"

"Yes, indeed. Mr. Worth gave them to us."

"And will Mr. Worth be here for Thanksgiving dinner, too?"

"Oh, my, yes. Mr. Worth hasn't missed dinner here in thirty years, Mrs. Harrington. He doesn't really live here but in a way he does, if you know what I mean. He *lives* in a hotel but he *stays* here. He was her baby sitter, so to speak. Mrs. H. could not stand to be alone. That's why she always had a cat to sleep with her. Moving art. That's what she called her cat."

Jill joined Keefe in the living room. He was sprawled on a gray linen sofa, staring at the coffered ceiling. "I could feel at home here, Jill."

"Well, don't get too used to it if you're really planning on coming back to New York with me."

"Of course I am."

"Why don't you stay? Get a good night's sleep? I'll probably be able to come back tomorrow or Friday morning, at the latest. Lie around the pool. Relax."

"Right. I'll talk to Lamby. If I'm good, he'll purr and blink his gigantic blue eyes."

"Okay, this is it. Mr. Joyner'll drive us to the airport."

"*I'll* drive us to the airport."

Jill kissed Bethy good-bye and promised to call tomorrow at dinner time. Thanksgiving dinner. What a rotten time to leave your daughter alone. She hated Brodhead. She hated BDK&C. But she really had no choice. Or did she?

"Maybe you can think of some wonderful words, Keefe?"

"I can think of lots of wonderful words for you and lots of not-so-wonderful words for Bonehead Kincaid. I think he's cracking up since Suzy took her swan dive."

As they stepped off the plane at La Guardia, an icy wind tore through them and it was raining. Mean, driving rain. The evening promised all the romance of a defrosting refrigerator.

Jill pulled Rose-Delia's sable cloak tight around her and slipped her arm through Keefe's.

She was so glad he'd insisted on coming back with her. He must be exhausted. An eight-hour round trip to Florida, with a dinner that tasted like wet paper.

At last, Bonehead's limo driver waved a sign with BDK&C scrawled on it. Jill waved back and soon they were curled up in the velvety depths of the warm back seat. Jill's eyes were closing as they pulled up in front of the agency.

Keefe insisted on going into the building with her even though the night man was on duty. He was so protective. So unlike Ian. He must have a hidden flaw somewhere. How could these two people both be members of the human race? Well, maybe Ian wasn't.

She was glad she didn't have time to think about it.

Keefe kissed her on the cheek. "Talk to you later."

When Jill got off the elevator, all the lights were on. Typewriters clattered. The Xerox machine ground on. Chip La Doza was moving as though he were on roller skates. Some of the wives were there, tired, grim faces set, manicured nails chewed.

Brodhead burst from his office. "Jill, is that you?"

No, it's Fay Wray, free at last. "Yes, Brodhead."

"Come in here. Get some coffee. We're in high gear tonight. Got any ideas as good as 'Wife Swapper's Week'?"

"Probably not, Brodhead. Do you mind if I go to the ladies' room? I'll be right back."

"Go to mine. It's closer."

She handed him her notebook. "Here's everything I could come up with on the plane. Why don't you glance over it?"

She let herself into Brodhead's sanctum. It was papered with labels from every product the agency had. It was dizzying. She closed her eyes. "Oh, Keefe, I need you so." Just thinking about him would get her through until morning, or whenever Brodhead decided he'd had enough. But lately, he'd never had enough. He had no one to go home to, so he stayed in the office around the clock. It was hell on everyone but Dorothea.

Jill glanced at her watch. Three-ten A.M. Oh, to be lying in Rose-Delia's Georgian bed, snuggled against Keefe. On impulse, she picked up Bonehead's red telephone and dialed his number.

"I thought you'd never call, darling," he said, laughing.

"I'm glad you're not asleep. I'd be jealous."

"Why don't you just come over here when Bonehead stops for breakfast? Don't call. Just come up."

"I don't have a key."

"Buzz. I'll let you in if the doorman's passed out."

"Jill, hurry up," Bonehead called. "I really like some of your ideas. I've got La Doza. He's raring to go." Bonehead was always talking about someone being raring to go.

Jill stepped into Brodhead's office. It seemed a century ago that she'd first come into this room, knees shaking, palms dripping, to stare at the stuffed crocodile. Now, it just looked

213

like an ordinary office and the Duncan Phyfe might have been sent over on approval from Bloomingdale's.

"'Raring to go,' the man says," sighed Chip, sinking to the carpet with his drawing pad and Magic Marker. "I haven't been raring to go for thirty-six hours. How was Palm Beach, Jill?"

"I'll tell you later. I think Brodhead's serious about Breathless. Got it, Chip?'

"Well, the bullshit has been flowing around here like Texas crude. Bonehead's called every writer who's ever worked here, who's ever done freelance here, whose ever even come in for an interview, and pulled them in."

"And?"

"Most of them haven't had a new idea since cigarette packs danced their way into the hearts of America."

"That means..."

"That means I hope you've got a magic wand that works."

"Okay. I know you're an art director, but tonight, you write."

"Tonight, I write. I write my resignation."

"You *do* know the problem, don't you?"

"Yeah. Twenty-five new storyboards for Breathless before anyone gets close to a drumstick tomorrow."

"Oh. I'm supposed to put new words into the mouths of those people in the yacht commercial and the fireplace commercial. It seems Chuckie Blum hates those commercials. Who did them?"

"Charlie Whitrock and Stan Marvin. Brodhead loved them on Wednesday morning."

"Then what happened?"

"Chuckie Blum. He's new on the horizon. Just bought the Breathless company. Doesn't know a thing about advertising, only what he likes. He says he has a nose for stinkers. And those two commercials are stinkers and if Bonehead can't fix them up, he's taking his business to J. Walter Thompson."

"I know Brodhead likes talk like that."

"What do you think of the commercials, Jill?"

"Chip, I've never even *seen* them. Soneone's racking them up now. I think we'd both better study them. Looks like lots of dubbing, I guess. Bonehead didn't say whether anything is voice over. Wouldn't it be a treat if they were *all* voice over?"

"Get the fucking magic wand and start waving."

Dorothea tore into Brodhead's office. "Everybody out. Out. There's a bomb in the building. There's a bomb in the building. It's set to go off at three-thirty exactly. Out." She ran down the hall blowing her London Bobby's whistle. "Everybody out. Out. There's a bomb set to go off in four minutes."

Bonehead ran behind her shouting. "It's Chuckie Blum! It's someone I fired last week! But it's not a bomb. I refuse to leave the building. There is no bomb. Do you all understand?" Brodhead raved on. Everyone was in the elevators.

Jill knew there was no bomb. She also knew who had phoned in the threat.

CHAPTER SIXTEEN

"*What happened* after all of you got down to Madison Avenue?" Keefe asked, yawning.

"Absolutely nothing. Three-thirty came and went. Four o'clock came and went. Then we all went back upstairs. Of course there wasn't any bomb. Only Brodhead and I knew that. Everyone else was hoping that Brodhead would let us go home. But he wouldn't, of course. If we went home, he wouldn't have an audience."

"How did you know there wasn't any bomb? Your ESP working overtime again?"

"Nope."

"Well, tell me."

"I can't."

"You can tell me anything, Jill. I feel as though I can tell *you* anything."

"Well," she began, reluctant to mention Ian's name.

"Ian did it, didn't he? Just to be a goddamn pain in the ass one more time."

"Ian might have done it. It certainly fits his pattern. But I secretly suspect Beth."

"Beth?"

"She's her father's daughter. And she was upset that I had to come back to New York."

"I guess I can't blame her."

"*And* she's jealous of her half brother. I have no idea what she thinks about Juliet. I have no idea what anyone thinks about Juliet, let alone Ian. It's my fault she loves Tansy. Now, she's in love with Mr. and Mrs. Joyner. By the time we get back down there, they'll probably be inseparable. I'm raising a stranger, Keefe. And I don't know what to do about it."

Keefe tightened his arms around her.

"I'm going to help you fix everything, Jill. I'm going to get you away from Bonehead, away from Ian. And now, you can move out of Pumpkin's apartment into your townhouse on Sutton."

"Oh, no I can't. It's rented for another year."

"To whom? Maybe you can get them out?"

"I don't know. It's all written down in that stack of papers Hogwood Worth gave me."

"Hogwood Worth. Now, that's a name."

"Hope Hogwood Worth. He's a sweet, courtly man, Keefe. The way you'll be when you're in your eighties."

"I might make it. My grandmother was ninety-seven when she died."

"No one in my family made it past fifty-eight. Twenty more years of BDK&C before I drop into my typewriter."

"Jill, why don't you quit?"

"Because I'm not a quitter. I thought I was for a long time. You know that. Now I know I'm not. I just can't go back, Keefe. Any more than you can."

"Why don't we go to Pumpkin's? She's having Thanksgiving dinner around four."

"And Noël St. Martin jumps out of a two-hundred pound turkey, naked as the day he was born."

"Noël St. Martin was not born naked. He emerged in a blue velvet suit with a white lace collar."

"Impeccably cut, of course."

"Of course. Now, let's have a hot shower and a cold bottle of something bubbly."

"Thought you'd never suggest it."

"How did you solve the problem with Breathless, Jill? I sure am glad it wasn't mine to solve."

"Well, in the yacht commercial, where the guy is trying to get the girl to come aboard, we just cut in some footage of flags spelling out Breathless and made the whole commercial voice over. The one with the sexy fireplace scene was a little harder. But essentially, we did the same thing... cut away from the couple talking to each other to the fire itself. Chip superimposed some flame-shaped type... sounds awful, I know, but it works. It spells out Breathless in the flames. And the new line is 'Get the Breathless message.' Bonehead says that if Chuckie Blum buys it, I'll be the newest associate creative director at BDK&C. And if Chuckie Blum wants to keep me on the account, I'll be the newest senior vice-president."

"Congratulations! But is that what you want?"

"Yes, it really is. Sometimes I can't believe it, but it is."

"Why do you want power?"

"What's the alternative?"

Who was this person speaking with her voice?

"Okay, okay. Bubbly coming right up."

"You didn't tell me what you think of the Breathless message."

"I've got the Breathless message." He kissed her. She kissed him back. "Make up your mind. Do you want to be late to Pumpkin's dinner? Or do you want to skip it altogether?"

"Just a little late, I think. But only because Pumpkin is a good friend. If it were Di and Charles or Indira or the Kissingers, I could skip." The phone rang.

"Shit," Keefe moaned. "Shall I get it?"

"I'm sure it's the bloodhounds."

It was Chip La Doza. Bonehead sent Chuckie Blum a telegram with "Get the Breathless Message" and Chuckie loved it so much, he asked Bonehead over to his Sutton Place townhouse for turkey and wasn't that great?

"Keefe, ask Chip Chuckie Blum's address on Sutton Place."

"He says it's thirty-one and enjoy your turkey."

"Well, now you know why we can't move into my townhouse."

"I think we should call Pumpkin and tell her a plausible lie. Wouldn't you like to spend the rest of the day in bed?"

"Yes. But it's rude to cancel at the last minute."

"You win. I'll be ready in ten." He leapt out of bed. Would she ever tire of his body? She didn't want to go to Pumpkin's either.

"I want to call Bethy. See if she's tried to burn down Frog's Leap." Jill punched several buttons. Eight rings later, Mrs. Joyner answered.

"Mrs. Harrington's residence."

"It's Mrs. Harrington, Mrs. Joyner. Happy Thanksgiving."

"Oh, Missus! Happy Thanksgiving to you. Your Bethy is taking a nap."

Bethy hadn't taken a nap since she'd been four. Bethy hated naps.

"Oh?"

"She was up very late, Missus. She made a very unfortunate telephone call early this morning."

"Did it have anything to do with...a bomb?"

"I'm afraid so. She said she thought it might stir things up at that place where you work."

"Well, tell her Mr. Kincaid was very angry and so was I. I'll call her when she wakes up."

"Very good, Missus."

The instant Jill hung up, the phone rang. "Shall I get it, Keefe?"

"Given the discreet hour, Jill, I think you're safe," he laughed. "Disguise your voice. Try Chinese."

It was Bonehead. "Jill, I'd like you and La Doza to meet me at Chuckie Blum's. He wants desperately to meet you both right away. I know you're dead on your feet but it's just this one time. Blum is ape for the Breathless message. I told him you were his A.C.D. Come on, Jill, don't make an old man beg."

"I'm dabbing on some Breathless as we speak," Jill answered, "but I must show up at Pumpkin's. And I'm already late. She *is* my dearest friend, Brodhead."

"Good friends are a dime a dozen. Good lines are hard to find and you've just come up with a winner for Chuckie Blum."

"Okay, *sir*. See you over there. Thirty-one Sutton, right?"

The Sutton Place house was an elegant townhouse with black shutters and a set of steep little steps going up to a black door with a big brass knocker. A maid opened the door, greeted Jill by name and ushered her into the living room.

It was Pumpkin Endicott-Osborne all over, from the Victorian parlor set done in plaid taffeta to the swaggered draperies and creamy lace curtains. Any minute, Violetta would sit down at the piano and burst into an aria.

"Well, waddaya think of the place, Miss Harrington?" asked Chuckie Blum. He talked gold chains but he wasn't wearing any. Everything he wore looked like it came from the Dior store.

"Built in 1879. A real antique, for New York. It's owned by some squillionare in Palm Beach who never comes here any more. Too bad. It was a wedding present from her mother-in-law. Some wedding present, huh? Back then, they had it made. No income tax." He took a breath.

"Lemme show you the dining room. Ya know, in 1879, only butchers lived here. This was strictly slaughterhouses over here. They'd bring the cattle over from Jersey and then they'd drive 'em crosstown for the moment of truth. You think ya got gridlock now, how'd ya like to get caught in a stampede?"

He shook Jill's hand. "Glad to know ya, Miss Harrington. Anybody who can get the Breathless message across is after my own heart. Where's your sidekick?"

"Coming up the front steps." Wait till Chip saw *this*. He would genuflect in front of the gilded harp; prostrate himself at the feet of the marble Psyche on the onyx base.

Jill wasn't too far from wrong, but Chip's admiration took a different form. He couldn't speak.

"Does something to you, right La Doza?" Chuckie clapped him on the back.

"Leaves me breathless, as it were."

Chuckie clapped him on the back. "Drink? I'm having a Black Velvet. Ever have one?"

Chip watched, fascinated, as Chuckie Blum poured iced Dom Perignon and Guiness Stout together into an enormous silver goblet. "Jill." He handed it to her with a flourish.

Then he turned to Chip. "And Chipper."

Chip hated to be called Chipper. He smiled broadly and raised the goblet in salute. "To the Breathless message."

"Mr. Blum, we had an idea on the way over," Jill began.

How they'd had an idea on the way over when they'd arrived separately was not lost on Chuckie Blum. Jill had had an idea.

"Shoot."

"I think Breathless is a fragrance that has more wife-appeal than..."

"Mistress-appeal?"

"Not exactly mistress-appeal...it has woman-appeal versus girl-appeal, if that makes any sense."

"The way you put it, Jill, it makes all the sense in the world."

"So, I think we should run your commercials in the daytime, on the soaps and not in Prime Time as we'd originally thought."

"I thought women didn't watch daytime TV anymore. That's what my subalterns tell me."

"Fire them," retorted Jill. "Haven't you heard of *General Hospital?* That's for openers. What about all the 'I love Soaps' T-shirts, tote bags, bumper stickers? Women love soaps." The wives had said so. That was their biggest problem in working at the agency. They were missing their programs.

"Keep talking." Chuckie sipped his Black Velvet.

"How about a different way to send the message? How about a way that'll really capture womens' imaginations?"

"Just what I'm paying you for. I may up the ante."

"I feel that Breathless is bought by the women themselves. It's not a gift unless it's a gift from a son or daughter. Mostly it's self-purchase. She's doing something nice for herself because she deserves it. And women who do something nice for themselves also do something nice for their homes. Right?"

"So far, so good."

"And who does nicer things for homes than Pumpkin Endicott-Osborne?" Jill gestured around the room. "You must think so." She'd wanted to do something nice for Pumpkin for ages. She knew she could never repay her completely, but at least this would be a stab in the right direction.

"Fascinating." Chuckie mixed himself another Black Velvet. Chip just stared. Jill had never seen Chip like this. He looked like the victim of a teenage crush.

"So, we can get Pumpkin to do some TV spots. 'How to leave 'em breathless.' Decor ideas based on underlying psychological feelings—the way horoscopes work on people's minds. We'll call it..." Jill turned to Chip, "What was your thought?"

"Psycho-Deco," he said tonelessly. "Christ, even *I* could fall for that."

"You guys are fantastic. I can't wait for Kincaid to get here so I can tell him how we've solved Breathless. Do you think we can get any mileage out of the fireplace commercial? The yacht commercial?"

"Pumpkin decorates rooms around fireplaces. She also decorates yachts. *Definitely* is the answer."

"What do you think about putting the fire up in lights in Times Square? We can really burn it in! Get it?"

"As a commercial bullshit artist, I agree!" Chip said.

God, Chip was loaded. No sleep. Working too hard. Probably didn't have any breakfast. And Black Velvets were lethal. Her head was beginning to whirl.

Chuckie Blum squeezed Chip's arm. "You guys are the greatest!"

Be still my heart, Chip thought.

Not counting the living room in Malmaison, this was the living room of Chip's dreams. Oh, to walk across that white bear carpet. Loll on the plaid taffeta. Play the harp under the John Singer Sargent of Maude Lithgow Harrington. He'd take lessons!

"What would it cost for a five-minute commercial? One to run in the afternoon?"

"Oh, about seventy-five thousand per spot."

"I wouldn't need more than one day, would I?" asked Chuckie Blum, crossing his legs and lighting a green cigarette.

Chip's eyes fastened on Chuckie's socks. Aubergine silk, with clocks. Heaven.

Five spots a week, seventy-five per spot. Even Chip's two-and-two mathematical mind figured that meant big bucks.

"So, where *are* we?" asked Chuckie.

"A series of taped Psycho-Deco, get-the-message spots, featuring Pumpkin Osborne, five times a week. That's where we are," Jill said with authority.

"One small thing," said Chuckie. "Do you think we can get Osborne? She *is* the biggest name in decorating, next to Parrish-Hadley."

"Mr. Blum, we're late for lunch at Mrs. Osborne's. May I use your phone? Don't want the turkey to get cold." Christ! How could one innocent-looking stout-and-champagne do this? All of her motor skills had suddenly been turned to low.

"Pumpkin, are you there?" Jill asked.

"Not sure," came a fuzzy reply.

"Are we still invited for turkey?"

"Turkey?" Pumpkin sounded sloshed.

"Is Noël there, Pumpkin?"

"Noël. No-el, No-el, born is the king of Is-ra-el," Pumpkin drawled. Jill hung up, laughing.

"I think we're still invited for lunch. Mr. Blum, we'll nail her down right away."

"I hope all of you feel like celebrating," said Chuckie. "I always feel like celebrating. And now there's something to celebrate."

"Bless us and save us, we love you, Bette Davis," Chip intoned.

"Listen, Jill, I think we need a song. Music. Lilting music. For Breathless."

"We have a song, Mr. Blum. Haven't you heard it?"

"Please, dear girl, call me Chuckie. Are you referring to all that panting? That group-grope on tape?"

"I think so."

"Nasty. Too much nasty aftertaste. Breathless cries for the crash of the surf, the sting of the wind in the High Sierras, the thrill of the chase." Chuckie's short legs measured the long room in five paces.

"Too bad they already overused the *William Tell* Overture," Chip sighed under his breath.

"That's it!" Chuckie stopped dead in his tracks. "*IT!*"

"No, Chuckie. Too obvious."

"Dear ones, there is nothing in this world that is too obvious for the American consumer. Tell 'em. Show 'em. Then sing it for emphasis."

Jill was puzzled. Brodhead had told her that Chuckie Blum didn't know a damn thing about advertising. That he was a money man, head of the conglomerate that bought Aromateria. If that were true, then he must have been taking acting lessons from Al Pacino. Where the hell *was* Bonehead, anyway?

"Correct me if I'm wrong," said Chuckie. "I don't understand a goddamn thing about advertising...oh, I know you folks do your best work in the shower, walking in the park, around the pool. Anywhere but in your office. So I guess you're really on send now, huh?"

"I'm on send," intoned Chip, staring at his Gucci loafers.

"What was it you said, Jill? Breathless is a wife-fragrance? What's a better word for 'wife'?"

"Gee. Uxor? Spouse? Although spouse sounds like an inedible Philadelphia creation made from the intestines of pigs or the necks of chickens."

"Chipper, you funny little devil, we need more laughs for the money. More humor in advertising. I ask you, who gives a shit about the Pepsi Duel? You'd think they were trying to sell an eighty-dollar bottle of Bordeaux. Trust me. People want to be entertained. Something to make 'em happy. Something to make 'em sing along. They even want to learn something, strange as it may seem. I learn something new every day. Couldn't go to sleep at night if I didn't."

"And what did you learn today, Chuckie?" asked Brodhead, strolling in from the hall.

"That you've got just about the smartest pair of brains on Madison Avenue." He pinched Chip's behind.

Oh, thought Jill, so it was "What time do you want it to be, Mr. Blum?" for something new and different. But she knew that Chuckie Blum liked the campaign. And so did she.

"Come to think of it, Jill, you're not any relation to that Harrington woman in Palm Beach, are you?"

"Chuckie, I cannot tell a lie—off the air, that is. She was my late grandmother-in-law."

She was so tired her mind was beginning to wander. I'm so glad summer is over and done with, thought Jill. Poison ivy, oak, sumac. Bees, wasps, hornets, mosquitoes, all waiting to sink their stingers into her. No more horse flies. No more house flies.

Jill hated summer. But maybe just summer in Badger Hollow.

Next week, that house was going on the market. In retrospect, she hated it. It wasn't the happy home of her childhood; of anyone's childhood.

In an instant, she knew she didn't want Rose-Delia's Palm Beach house, Frog's Leap, either. Maybe Ian would. He'd spent part of his childhood there. Maybe it held secret memories for him. She would certainly never know if it did.

She needed something new. Somewhere new. And it had to be a happy house.

In one of Ian's crossword puzzles there had been a definition: verb for Jill. The answer had been, of course, tumble. Ian had found it inordinately amusing; she'd locked herself in the bathroom. That had been last summer, in someone else's life.

She inhaled the leaf-scented air. "I think it's going to snow!"

Chip and Chuckie were holding hands behind their backs. Brodhead was looking for a cab.

"Why don't we walk? It's only ten minutes away."

No one answered. "Then I'll walk," she said. "See you over there. Just down Sutton."

Two blocks away from Pumpkin's, Jill turned and ran back to Keefe's apartment. To hell with dinner. To hell with everything else. She had nothing more to give BDK&C, Bonehead or Chuckie Blum.

CHAPTER SEVENTEEN

"*Hello, Jill,*" a distantly familiar voice said. "I hear you're quite the success on Madison Avenue."

Who was it? All those pear-shaped tones right out of bad old English drawing room comedies. Jill looked around her office nervously.

"Hello, there," Jill answered brightly, searching for the identity of the mystery caller. It wasn't a client. No one from Laurel Hall. Someone from Badger Hollow? She'd heard that voice somewhere, but not in years.

"Hope you haven't forgotten me."

Forgotten him? Who the hell could it be?

"It's Jason. Jason...Picker."

This is your life, Jill Harrington. "How are you, Jason?" she asked evenly.

"The burning question, my dear, is how are *you?*"

"Fine, Jason. Just terrific."

Ian had been arrested for drunken driving and Mr. Worth had just called her from Palm Beach to discuss bail. Bethy had thrown a tantrum, screaming that the math teacher was a lesbian, insisting that she be sent home from Laurel Hall.

Beth hated math and had cut ten classes before they'd called Jill, right before Hogwood Worth had called. And to top things off, Chuckie Blum had asked Chip to move in with him, apparently last night, and Brodhead had found out about it, *all* this morning. He was livid.

He wanted her to evict Chuckie from her town house. After which he would tell Chuckie to take Breathless and shove it.

So far, it had been a morning to remember. And it wasn't even ten o'clock.

"I thought we might have a little cocktail or better still, dinner. How about it?"

Jill hesitated a moment too long.

"Why don't you come to my flat, Jill. We could have some hors d'oeuvres in front of the fireplace and then go somewhere in the neighborhood for a little supper."

"How about lunch," Jill suggested. A little too fast?

By twelve, things would have heated up to an intolerable level. The idea that Bonehead wanted to give up Breathless had left her dumbfounded. So what if Chuckie asked Chip to move in? It was none of his business. But since Suzy died Brodhead was into everybody else's business. He'd even given the Badger Hollow Clarkes a run for their money. It was only a matter of time until he got around to her relationship with Keefe.

"Lunch?" Jason asked. "Lunch! Well, well, what a splendid idea, Jill. What do you crave?"

What did she crave? Peace. Quiet. Two weeks of sleep therapy in a clinic in Switzerland.

"Uh, Jason, there's a quaint little Italian restaurant right in my building. Chez Venezia. I hope it isn't too inconvenient for you, but I'm being a little selfish today. Things are hectic."

"They won't let you out of the yard, eh? Well, I can't say as I blame them. We have lots of catching up to do, Jill. I'm sure I have as much to tell you as you have to tell me."

"Twelve-thirty sound good, Jason? See you then. I'll book a table."

"À *bientot*."

Jason sounded a little silly. But maybe he always had. She

probably wouldn't have noticed it before. What did he look like? It must have been six years since she'd seen him. Well, she hoped he was prepared for a shock when he saw her. She'd certainly changed. Would they even recognize each other?

There'd been a time when all she wanted from life was to spend an entire night in Jason Picker's pale, freckled, muscle-less arms.

Had she been in love with him? How pathetic their frantic little pawings seemed now. But it had saved her then.

"'All real living is meeting,'" Jason had loved quoting Martin Buber. Even back then, in her dumb period, Jill had been sure that Martin Buber had had something quite different in mind than their ribald trysts when he'd written that.

"Jill! Jill!" Chip's panicked voice called. "Quick. Mary-Sue Cratchitt is giving a lecture on women's lib and God-knows-what-else in the conference room. To the *wives*."

Mary-Sue, her Anglo-Saxon good looks stormy and agitated, paused to rearrange her resentments.

"And that, my friends, is only the beginning. Even in supposedly enlightened advertising, medieval inequalities exist. We do *not* get equal pay for equal work."

Chip grimaced. "When Bonehead gets wind of this, I hope I'm out to lunch. He hates rabble-rousers."

The wives and most of the women employees at BDK&C listened intently. Some of them took notes. They seemed to be fascinated by Mary-Sue's controlled angst.

"Men in advertising earn sixty-two percent more than women," Mary-Sue reported. "Sixty-two percent more for the same work, in all branches. Account service, creative. Everywhere, they're out to exploit us!"

"Mark my words," said Chip, nudging Jill, "a peasant will be hanged for this."

"We've got to act. Now. Today. I suggest we strike. Over at Ogilvy & Mather, women are suing!"

Mary-Sue's huge blue eyes roved the room. "Well?" she demanded, "who wants to strike a blow for womankind?"

A hand shot up. Carla De Santo, wife of an executive art director from Staten Island.

"Ms. Cratchitt, I'm sorry you feel underpaid here at BDK&C. I'm sure you are."

Murmurs.

"But we don't work here; our husbands do. And I'm glad Mr. Kincaid pays him as much as he does. He's probably worth more," she giggled nervously. "But I don't think anybody should go on strike. My father was in construction. There were strikes all the time. But that's no way for here."

"Mary-Sue is lucking out." Chip nudged Jill. "History in the making."

Jill had been listening half-heartedly. Tomorrow, she was going up to Badger Hollow, along with Tansy, to pack up everything she wanted and send the rest to auction.

Pumpkin had convinced her to do it. But she really hadn't needed too much convincing. Who wanted to look at the fake Louis XVI chairs with their food-stained needlepoint seats? If Ian wanted them, he could have them. Along with everything that reminded her of life at the bottom. Especially their queen-size bed.

"Jill," Chip whispered, "have you read the *Times* this morning?"

"Uh-uh." She hadn't had a second even to open the paper, let alone read anything. Had Ian's antics made the *New York Times?*

The wives were beginning to move restlessly in their chairs. As far as they were concerned, the meeting was over. Mary-Sue had had no supporters among the wives because they were afraid for their husbands' jobs, and no supporters among the women employees because the wives were in the room.

"What's in the paper?" Jill asked, not at all sure she wanted to know.

"You!"

"Me?"

"You made Phil Dougherty's column!"

"I did? This morning?" She had been interviewed a couple

of weeks before, but so much had happened that it had gone completely out of her mind. She hoped she looked all right in the photograph.

That was it! Jason Picker had read the advertising column. That's why he'd called to invite her to lunch. She slipped out of the conference room and dashed back to her office. Two enormous bouquets, one of red roses, the other of celery, carrots, parsley, watercress and leeks, grew from the center of her desk.

The roses were from Keefe. The card read simply "I love you." The vegetables were from Ian. The card read "Congratulations to an embattled ex-housewife. See you in court re: Alimony. Cheers!" It wasn't signed.

The hell with him. She grabbed the newspaper and turned to page D10. Her hands were shaking. She almost didn't want to read the article. What if it made her sound like an idiot? But he wouldn't have written about an idiot.

She was the lead story. Next to her picture—glamorous and not too businesslike—Jill read:

> A totally new and revolutionary concept was launched in Ad Land today, according to Brodhead Kincaid, that perfect model of a modern major general CEO at BDK&C.
>
> "Turn About is fair play, I like to say," gushed slyboots Kincaid, as he introduced Jill Harrington, BDK&C creative guru credited with the breakthrough concept which encourages wives to exchange agency jobs with their husbands for two weeks to a month.
>
> "We wanted to see what wives had on their minds," said the Titian-haired former homemaker, who has taken Madison Avenue like a pink tornado. "After all, who buys the products? Not the husbands."
>
> Rumor has it that Kincaid had wanted to dub the program "Wife Swapper's Week," but was cut off at the pass by the disarming Mrs. Harrington.
>
> No one said anything about art directors being replaced by wives who can't draw. Stay tuned!

Oh, Jill sighed. There were worse things than being described as a creative guru and Titian-haired former homemaker. Pumpkin would love it. And, obviously, Ian had loved it even more.

"Well, instant celeb, how does it feel to be quoted in the *New York Times?*" smiled Chip.

"I can't believe it. I feel like I just won an Academy Award, or something. Like I ought to start thanking everybody, starting with you, Chip. You've been so terrific."

"Ah, modesty doesn't become me," he laughed. "But I had nothing to do with Turn About. That was all yours, Jill."

"If I hadn't been working with you, I never would have come up with it."

"Oh, yes you would have. You're the former homemaker, remember? *Pas moi.*"

"But you helped me, Chip."

"Come on, Jill. We all owe each other."

Maybe he's right, Jill thought. I'll file it for now. She had ten minutes to call Keefe before she went to lunch. He'd mentioned that he'd go up to Badger Hollow with her, to help her close the house. The more she'd thought about it, the more she knew it was a bad idea. She had to keep him apart from her other life as much as possible.

And now, the house was sad and unloved. Littered by Ian. Musty. Too cold. Had they fixed the living room window where she'd thrown the Waterford lamp?

At three, Bonehead was giving a talk in the little theater about striking the right balance between the creative need for independence essential for artistic integrity and financial control essential for corporate health.

It sounded an awful lot like something he'd stolen from someone else. It certainly didn't sound like Bonehead. What the hell. As soon as the speech was over, she was driving to Badger Hollow.

On her way to the elevator, Jill overheard Bammie Pomino talking frantically on the telephone.

"I've always wanted perky tits," she was saying, "and I'm

stuck with Sagamore Hills. Yeah. I've heard about that *test*. If you can hold a pencil under 'em, it's supposed to mean you've reached the point of no return. Well, how about if you can hold an IBM Selectric under there?"

Who was the wizened choirboy sitting alone, nursing a Kir, staring into the smoke-filled red interior of Chez Venezia? Jason Picker had aged a millennium. He seemed to have shrunk, his bones first and now his skin was trying to catch up. How old was Jason? He'd told her that he was on the sunny side of fifty. And that had been seven years ago. Now he was definitely on the foggy side of seventy. Maybe more. As Jill neared the table, Jason rose to kiss her.

His kiss was dry, dusty, on her mouth. His jacket smelled of camphor. His cologne was more alcohol than scent. His teeth were the color of Pumpkin's ancient ivory netsukes.

"Jill, my dear, let me look at you. You've done it. Done it, I say. You were always exquisite but now...now..." his voice cracked and he coughed. "Somehow, Jill, you've turned back the hands of time."

"Oh, nonsense, Jason, I just went on a diet. Should have years ago. I've never felt better."

She could feel herself slipping back into her old conversational habits with Jason. Next, he'd ask about the girls. Was she up to it? And then about Ian. Had she *ever* been up to that?

Then, he'd ask what books she'd read lately and she'd tell him. He'd say he hadn't read any of them. Then, they'd have a second drink and he'd start telling her how he longed to go to bed with her.

"How's Bethy, Jill? Acting in school plays?"

"Yes, of course." Bethy refused even to try out for any plays. Jason had listened to all of her troubles for years. He'd tried so hard to make her strong and smart. He'd tried to tell her how to survive. And she had worshipped him.

"Tell me all about advertising, Jill. I've wanted to call you for months. Ever since...well, you know."

"Why didn't you, Jason?"

"I thought it might prove too difficult for you."

Correction, it might have proved too difficult for you, old dear. Jason liked his drama on stage.

"It wasn't easy. I won't pretend it was. And Ian's been a pain."

"Jill, sweet, Ian was *always* a pain. I wish I could have afforded to take you away from him."

Ah, that again. Jason never had any money. Just what he earned from teaching history and drama and five thousand a year from a ancient aunt's trust.

Watching Jason, listening to him, she began to feel sorry for him. Had he felt sorry for her, so long ago? Or, had he really loved her? He had always been so mysterious. All the better to intrigue a dowdy, plump *hausfrau* with just a demitasse spoonful of star quality.

She didn't deserve pain. Why was she re-opening bad old times? A waiter loomed toward them. Good. A drink. A luscious big, extra dry Russian vodka martini with a twist. No rocks. Straight up. Tiny beads of lemon oil from the twist floating on the clear, icy crystal surface.

"Mrs. Harrington, you're wanted on the telephone," the respectful young waiter said. "Your office."

"Did they say who in my office?" Jill asked, always expecting the worst. Chip wouldn't do that to her. Not of his own volition. Whatever it was, it was either Bonehead or Bonehead was behind it. His new-found nosiness was getting to her.

It *was* Brodhead. He wanted to practice his speech on her. To get her opinion. Was it too long? Too short? Clear enough? Could she add anything? Delete anything? Jill was sure he'd had the speech written for weeks; had probably given it a dozen times before.

"I'm having lunch, Brodhead."

"I know. That's why I called you at the restaurant."

"How about in an hour or so?"

"Are you lunching with a client, Jill?" He knew damn well she wasn't.

"No. A friend."

"Excuse yourself. The agency comes first." (*I* come first.) "See you in my office in ten, okay?"

When she returned to the table, her martini was waiting. It looked just as good as she'd imagined it.

"Jason, I'm sorry but I have to go back up to the office. There's some emergency." She knew it didn't sound too convincing. But maybe Jason Picker didn't know that BDK&C had 850 employees in the New York office alone and that any one of the 849 could have listened to Bonehead's speech.

"Well, well, well, Jill, you certainly are the important executive these days. Much too important for me, I guess. Think I'll have to call you Dolley Madison Avenue."

"Next week, Jason. I promise," Jill said, gulping her drink. "Thanks for the drink." She took his hand. It was parched as the rest of him looked. The skin seemed to slide away from the bones. Was he ill? Maybe that was it. But she just didn't have time to go into it now. Just as she hadn't had time to get involved with Mary-Sue and her crusade. Brodhead had given her the raise and the double promotion. She owed him anything he wanted to ask of her. And right now, it was help with the speech.

Jason kissed her cheek. "I've always said that the world has produced more millionaires than masterpieces. I see you've traded in the latter for the former."

Did he know anything about Rose-Delia's will? Probably not. Maybe he was referring to the article in the *Times*.

"I'll watch the papers, Jill. You're the only celebrity I know. Take care."

She ran out the side door and around to the back of the building, to Brodhead's private elevator. Stooped little Jason Picker moved to the bar and ordered a double cognac. No rocks. No water. No pretzels.

CHAPTER EIGHTEEN

Badger Hollow.
    Its familiarity had become unfamiliar. So quickly. The important old buildings had pulled in their shoulders. The low, new buildings were swallowing up the hills.

Brodhead had said it in his speech: The village green has been replaced by the shopping mall. True. Badger Hollow was becoming uglier, faster, than most of the neighborhoods in Manhattan.

What did Jill feel? Nostalgia? What was it? A vague headache?

Jill hoped that Tansy had gotten to the house with no mishaps. She'd asked her to pick up everything she needed to clean a house. Tansy had been delighted. She loved new products. Loved to buy them, test them, write to manufacturers about them. Maybe Jill could get Tansy on the payroll at BDK&C. She'd make a note of it when she got to the house. The house. She was dreading it.

This morning she'd told Tansy to go full steam ahead and she'd join her as soon as possible. As soon as possible was *now*. Five-thirty. It was dark and cold and the wind bit deep as Jill stepped out of Rose-Delia's Rolls. She had to stop that. *Her* Rolls. She started up the path. Frost clung to the flagstones, making the walking treacherous.

Lights blazed from every window and the radio was blaring from the kitchen, with Tansy's contralto singing along.

Jill hung her coat in the hall closet and walked into the dining room. No Tansy.

She crossed to the living room. The paneling cried for wax. The sofas and chairs were beggars in silk. The draperies had grown a coat of threads.

How Mrs. Cavanaugh from the real estate had managed to unload this mess for three hundred fifty thousand dollars was a mystery to Jill. But unloaded it was. Tomorrow at eight, the movers would be here.

Tansy had washed every glass, dish and piece of ugly crystal in the house. For some inexplicable reason, the new owners had fallen in love with all of it. Good. It had saved Jill a call to the Salvation Army.

She knew she could never again sip coffee from one of those ceramic bunny mugs or scotch from one of the hideously etched hi ball glasses Mother's husband had abandoned.

She never wanted to re-heat stew in those pots, bake a cake in those pans or eat ice cream, standing in front of the open freezer, with one of those spoons.

Somehow, though, the rest of the house didn't evoke the same feelings. The living room was fairly impersonal. It was meant for entertaining, but since she and Ian had given up entertaining after Beth was born, it just existed. It might as well have had a velvet rope across the door with a small sign proclaiming "This room, Tudor in feeling, furnished in the style immediately preceding Art Deco, has remained untouched, except for occasional dusting and vacuuming, since life came to a halt sometime in the Seventies."

Bethy had asked her to store her bedroom furniture, in a rare burst of sentimentality, in case she ever had a little girl of her own. Jill had been so surprised that she'd immediately agreed. Beth's canopy bed and matching French provincial chest, desk, chairs, night tables and faded Aubusson—a relic from Jill's mother's room—had already been taken away. One thing less to face.

The library had been returned to pristine neatness. Ian had taken all of the books. Many of them were Jill's but she didn't care about them. Ian had used them to humiliate her, to test her knowledge of their contents. The hell with them.

A chill went through her. The place was freezing. Tansy had laid a fire in the library fireplace. Jill struck a match and it burst into life. How about a drink? Had Ian left anything? Probably not. It hadn't occurred to her to stop at a store.

She returned to the kitchen.

"Now, then, Miz Jilly, hows 'bout a nice taste?"

"Where'd you find that vodka, Tansy? I can't believe Ian left anything behind."

"Uh-huh. He din. Brought it mahself. 'Long with some chicken, potato salad, green beans an' some apple pie. Knows you's on a diet, Miz Jilly, but ain' nothin' like apple pie to give strength fer a long haul."

Jill accepted the drink gratefully and climbed the stairs. No use putting it off any longer. She had to face Wendy's room. She must open her drawers, her closet. Go through her desk. Clean it out. Keep things; throw things away. How could she throw anything of Wendy's away?

Her mother had thrown her father's things away. Lady Hamilton had thrown Lord Nelson's things away. Others had done it.

How easy it had been to scold the girls for harboring rats' nests of old comics, worn-out sneakers, smelly stuffed animals leaking sawdust.

Jill turned the doorknob. The door in Wendy's room eased open. Jill felt for the little frog lamp on the bureau. It wasn't there. Neither was the bureau. She walked into the room. Her heels echoed on the naked oak floor. She felt along the wall near the door, searching blindly for the overhead light switch. The room had been stripped.

Everything was gone. Like Wendy.

Someone was leaning on the door bell. Didn't Tansy hear it? Maybe not. Her singing could lift the proscenium at the Met.

A man's voice. Who? Bonehead with another project? Impossible. But nothing was impossible. Not at BDK&C. She heard footsteps on the stairs. It was Keefe. She ran into his arms.

"You did this, didn't you?"

"Yes. I hope it's, well, okay."

"It's more than okay. I didn't know how I was going to face her things."

"I sent it all to storage. That is, everything except the stuff in her desk. Compositions. School work. Photographs."

"Storage?" said Jill, not quite trusting her ears. "How did you know? I mean, where did you send everything?"

"Remember? You were so amazed that Bethy wanted to keep her furniture that you arranged to have it stored?"

"Yes." Had she told him about that? She couldn't remember. But then, everything had been racing along.

"I wrote down the name of the place and called them. Told them you were storing two rooms instead of one. Simple."

"Keefe, how did you know?"

"How did I know? I know I'm an insensitive clod at times, but give me a little credit."

Oh, God, she'd give him credit. Credit for compassion, for smarts, for looks. Why hadn't someone else already trapped him?

There! She thought it. The martini had given her a soupçon of courage.

"If I gave you any more credit, I'd bankrupt myself."

"Never, Jill. Never. The instant you give, twice as much comes back to fill the void. Christ, I'm getting sentimental."

"I think you're working too hard, Keefe. I think the toilet paper and the roach killer and the lemon-scented dishwater detergent are taking over your head. And believe me, I understand." She hugged him.

"I think I should take you out to dinner. Now."

"But Tansy. And the house. And the movers."

"Madame, may I take you on a complete guided tour?"

All of the upstairs rooms were empty. The windows were washed. The floors were waxed. The bathrooms were whiter than white; cleaner than clean. No spots, stains, mildew or funny bathroom odor.

"You. And Tansy. And Pumpkin, right?"

"Listen, Jill, you've had a lot on your mind."

"I guess so."

"And you didn't want to admit it. You didn't want to ask for help, because under that Titian hair, under that mantle of a creative guru, beats a heart of steel."

"Beats a heart of Ida-Ho mashed potato."

"Speaking of which..."

"But Keefe, Tansy has fried chicken and potato salad. A whole feast downstairs."

"Right. And Tansy and all her helpers are going to eat every bite. *We* are going to dine in style. At the Box Tree."

"You're spoiling me again. And *what* helpers?"

"You deserve it. An army of gnomes whose specialty is wiping and shining have been here all day."

"Oh, Keefe! So all the movers have to do is pack up the living room, dining room and library."

"You got it."

"Where is Tansy going to sleep tonight?"

"In the maid's room."

"The maid's room? But it's only been used for storage. For...ever."

"Well, it looks like a Plaza suite at the moment."

"Keefe, where were you today, if I may ask?"

"You may not ask."

"Where am I...where are we spending the night? We're not driving back to Pumpkin's, are we?"

"You may not ask that, either. It's a surprise."

"I'd forgotten that most surprises are fun."

Keefe took her hands and kissed them. "Especially when you deserve them."

As they turned out of the driveway onto Badger Hollow Lane, Jill realized she had no regrets. Not about selling the house. Nor electing to work like a demon at the office. Nor pushing ahead with the divorce.

And certainly not about falling in love with Keefe. If they got married. If they didn't get married.

No regrets.

They had to be the two most beautiful words in the English language.

CHAPTER NINETEEN

he competitive lawns of Badger Hollow couldn't hold a candle to the non-competitive, rarely-seen-except-by-the-gardener-and-close-friends lawns of the North Shore.

It was breathtaking. Locust Valley. Muttontown. All the Brookvilles. Oyster Bay. Supposedly sleepy little villages that all ran into each other. Manicured. Elegant. The garden and lawn services never slept. Neither did the police.

Once Jill had made up her mind to dump Badger Hollow, she'd moved right ahead. When she'd read the ad in the Sunday *New York Times*, it sounded too good to be true:

> Pool house and Olympic-size pool. 3 perfect acres. Absolute privacy. 2 WBF, 30' LR, DR, kit, wet bar, maid's, 2-car gar. Foxpoint Realty. (516) 671-6110

She'd called Foxpoint at ten and made an appointment for noon.

Whoever had written the ad had forgotten some of the best points. There was an underground sprinkler system with five settings. A twelve-foot hedge around the entire property. And a driveway a quarter-mile long. Absolute privacy was right. Yet, it was less than three-tenths of a mile from Northern Boulevard, and just a little farther to Gristede Brothers, the drug store, the post office and the cleaner. Completely unsuburban suburbia. No Clarkes next door to tell her how and when to cut the grass. No one could even *see* her grass unless they were sitting in it. The house had been designed by Edward Durrell Stone before he'd gotten involved with concrete filigree.

She couldn't wait for Chip and Pumpkin to see it. She'd let Pumpkin "do" it. Another way to pay her back.

Mrs. Tucker from Foxpoint Realty met Jill in the driveway.

She opened the gate at the top of the stairs. Beneath them sprawled a fifty-foot pool. An enormous lawn. There was room for a tennis court. And the house!

Mrs. Tucker said it had been built in 1950 but it looked more like 1930. U-shaped, mostly glass, with the long, main part of the "U" comprising the living room. The living room had once been a ballroom for a main house, with the rest of the Gatsby-like estate still intact at the top of the hill.

The two bedrooms had been guest rooms. The house was made for entertaining. There had been good times here. Jill felt it as she wandered from room to room. There was a sensation of time suspended. It could have been the Twenties or the Thirties. Or any other time except the present. Jill wouldn't have been surprised to see Rose-Delia pull up in her 1927 Reo.

"Well, Mrs. Harrington, is there anything else you need to know about the house?"

"Only when I can move in."

"Well, well, well! This is not a house for everybody."

"That is exactly what appeals to me about it, Mrs. Tucker."

"The owners will move out their furniture within two weeks. We can probably arrange the closing for right after Christmas. What a nice Christmas present, Mrs. Harrington."

What a nice Christmas present for her *and Keefe*, Jill thought.

She couldn't wait to show it to him. It was exactly the kind of house he'd love. The fireplaces. The gigantic pool. The lush hedges. She imagined them sunbathing. Skinny-dipping.

It had been a little over a month since anything had gone dreadfully wrong. In fact, at long last everything seemed to be going all right.

Ian had stopped polluting the mails with nasty letters to her and to Ralston Rhodes. It seemed like he was conceding defeat, though Jill was afraid to say so out loud.

And the office, thank God, had cooled off for the holidays. Only one or two crises a day.

All of the wives except one, Jeannie Eaton, had gone home to their soaps, loaded down with gift packs of Breathless and cases of ersatz cake mix, expensive vodka, tons of detergent and crates of instant potatoes.

Jeannie had decided that she'd always wanted to be a television producer, and so, at forty-nine, she became the oldest, lowest-paid gofer in the history of BDK&C. She maintained that Jill had inspired her. And Jill, who barely knew her, took her to lunch at, where else, Chez Venezia.

Breathless, because of Jill's campaign, was out-selling the frozen Pizza Raisin Bagels in selected supermarkets all over the Great Mid Waist, as Chuckie called it.

Charlie and FiFi Woolverson had revved up with even greater feats of espionage. Charlie's new spy, Juan, made Xerox copies of absolutely everything anybody left on his desk during lunchtime. And nobody cared. Things at BDK&C had almost become boring.

The elevators hadn't broken down. There had been no bomb scares. Bonehead was on vacation in Hobe Sound. Rumor had it that he'd "met someone." Chip was on vacation at Chuckie's house in Barbados.

Jill had thought about a vacation, but there were still a few details to be ironed out in connection with the sale of Frog's Leap, Rose-Delia's house in Palm Beach. Ian had decided that he couldn't afford to keep it up.

Soon, all the pieces and parts would fit together and she could live happily ever after. Jill yawned.

She was on the verge of asking FiFi to have lunch with her, even though one had to be pretty hungry to lunch with FiFi. Instead, she called Keefe to ask him to lunch before she caught the plane to Florida.

His secretary told Jill that Mr. Neuman had gone to Southampton early that morning.

"Southampton? Are you sure?" Jill had asked. She didn't mean Southampton, England, did she? Jill hoped she didn't sound too anxious.

"Maybe it was East Hampton? I'm sorry, but Mr. Neuman's secretary is on vacation. I'm the temp. Anyway, I don't see any number here where he can be reached. He'll be back in on Monday. Any message?"

"Well, if he calls in..." Jill began. "No. No message. Merry Christmas." Jill replaced the receiver slowly. Funny, she thought. Funny that he hadn't mentioned any trip to Southampton or East Hampton or anywhere when they'd had dinner last night. Keefe wasn't that impulsive. Another surprise? For her? For Christmas? *He* knew she was going to Palm Beach. Oh, well, he'd probably call her tonight. She grabbed her under-the-seat Vuitton bag. Maybe Beth would be happy to see her. One could always pray for miracles.

Keefe Neuman turned into the narrow macadam, sand-whisked road that led to the East Hampton airport. He'd bought himself a very special Christmas present and he couldn't wait to try it out. He also couldn't wait to take Jill up.

Keefe had discussed it with his psychiatrist.

He felt he was strong enough to take Jill for a ride without mishap. But first, he had to see what it was like to fly the new plane, by himself, down to Palm Beach.

Jill loved to fly. She'd told him often that if she had more time, she'd take flying lessons herself.

She didn't suffer from agoraphobia. She didn't seem to suffer from anything these days. He hoped he was at least partially

245

responsible. She loved him. It had taken him a long time to believe it. He hadn't been loved as a child. He'd been hideous. Fat. With a harelip. And even after his lip had been repaired, badly, and he'd starved himself to near-perfection, he still felt ugly. He'd taken speech lessons. They'd helped. He'd had his lip done over by Dr. Hogan, the most famous plastic surgeon in New York. But he still didn't feel like the Brooklyn Adonis of his secretary's dreams. Would the self-doubt ever leave him? Only Jill's magnificent face, turned up to his, made him think that maybe it would. Someday.

There it was, gleaming in the bright winter sunshine. His Cessna Cardinal R.G.

With the right wind, he'd be in Palm Beach in nine hours. Four hours from East Hampton to Myrtle Beach, South Carolina. An hour to re-fuel, get a cup of coffee, and take off. Four more hours to West Palm.

He'd breeze through the front door of Frog's Leap as though he'd been expected. He longed to see the expression on her face. Jill was so like a child sometimes, her reactions fresh, natural. She was the most creative person he'd ever met. No wonder Bonehead and the motley crew at BDK&C were so in love with her.

He hadn't mentioned it to Jill, but he'd been flying every Saturday afternoon for months, getting ready for this moment. The moment when he could fly into her arms, as it were, and steal her away to the Caribbean. He had another surprise for her, too. Her real Christmas present: an engagement ring.

There was no way he could top the jewels Rose-Delia had left to Jill and so he hadn't bothered to try. The ring he'd gotten at James Robinson on Fifty-Seventh Street was from the reign of Charles I. Huge, intricate, romantic. A massive amethyst, surrounded by mine-cut diamonds and set in rose gold. She had to like it. She *had* to.

He took off, the beach and ocean looking like a paint-by-numbers canvas beneath him. But something was wrong. As soon as he cut back to cruise power, there was a wild fluctuation in his oil pressure. What was it? The plane had been behaving beautifully. He had to go down. Shit. He didn't want to waste the time. But the uncertainty was too great. What if he couldn't make it to Myrtle Beach? It was probably nothing, but what if?

Fear gripped him. Out of nowhere.

This wasn't like the Saturday flying he'd been doing.

His head began to throb. The trees and high tension wires that ringed East Hampton airport rushed to meet him.

He woke up in Southampton Hospital, much of his body encased in bandages and plaster. He fumbled for the buzzer. He couldn't reach it. A nurse, big and fat and jolly, rose from her post in the depths of an armchair.

"Welcome back, Mr. Neuman."

"Where've I been?"

"Wild blue yonder, I guess. Feel like a visitor?"

A visitor? Who knew he was here? He'd told the office that he was going to Southampton but he hadn't said where.

"I don't know. I feel like... shit. My leg. Can I have a shot or something?"

The pain traveled from his toes to his eyes. It was the worst pain he had ever felt. The plastic surgery on his lip had been nothing compared to this. He began to shake.

"Try one of these." The nurse handed him a pill and a little paper cup of water. "And if that doesn't help, we'll get you a brick and I'll give you a good whack on the head." She laughed. "By the way, your visitor is a lady. She's been here a long time, waiting for you to wake up."

Jill? Christ. She couldn't see him. Not like this. He touched his face. No stubble. No bandages on his head.

"You look dandy, Mr. Neuman," the nurse said. "And your friend, Mrs. Harrington, will think you never looked better. We almost lost you, you know."

He knew.

"Did you find anything in my pocket?"

"It's in the safe, Mr. Neuman. All of your money and credit cards. Absolutely everything. It's all okay. Now, if I don't let

Mrs. Harrington in, I'm afraid we're going to have to sedate her."

"Get her, please."

Jill had never looked more beautiful. Lack of sleep added a translucence to her face. She appeared angelic. From a dream. A cathedral. She'd been crying. She wore no makeup.

"Oh, Keefe," she tried to scold, "what the hell kind of a Christmas present is this?"

"You probably won't believe it, but I hadn't planned it like this." He tried to smile. Pain.

Charlene and her accidents that steer our lives.

When the phone call had come, that's all Jill could think about. Goddamn unfair accidents. Wendy. Rose-Delia. She'd never believed for a minute that Rose-Delia had committed suicide. Rose-Delia was the strongest person she'd ever met. And besides, Rose-Delia had been much too meticulous not to have left a suicide note.

Now, Keefe.

What had he been doing? What had he been trying to prove? That he was macho enough to go up again? She wished she'd never discussed flying with him. Maybe she was responsible for doing to him what he thought he had done to Didi.

How much more was she meant to endure?

What if he died? Just because he was alive now didn't mean... She couldn't think about that now. He'd been in surgery seven hours. He had better than a fifty-fifty chance of complete recovery. There was no brain damage. Which was incredible.

The only thing she'd gotten used to was doctor talk.

We're doing everything possible. His heart is strong. His vital signs are good. It's touch-and-go, wait-and-see. Why couldn't a body be more like a machine?

Oh, God, why had she thought *that?* Hadn't that goddamn plane been a machine? And the goddamn bus? And the goddamn bike? And the goddamn boat on Lake Worth?

Be cheerful, Jill. Try to act like a human being with her

wits about her. Try to speak to him. *Try to act act as if nothing had happened.*
That's what they'd done in the movies of her childhood.
"When are you going to stay out of airplanes, darling?"
"Never. I love airplanes."
"So I figured. Is it permissible to kiss the remains?" she asked, moving closer to the bed. She was half afraid to touch. She couldn't bear to hurt him any more.
He'd been so strong, so full of energy. He'd seemed to have plenty left over. Plenty for her. But not now.
Please, God, make him have just a little of that spark. I need it. More than ever. Jill prayed silently.
Prayers had never helped her before but now she was desperate. What if she lost him? What if...he...died?
She couldn't go on. Not now. She touched him. He didn't fall to pieces. She sunk onto the foot of the bed.
They'd warned her, in their creamy lowered voices, about his leg. She couldn't look at the covers, covering nothing. They hadn't told him. They had asked her to.
How could she tell him? *How?*
"Keefe, when you get out of here, I think we should get married. If I can elude Ian, then you can extricate yourself from Didi." There. The first step. If she could get him to talk about getting married, he couldn't change his mind when he found out that his left leg stopped at the knee.
"Tell me about good old Ian. I haven't had a laugh in hours. Any bomb threats? Streaking at the Metropolitan Museum? Any new wives? Mistresses? Is he living on his allowance?"
In spite of herself, Jill had to laugh.
"He's invented something, Keefe. As a matter of fact, he was planning to discuss it with you. Calls you 'that marketing genius.' Of course, Ian thinks marketing is only what you do in the A&P."
"What did he invent? A fly shooter?"
"A fly shooter exists, oh marketing genius. It's a reloadable little gun thing that shoots a disc at the fly. Spring action.

Pumpkin's housewares store sells them."

Keefe tried to shake his head. It hurt too much. "What did he invent? You can't keep an accident victim in suspense like this, Jill. It's unfair."

"Blowup famous art."

"Come again?"

"Rubber balloons. And when you inflate them, *voilà*, a bust of Queen Victoria, Michaelangelo's *David*, the Christ of the Andes."

"You made that up. You're going to cheer me up if it's the last thing you do."

"Even *I* couldn't make *that* up, Keefe."

"Ian is crazy. But you know, something like that might just catch on."

"If it doesn't, he's going to the University of Guelph. To study architecture."

"Je-sus. Listen, you don't happen to have a martini or a vat of scotch in your bag, do you?"

"Yes. But we'll have to ask if you're allowed to drink."

"Come closer. I want you to buzz for the nurse and then kiss me."

Jill could see the pain in his eyes. She took him into her arms without actually moving him.

If only she could give him some blood or strength or some *anything*. She closed her eyes.

"Just as soon as you get out of here, I have a big surprise for you."

"Can I guess?"

"You'll never guess. Not in a million years."

"Let me try. Does it have anything to do with a swimming pool? And fireplaces? And twelve-foot hedges?"

"You bastard. How did you find out?"

"Bethy has turned into quite the little letter writer."

"I'll kill her."

"She didn't know it was a surprise. You didn't tell her it was because you didn't know she writes to me. For once, Miss Beth is in the right."

"Well, Keefe, what other surprises are lurking around here?"

The nurse appeared in the doorway.

"Will you bring me the little box? You know, the one from James Robinson in the safe?" He tried to smile.

"Keefe, I really do think we should get married. I have to keep an eye on you. It's perfectly clear you don't have any sense at all."

"Will you stop stealing the snake's best lines? Just wait until Nursey gets back with the box."

"I'm worried about... other women. There, I've said it."

"Are you kidding?"

She stared at him. Even in pain, he had never been handsomer. How she loved him.

"You honestly believe you can do anything once you make up your mind to it, don't you, Jill?"

"Facts prove, as we say on Madison Avenue. If I hadn't told myself that about ten thousand times today, I wouldn't be here now."

Gently, he took her hand. There was nothing left to say.